METAWARS

ORCHARD BOOKS

338 Euston Road, London NW1 3BH
Orchard Books Australia
Level 17/207 Kent Street, Sydney, NSW 2000

This edition published in 2014 by Orchard Books

ISBN 978 1 40831 462 3

Text © Awesome Media & Entertainment Ltd 2014
With special thanks to Steve Lyons

A CIP catalogue record for this book is available
from the British Library.

1 3 5 7 9 8 6 4 2

Printed in Great Britain by Cox & Wyman

Orchard Books is a division of Hachette Children's Books,
an Hachette UK company.

www.hachette.co.uk
www.jeffnorton.com

METAWARS
THE FREEDOM FRONTIER

JEFF NORTON

ORCHARD

For Torin.
Welcome to the world. Welcome to our family.
Let's live for real.

Prologue

Sal Vator reached down and hoisted his two children onto the roof of their creaking bungalow. The tsunami was coming fast, and it was coming high. The black wave was sweeping over everything, drowning southern Louisiana in a toxic mix of crude oil and sea water.

'Why are we on the roof, Daddy?' shouted his six-year-old boy, Peter, over the sirens.

'The levee finally burst,' he replied calmly. Sal had tried to warn the oil companies and the government that drilling too deep would crack the floor of the Gulf of Mexico. But no one listened to his 'troublemaking' science.

'What's tha' sound, Dadda?' asked Luisa, not yet four.

'Close your eyes, my children, and I'll sing to you,' he said. Sal hugged his children closer as the thunderous roar of the wave grew closer. He wanted his voice to be the last thing they heard before they died.

'*Today was fun but tomorrow is another one*,' he began to sing. It was a lullaby that his mama had sung to him when he was a boy. That was a long time ago, but Sal never forgot it. '*Today's children play and sleep, then rest for God to keep. When it's time to rise, I'll tell you when; tomorrow's children will rise again.'*

The wave slammed into him, ripping Peter from his arms. As the furious water rushed over him, Sal clutched his baby girl with all of his strength, but he was no match for nature. Drowning in darkness, Sal Vator lost his grip and was suddenly alone. Tossed under an unforgiving current, he kicked and fought blindly, hoping to find his children.

Pain shot into his shoulder as he slammed against something hard. Metal. He reached out and grabbed hold of a strut. A hydro tower. He tightened his grip and pulled himself above the raging waters, gasping for oxygen as he surfaced. He climbed the structure to survey the watery wasteland below. Everything and everyone was submerged by the great flood.

He didn't cry. He didn't flinch. Sal Vator simply looked to the horizon and made the world a promise.

'Tomorrow's children will rise again.'

1

Jonah Delacroix soared over the Arctic desert.

The icy expanse of the Canadian north stretched out to the distant horizon. It was hard to believe that it was real. He was astounded that in a world so crowded, so crammed full of people, so much nothingness could still exist. But of course, even in an over-heating world, the icescape this far north was too cold to be liveable most of the year.

Jonah's body was protected from that cold by Kevlar body armour, and his head shielded by a helmet that drew oxygen from the small tank on his back. At ten thousand feet, the air was getting thinner. He heard the echoes of his rhythmic breathing as he clung to the undercarriage of the Guardian airship. The huge flying dirigible, at least one hundred buses long, was creeping across the freezing sky towards the final front in the battle for the future.

Under its skeletal structure, directly under the pressurised cabin where four hundred soldiers waited to wage war against their enemy, the Millennials, Jonah balanced his body above the Earth. As he stabilised himself across a pair of parallel beams that made up the lattice-like cage that enveloped the blimp, with nothing but icy air below, he wondered if the battle was inevitable.

Jonah should have been readying himself for war, but all he could think of was peace.

There has to be a way.

He had raced around the world to fight in the MetaWars on the side of the Guardians. At stake was the very future of the Metasphere, the global, immersive virtual space where over seven billion people interfaced with one another every day for work and play. But the Metasphere was so much more than a 3D social network or a massive role-playing game, it was an alternative to the crowded, violent and exhausted planet that carried too many hungry and thirsty souls on its shoulders. It was an escape.

The Guardians were a secret society dedicated to keeping the Metasphere open and free. They opposed Matthew Granger, the founder of the Metasphere, and his Millennial organisation. The Millennials believed in controlling the virtual world as their own monopoly. Neither side would compromise, compelling both into a bloody, zero-sum game.

With Jonah's help, and especially with his knowledge of the locations of the four server farms that powered the Metasphere – the Four Corners – the Guardians had taken the first three in violent attacks. Jonah had led the Guardians to Australia to secure the Southern Corner, to the Republic of Manhattan to take the Western Corner, and just three months ago to Cuba to win the Eastern Corner. Now, the Guardians were about to take back the Northern Corner.

Three down, one to go.

In recent months Jonah had left the Eastern Corner in allied hands and travelled north with his best friend, Sam, to the Atlantic port city of Halifax, Nova Scotia. There they'd reconnected with the Guardians to plan this assault in Canada's North West Territories. It was the final push of the MetaWar that had consumed both sides. Around the world, Jonah had seen too many people die in the struggle for control over web 4.0.

Jonah knew the locations of the secret server farms that powered the online virtual world from the inherited memories of his father. His dad was once a Guardian double-agent who'd infiltrated the Millennials as Matthew Granger's private pilot. And the Guardians' intelligence confirmed that Granger still ran the servers of the Northern Corner from the same abandoned, ice-trapped diamond mine that Jonah's dad used to fly in and out of.

The airship was part of the stealth attack from above. The plan was for the Guardians to parachute down to the disused mining complex and secure it for the ground forces that were approaching on snowmobiles. Together, the air and ground attacks would take the Millennials by surprise and put an end to Granger's grip over the virtual world.

Jonah had once looked up to Matthew Granger, the brilliant and enigmatic founder of the virtual world; but now he had come to see him as his enemy. Granger fought and killed for control over what he considered to be 'his' virtual world. He'd had the Metasphere taken away from him by various governments and was imprisoned for years. But when Granger escaped and recaptured his creation, the Guardians assembled across the world and both sides clashed in the MetaWars.

The Northern Corner was the final front in a war that had raged across both worlds. And once the attack was over, the Northern Corner servers safely in Guardian hands, the Metasphere would be free.

But to Jonah, it had come to feel like freedom at any price. He had finally joined this group, a network of 'terrorists' he'd once loathed, because the Millennials murdered his mother and he believed that Matthew Granger killed his father. Jonah had joined the Guardian cause, reluctantly at first, and then with increasing conviction, hoping to end the cycle of violence that defined the battle for humanity's digital future.

The Guardians wanted *freedom*. The Millennials wanted *control*. And both sides were willing to kill for their goals. He wondered how different they actually were. Whose side was he really on?

Hanging high above the desolate landscape, the Earth slowly sliding beneath him, Jonah Delacroix decided that he must end the MetaWars.

2

Jonah smiled when Sam's voice filled his helmet.

'Jonah, are you finished with your moping?' she teased. 'You've been hanging down there for hours.'

To Jonah, alone with his thoughts and the mesmerising Arctic landscape, it had only felt like minutes. But Sam's intrusion was a welcome interruption. In the past few months, she'd gone from suspicious enemy to trusted friend. And increasingly, Jonah hoped, there might still be more to their relationship.

He had nearly lost Sam too many times to ignore the way he felt about her. It wasn't just the physical attraction, though that didn't hurt; there was something deeper, something visceral that connected them. They had protected each other, cheated death together, and survived against impossible odds. They had watched over one another and had become inseparable.

Jonah loved Sam in a way that he couldn't understand, and certainly couldn't articulate. He had only ever felt familial love before; love for his parents that ended in a shattered heart. Twice. He'd been so overwhelmed by the painful anguish of losing his father, then his mother, and then his father again, that he was completely unprepared and uninitiated for the way he felt about Sam. He could barely comprehend the way he loved her; the way he needed her. He was terrified of losing her. But Sam was insistent on being on the front lines. As long as the MetaWars raged on, she could be ripped away from him at any moment. Every battle made that terrifying possibility more probable.

And Jonah couldn't face that.

He couldn't face losing her and never being by her side. Ultimately it was that realisation, and not the politics of the Metasphere or the battle between freedom and control, that had led him to a radical notion.

After hanging below the inflatable airship for hours, thinking through all of his options, Jonah concluded there was only one way to keep Sam alive. Only one way to keep them together. He would have to end the MetaWars before Sam became a casualty. Jonah would need to broker a truce with his enemy.

'I'm *not* moping,' he replied. 'I'm thinking. And I always think better when I fly. You know that.'

Jonah loved to fly. Originally, he could only fly in the Metasphere. But since absorbing his father's memories, he'd learned to fly aeroplanes in the real world. To Jonah, there was nothing that could compete with the sensation of flight. It was the one thing that made him feel alive and free. Slipping the surly bonds of gravity, be they real or digital, brought him peace, tranquillity and clarity of thought. He felt at home in the space between Heaven and Earth. He didn't know if it was from his own experiences, or from the borrowed, integrated memories of his dead father that now lived on in his head, but the effect was profound.

Jonah's father, Jason Delacroix, had been a life-long pilot. He'd first flown for the RAF, then for commercial airlines when they still existed, and then as a private pilot for Granger. When Jonah filtered his father's avatar, assuming his identity in the virtual world, he'd also gained all of his father's memories, allowing him to draw upon the experiences of two lifetimes.

'And I've been thinking a lot,' Jonah continued to Sam. 'I need to talk to you.'

'We're talking now,' Sam replied.

'No, just us,' Jonah insisted. He knew that any one of the Guardians, and Sam's father, especially, could be listening to their conversation. 'I'm coming up.'

Jonah shuffled himself backwards on the parallel beams of the airship's outer frame. He wanted to talk to her face to face.

'About time too,' she said with a smile in her voice. 'I'll open the hatch.'

Jonah looked back as the circular hatch opened

under the belly of the steel-grey cabin. Sam's hand, clad in an insulated white glove, waved him in.

Jonah shimmied himself under the opening. He kept hold of the beams, careful not to become gravity's victim. He might have loved to fly, but he didn't want to fall. Once he was in place under the hatch, he pulled himself up into the small utility room at the aft of the cabin.

Once inside, Sam shut the hatch and sealed it by spinning the door-wheel. Her red hair touched the shoulders of her white, tight-fitting jumpsuit. She had an athletic body that was built for killing. Sam was fierce, but she was beautiful.

Jonah took off his helmet, breathing in the re-circulated air of the cabin, and looked into Sam's green eyes. He knew she wouldn't like his proposal. But before he could confide his plan, she reached out and tousled his hair.

'That helmet presses your hair down,' she said. 'It's not natural; well, not for you.'

Jonah had always had a wave of unruly hair with a mind of its own. It was something that had often embarrassed him, and it had followed him into the Metasphere, where unlike most users who had fantastical online avatars ranging from animals to geometric shapes, Jonah had a boring 'humatar' – a digital mirror image of his real-world self – complete with unruly hair.

'Well, *I* still can't get used to *you* with long hair,' Jonah teased back.

When he'd first met Sam, when they'd literally slammed into each other in the street, her hair was short, close-cropped, but she'd grown it out since then. He had been racing in an illegal roller derby that night, planning to win enough money to pay for food for him and his mother. Sam had been on a Guardian mission with her dad: blowing up a building. It suddenly dawned on Jonah that he'd been trying to stay alive ever since.

'It's not that long,' she said defensively, whipping it back with a flick of her gloved hand. She helped Jonah remove the upper part of his auto-camouflaging body armour.

'It's, you know, mane-length,' he said with a smile. In the Metasphere, Sam's avatar was a pearly white unicorn with a bright red mane.

'Yeah, well, you're a horse's—'

'You two!' shouted a gruff voice from the door. 'What are you doing?'

'Hi, Dad,' said Sam.

Axel Kavanaugh blocked the entire metal doorframe. He narrowed his hardened eyes and glared at Jonah. 'Teenagers,' he muttered under his breath, scratching his grey beard.

'Dad, it's not what it looks like.'

Axel rolled his eyes and then stared straight

through Jonah.

'What?' Jonah asked. 'What does it look like?'

'C'mon, you two,' Axel said, shaking his head. 'T-minus thirty to deployment. We're approaching the drop zone and I want everyone on the same page. It's time to end this war.'

Axel turned and marched into the main cabin.

Jonah watched Axel stride through the bustling mission command centre, with its banks of flat-screen monitors and terminals, to the far forward section of the cabin, where the white-clad Guardian paratroopers sat in fifty rows of airline-style seating, awaiting their final instructions. Jonah wanted to be sure he was well out of Axel's earshot before sharing his intentions with Sam.

'Not like this,' Jonah said to Sam. 'I think there is another way to end this war...' He almost added 'before it's too late', but didn't. 'I'm not going to jump down there to fight, and I don't think you should either.'

Sam put her arm on Jonah's shoulder. 'We've been through this, Jonah. You make your decisions and I make mine.'

'I've made mine,' he said. 'I want to make peace with the Millennials. I'm going to propose a truce.'

'Um, did you get your O_2 mix wrong while you were dangling down there?'

Jonah swallowed a nervous laugh. He knew a truce

sounded crazy, even as he said it to Sam. But he'd convinced himself that it would be crazy not to try. There had been too much violence, too much death – on both sides. And he couldn't live with himself if something happened to Sam in the final fight.

'I'm going *in*,' he said. Jonah knew Sam understood. He was going to log into the Metasphere.

'You heard Axel,' argued Sam. 'We've got less than half an hour until we deploy. Thirty minutes until we end this war, for good.'

It wasn't long, but to Jonah, it was a chance. A chance to put a stop to violence, bloodshed and the possibility of losing Sam.

'I'm going in,' he repeated. 'I'm going to talk to the one person who can stop all of this.'

3

Matthew Granger stood on a windswept platform overlooking a scar in the Earth.

He surveyed what used to be a diamond mine. Granger wore a synthetic cold suit under a thick blue parka and clutched a thermos of real coffee, an unaffordable luxury to most people. It was well below zero and though the Arctic wind whipped at his body, he was shielded from the temperature. Of course, the suit only needed to protect his body down to his upper thighs. His prosthetic legs were titanium, replacements for the ones he had lost as a child.

Sometimes, like now, he felt the legacy of those two missing limbs. His legs actually felt cold. But he told himself that was impossible. He was probably conjuring some distant memory, perhaps the first time his parents took him skiing at Lake Tahoe. The human body, he realised, had a way of never forgetting.

And never forgiving.

Granger was overseeing the extraction of the Northern Corner, his last foothold in the Metasphere virtual world he'd created and once ran. He was standing on the precipice of a new world order. And that, and not the Arctic wind, sent a chill rushing through him. Until this day, the computer servers of this fourth corner, the real-world home of the data and code that housed over two billion users, operated secretly in the tunnels and cavities beneath the frozen surface.

Granger's black-clad Millennials transferred the last of the data from the underground servers onto the new micro-servers aboard the armada of waiting trucks. Time was of the essence. He knew the Guardians meant to attack.

Unlike sunny Havana, where the terrorists stole the Eastern Corner from him because his own people had failed to move the data, Granger was now supervising the transfer personally. He would ensure that the code that ran his remaining quarter of the Metasphere would be long gone before the Guardians attacked. All they would find would be an abandoned diamond mine.

'They're nearly here,' called a low voice. Granger turned to see a man in black body armour with tattoos peeking out behind his goggles and scarf. Jeremy Trundle, or Jez as he demanded to be called, pointed to the sky. Jez was once a Millennial who'd defected to the Guardians but secretly kept his loyalty to Granger, a loyalty Matthew Granger had exploited by playing the long game, waiting to activate his sleeper agent in his enemy's camp.

'They're on schedule,' Granger said. 'Are we?'

'Of course. The last of the data has been pulled from the old servers and Alexa has transferred everything onto the ice trucks without any interruption or outage in the Metasphere. Those micro-servers are humming and satellite uplink is live. They're ready to move south.'

Granger looked to the sky and saw the airship approach in the distance, like a tiny light bulb hanging in the air. His enemy was coming, but Granger was one step ahead.

'And the Guardians?' asked Granger. 'What do they think you're doing here?'

'Advance sniper recon,' Jez laughed. 'But they've got no idea that I'll be sniping at them. I'll pick 'em off one by one.'

'So everything's to schedule?' confirmed Granger.

'It's all in place,' said Jez. 'To end this war.'

'Then why are you talking to me?'

'Because of this,' snarled Jez, handing Granger his datapad. An encrypted message flashed on-screen in unintelligible gibberish. But the sender's avatar was unmistakeable: a teenage boy with a wry smile and unkempt black hair.

Jonah Delacroix.

Granger placed his hand on the datapad and the screen read his palm print. The gibberish turned to English. Granger stared at the strange message from his young adversary:

I PROPOSE PEACE.

'Keep a watch,' Granger ordered. 'They're coming.'

Granger turned from the platform, pushed past Jez, and descended the stairs two at a time. His titanium feet clanked against the steel steps.

'Where are you going?' Jez called.

Matthew Granger didn't need to explain himself to anyone. He was a maker of worlds, the founder of the Metasphere. He was humanity's only hope for a safe, stable and secure online future.

'I'm going in,' he said to himself. 'I'm going to talk to the one person who thinks he can stop all of this.'

4

Jonah opened his digital eyes to survey the wispy cloud he was floating on.

Of course, there was no cloud, and he wasn't really floating. It was a digital illusion. Jonah was experiencing a digital reality created by the interface of his brain's neural-synapses and the Metasphere's programming code. When the brain connected directly to the Metasphere, the brain believed that Jonah Delacroix, the digital humatar, was standing on a soft tuft of greyish white cloud. It felt real because the Metasphere was a five-sensory experience. It looked, smelled, tasted, felt and sounded real. That's what made the Metasphere so compelling, and to some, so addictive. That's what made it a better alternative to the crowded and confusing real world.

Jonah's exit halo, a golden ring that hovered nearby, was his only doorway back to the real world. It hung in the air behind him as he waited for Matthew Granger to appear.

Jonah didn't have to wait long. A second halo materialised, hovering opposite him above the cloud. And through it crawled a large, black spider. This was the most famous – most infamous – avatar in the virtual world; that of its founder, its creator, Matthew Granger.

The spider walked slowly towards Jonah and pressed its hairy face into his. Jonah wanted to step back from the grotesque, giant insect, but he was determined to show no fear and no hesitation.

'I accept your proposal,' said Granger's avatar in the calm, calculating voice that Jonah had come to fear and resent.

'What?' choked Jonah.

He had been expecting a debate, a negotiation. He'd been expecting Granger to spring one of his logic puzzles; twisting the truth and attempting to make Jonah question his resolve.

'You propose peace,' said Granger, 'and I accept.'

Jonah didn't know what to say. For a moment, he simply stared at the spider and wondered if he could have ended the fighting months earlier. Too many people had died on both sides of the war in the conflict for control over the Metasphere.

'Now, shall I outline the terms of the truce?' Granger asked. But it wasn't really a question.

'Terms?' asked Jonah, his mind still reeling from Granger's sudden, if conditional, acceptance of peace.

'Did you expect an unconditional surrender?'

'I didn't know—'

'I thought I taught you to play the long game, Jonah.'

Jonah had gone to Granger for help when he fled the Reborn in Miami Beach. The dead had risen. Thousands of Uploaded – the immortal avatars of people who'd chosen to sacrifice their real bodies in order to live forever online – had escaped the Metasphere and usurped the bodies of the living, calling themselves the *Reborn*.

They had stolen the bodies of living users, including Sam. It was a conflict that pitted Jonah against his father, who had stolen a body to 'live' again in the real world.

Out of desperation, Jonah had turned to Granger to contain these new immortals. On board his superboat, the *Marin Avenger*, Granger had lectured Jonah on the virtue of patience and the foolishness of acting impulsively (as Jonah often did), to play, as Granger put it, 'the long game'. But back then, Jonah was too late to understand the nature of his long game. The Millennials weren't interested in containing the dead; they were interested in exterminating them.

'I just want peace,' Jonah said. He was tired of war. He was sickened by death and dismemberment. He wanted the world, both worlds, to be free; but he desperately hoped there was another way to achieve it. 'I want the fighting to end.'

'As do I,' said Granger. 'Peace is the long game, Jonah. It's the natural state of things. An object in motion is in conflict with its environment. It will eventually come to a rest. As will this war between the Millennials and Guardians. It will eventually come to rest. I believe the Millennials will prevail. The Guardians believe they will prevail. It's what is called asymmetry.'

'A-what?' asked Jonah.

'A-sim-meh-tree,' enunciated Granger as if he were speaking to a child. 'So much for the world-famous Chang Academy education,' he scoffed. 'Each side believes something different and is willing to continue to fight, to kill, to murder, until they are proven right. But you, Jonah – you and I together – can stop all of this. Right here, right now. We can put the object to rest. We can achieve the natural state.'

'How?' asked Jonah, waiting for the catch. With Granger, there was always a catch. He knew Granger was still playing his own long game.

'I keep the Northern Corner, and the Guardians can keep the rest.'

'That's it? And we just stop? Stop fighting, stop—'

'I know the Guardians have forces approaching the Northern Corner right now. Perhaps, Jonah, you are with them?'

Jonah forced himself not to speak.

It would be a mistake to reveal his RWL, his Real World Location. He'd learned the painful lesson of revealing his physical whereabouts to the virtual world. It was that very mistake that led Granger's assassins to shoot up his bus-flat, and to destroy the City Tower where he'd logged in. It was Jonah's mistake that buried his mother in rubble while he soared to safety.

And now Jonah was negotiating peace with the man who was responsible for sending the bombs that murdered his mother. A dark part of him felt as Sam did, that he wanted to kill Matthew Granger. He was still angry, still furious; and he wasn't sure these emotions would ever leave him. He wasn't sure he even wanted them to. But Jonah had seen so much violence, so much death, that he knew in his head – and in his heart – that more death would only lead to more murder. It was a seemingly unstoppable cycle that Jonah knew he had to stop.

'It doesn't matter where I am,' said Jonah. 'But there is no need for death today.'

Jonah wanted to fight for a future where nobody had to lose their family to violence. He wanted a future free from battles, wars and the perpetual cycle of hatred. He wanted the world to cross the frontier from war to peace. He wanted to push the world across the freedom frontier. And stopping himself from killing his enemy, Jonah decided, was the first step.

'Let me get this right,' said Jonah. 'You keep the Northern Corner, and the Guardians keep the servers we've already acquired—'

'Stolen.'

'Stolen from a thief,' said Jonah. 'You took those servers by force from the governments that were—'

'Bankrupt,' spat the spider. 'Financially and morally. They were running the Metasphere, the world I created, into the ground. I saved the Metasphere from certain system-failure and to repay me for my salvation, the Guardians attacked and stole three-quarters of my world from me.'

'That's the way you see it,' said Jonah.

'That's the way it is!' shouted Granger. 'You killed and you slaughtered to take those servers. You sully the memories of the people you've murdered and you—'

'Since when did you care about *the people*?'

'Jonah, that's all I've ever cared about. I created the Metasphere to give the people of this ruined planet an escape, an alternative to the real world. I created the Metasphere for the people. My world is free from hunger, from pain, and while the Uploaded were with us, free from loss. It was a perfect world until the Guardians decided to rip it apart, corner by corner. And if I can hold onto even one quarter of that world, to give shelter to humanity from a real world that only offers suffering and cruelty, then I accept your proposal of peace. I accept, Jonah, because I can still provide my perfect world to the people.'

'OK,' said Jonah, taken aback by how passionately Granger spoke about his purpose. That was the thing about Matthew Granger, he kept surprising Jonah. 'I accept those terms.'

'Of course,' added Granger, 'I am assuming you speak on authority. I am assuming you are sanctioned to make this settlement.'

Jonah willed himself not to blink, but his digital doppelgänger betrayed him.

'You're playing a dangerous game, Jonah. You wanted to see what I'd say before proposing peace to the Guardians. You know, deep down, they are warmongers. They would rather fight than settle.'

Jonah caught himself nodding. He knew Granger was right. He believed he had a better chance of convincing the Guardians to cease their attack if Granger was already at the table.

'Did you know, Jonah, that the Millennial Corporation is a private company?'

A look of confusion and indifference crossed Jonah's face. 'What are you talking about?'

'It's a private company,' Granger repeated. 'With just one shareholder: *me*. It's not the most valuable company in the world, that's SynCorp, the oil sands company run by my…by my friend. The Millennial Corporation is the world's most valuable *private* company. But what if it weren't?'

'Valuable?'

'Private,' replied Granger. 'The Guardians have long argued that they fight for freedom, for openness and for transparency. Well, Jonah, today I'm going to beat them at their own game. I'm going public!'

Jonah had no idea what Granger was talking about. He'd heard of SynCorp, of course, the company that controlled most of the world's remaining oil; but Jonah didn't know anything about business or how companies were owned. His confusion must have shown on his digital face.

'I'm going to offer one share in the Millennial Corporation to every Metasphere user online today,' Granger explained. 'I am going to do the one thing that Guardians promise but never deliver. I am literally going to hand the Metasphere over to the people. This is my legacy, Jonah. This is my greatest gift to humanity; my perfect world for the people, in the hands of the people, owned by the people.'

'You're going to bribe everyone to your way?'

'No, Jonah, I'm going to give every user a stake in their future. You could say I am now more Guardian than the Guardians. And if you and your army attack the Northern Corner, then you'll be more Millennial than the Millennials.'

Before Jonah could argue, the spider turned and dived through his exit halo. The golden ring quickly depixelated and disappeared, leaving Jonah alone on his cloud, his head spinning with confusion.

5

Jonah tried to shrug off the familiar wave of nausea.

But the dizziness and disorientation that marked the transition between virtual and real worlds shook him every time. Although he'd passed between worlds enough times to know that the feeling would soon fade. He blinked his eyes, readying them to see again.

Slowly, Sam's face blurred into view. She was just an inch from Jonah's cheek and he could feel her breath on his neck. She held her hair back from her face as she reached around Jonah's body to disconnect his Direct Interface cable from his back.

'Thank you,' Jonah said quietly. She was being kind to him and he was overwhelmed by the urge to kiss her. But he didn't.

'Don't thank me,' she said, pulling back to reveal Axel, Bradbury and four other angry-looking Guardians standing over him. 'They heard every word.'

'Traitor,' barked Bradbury. He was a burly man with a moustache and permanent scowl. Bradbury was the Guardian's security expert, and Jonah always suspected that he viewed him as a threat to that security. Perhaps Jonah had just proved him right.

'We should throw him off this airship!' growled Yansen, one of the Guardian commanders.

As he blinked the last of the nausea away, Jonah spotted Mallia, Reilly and Torek as part of the lynch mob flanking Axel and Bradbury. The senior Guardian operatives were staring at Jonah with a mix of disappointment and disgust.

'He's either a traitor,' stated Reilly, pushing up his glasses, 'or hopelessly naive.'

'Either way he's a liability,' declared Mallia. 'And he's got to go.'

Sam stood between Jonah and the seething group. 'Not one of you touches Jonah!' she said, staring them down.

'Sam's right,' added Axel. 'If anyone's throwing the kid overboard, it's me.'

'Dad!' protested Sam. She helped Jonah to his unsteady feet.

'Jonah,' said Axel, pushing his face to Jonah's nose. 'What were you thinking in there? Wait, don't tell me: you *weren't*.'

'That's not fair,' said Sam. 'Jonah was just—'

'You knew about this?' Axel asked his daughter. 'We're on the cusp of taking the Northern Corner, ending the Millennials forever, and you let him attempt appeasement?'

'Granger wants peace,' Jonah said, planting his feet firmly on the floor. 'And we should too.'

'Granger wants *control*,' Axel shouted. 'That's what he's always wanted. And when one man wants control so badly that he'll kill for it, well…that's what we've all pledged to guard against.'

'Or are you not a Guardian?' asked Bradbury.

Jonah wanted to explain why peace was worth pursuing, but deep down, and maybe not even that deep, he feared that Matthew Granger's accusations might be right. Maybe the Guardians were warmongers who would rather fight than settle. But there was no more time to consider this; shouts of excitement from the forward cabin interrupted the discussion. Torek darted to the screens of the command centre and pulled up a dozen news feeds.

'Something's happening in the Metasphere,' he confirmed. 'Something big.'

'Granger's going public,' said Jonah. 'Just like he promised.'

'*Threatened*,' snapped Axel.

'Why would he give away control in his company if he's so obsessed with controlling everything himself?' asked Bradbury, studying the screens.

'IPO,' confirmed Mallia from the opposite terminal. 'And it's gone viral.'

Jonah looked over her shoulders to scan the announcement on-screen:

MILLENNIAL CORPORATION INITIAL PUBLIC OFFERING

MATTHEW GRANGER WILL GRANT ONE SHARE IN THE MILLENNIAL CORPORATION TO EVERY REGISTERED METASPHERE USER ONLINE.

EACH SHARE SHALL CARRY FULL VOTING RIGHTS AND PROVISIONS.

READ FULL TERMS & CONDITIONS.

CLICK <u>HERE</u> TO ACCEPT.

Reilly clicked through to a page of legalese language that Jonah didn't understand.

'It looks legit,' confirmed Reilly. 'I used to work in finance, and I can tell you this is the IPO of the millennium.'

'And it's live,' said Mallia.

'An initial public offering right before our attack,' growled Bradbury. 'It's not a coincidence.'

'Nothing is with Granger,' said Axel. 'He's not naive or idealistic like some people.'

Jonah ignored the jibe, but still felt its sting.

Torek tapped a screen, enlarging a bar graph that was growing exponentially. 'That's the total Metasphere population,' he explained. 'People are flocking online at rates I've never seen. Everyone wants a share.'

Jonah watched as the troopers in the forward cabin scrambled for their datapads and started to plug themselves in. He couldn't believe the Guardians were salivating at the chance to own part of the very organisation they despised.

'Everyone, indeed,' repeated Sam. She strode towards the seating area and yelled at the soldiers. 'Are you crazy? Don't go online, we're minutes away from the drop zone!'

But the Guardian warriors ignored her warning as they rushed to snag a share of the Millennial Corporation.

'This is our chance,' claimed one man, plugging himself in. 'Back in a jiffy.'

'Don't do it!' called Axel, but his command was drowned out by the greedy troopers.

As the paratroopers spoke over one another, defending their choice to log on, Jonah realised they had a reason to take up their share of their enemy's company:

'—we can take over from within—'

'—full voting rights—'

'—and then vote him out, not smoke him out—'

The stir of excitement was quickly replaced with the silence of metatrancing as over half of the soldiers logged in and slipped away from the real world.

'Idiots,' cursed Axel.

'I can't believe these guys,' said Sam, shaking her head.

'Maybe they're right,' said Jonah. 'If every Guardian owned a share of Millennial then we could change it from the inside.'

'It's a ruse,' said Axel to his command team. 'Granger's up to something, and it can't be good.'

'Granger wants this all to end,' said Jonah.

'It's a distraction,' sneered Bradbury. 'One we don't need on the cusp of battle.'

'But maybe this is his way of stopping the battle,' said Jonah.

Even as he uttered the words, it dawned on Jonah – from experience – that there was always more to Matthew Granger than his surface intentions. He played the long game, and Jonah wished he knew what it was.

Alexa Cannon looked out over the endless ice road stretching south.

'We're en route,' she said into the radio. 'See you tomorrow.'

'Tomorrow is our day,' replied Jez, his voice crackling over the radio, but his tone unwavering.

Alexa sat in the passenger seat of the first of twenty-four modified freight trucks carrying the entire Northern Corner data-set. Behind her, her boss, Matthew Granger, metatranced in the sleep-space of the cab. He had joined the convoy in a hurry, eager to log on. The trucks, of course, had a continual satellite uplink so that the Metasphere service was seamless and uninterrupted during the transition.

Alexa was curious about what he was doing inside the Metasphere, and was tempted to spy on him though his datapad, but she kept her temptation at bay. He was obsolete software, a relic of a soon to be exterminated era.

Matthew Granger might have been her boss, but she served another master.

She smiled to herself, spreading her ruby grin wide, as the truck rumbled south. After twenty years of following, the latter four-fifths of her entire life, she could reveal to the world whom her true master was.

Alexa peered back at Granger's helpless body, twitching gently as his mind interfaced with the virtual world he'd built to be an escape from the real world.

I could kill him now, she thought to herself.

Granger would never see it coming. His body would die and his avatar would simply depixelate out of existence. She'd spent many hours, over many years, fantasising about ending Matthew Granger's life. But her master, her 'father', had forbidden it.

Alexa was part of a bigger plan, a larger purpose. Her master's instructions were clear and she would not violate them. For Granger was about to finally help usher in a new era and her master needed him alive, for now. There was a great flood coming and Alexa had a place on the Ark. Granger had no idea that she, and many of her people, had infiltrated the Millennials at a young age. They'd risen in the organisation and earned the trust of their boss. Meanwhile others had infiltrated the Guardians and fought in the MetaWars. But their allegiance was to a higher calling, and thus they would be saved when the new era began.

They were Tomorrow's Children.

6

Granger's arachnid avatar materialised in a vast, sand-swept desert.

The only feature on the bleak, sandy landscape was a massive stone pyramid. It was a secret location hidden on the Northern Corner micro-servers. At Granger's arrangement, those physical servers were en route, via the ice-truck convoy, to Banff, Alberta – hundreds of miles south of the diamond mine.

As soon as they arrived in Banff, a once popular winter playground resort in the Rocky Mountains, the servers would be loaded onto a train to pull them through the mountains to the port city of Vancouver, where they'd be transferred to a cargo ship to sail for their final destination of Hawaii. Granger had commissioned a fortress on the island when he'd bought the state from the Chinese government, the former United States of America's largest creditor.

While Granger's physical body metatranced in the warmth of the truck's cab, guarded by his one of his most loyal Millennials, his online avatar scurried across the cracked desert.

As he approached the pyramid, a single scorpion appeared midway up the sloped side. Its stinger pulsed blue with a dangerous deconstruction virus. But it was no threat to Granger. The scorpion, an artificial intelligence of Granger's creation, scanned the spider and allowed the avatar to pass. Other intruders, if any could find this secret desert, would not be so fortunate. If an avatar hacked into this closed system, the scorpion would sting. The deconstruction virus would depixelate the user, breaking apart the avatar pixel by pixel until there was nothing left. The pyramid had an unlimited supply of scorps, and was programmed to generate one for every invading avatar. Like everything Granger designed, its elegance was in its simplicity.

He crawled up to the pinnacle of the pyramid and slid open the dusty capstone. He jumped into the dark cavity and landed on his eight legs in a vast chamber deep inside – the Imprint Chamber.

At first, the only light came from the hole at the top, but when the chamber sensed Granger's presence, the room's four stone walls, each sloping inwards to the apex above, lit up with a near-infinite number of scenes from the Metasphere. Surveying the scenes, he spied glimpses of avatars across the virtual world, in both Millennial- and Guardian-controlled territories. Here, he could watch his world through the all-seeing eyes of the exit halos.

The only furniture in the room was a massive, reclined metal chair with a red ring in place of a headrest. Granger settled his arachnid body into the chair and the ring adjusted to cover his head. Not only could the chamber show the view from each and every exit halo hovering throughout the Metasphere, but the Imprint Chair had a direct neural link to every single one. It meant that by simply thinking a thought, Granger could imprint that thought into the halos of every online avatar. He could slip a notion into a user's subconscious without them knowing.

It only takes one thought. Mine.

Once an avatar logged off through its halo, Granger's thought would be indelibly imprinted in its mind, forever.

Granger had lured over seven billion avatars online, over seventy per cent of the Earth's population. While the greedy users waited for their unearned piece of his Millennial Corporation, Granger cleared his mind and prepared to tell the world how to think. He would imprint the population with one simple notion.

Matthew Granger is in control.

That one thought, copied over seven billion times, would be his gift to the people. It would assure his command of this world and, in doing so, end the strife and struggles of the MetaWars forever. His offering wasn't just granting one share of the Millennial Corporation to the public, it was offering a piece of himself to the people. Everyone online would be under his control and would believe it so deeply, so viscerally, that they would (through persuasion or force) ensure the off-liners fell into place. *An object in motion is in conflict with its environment*, Granger reminded himself. It was time to set the world to rest.

'Population report,' he commanded to the invisible software.

A pop-up window opened beside him, showing him that the current online population of the Metasphere was 7,298,482,113. Nearly seven point three billion users online. And now Granger was going to keep seventy-five per cent of the world's human population online long enough to broadcast the imprint command.

'Access halo protocol,' he called to the air. Another pop-up opened, an operations panel that governed the exit halo operating system. He swept his spider's legs over the pop-up, indicating that he meant to issue a command to every halo. Even though the Guardians had taken control of three of his server farms, the exit halo protocol ran through the underlying code of the Metasphere and was powered from the Northern Corner servers.

It was time to reassert control.

He looked at the glowing icon of a single halo, a golden circle. With two of his furry appendages, he pinched the circle closed; sealing shut every single exit halo. He had just trapped 7,298,482,113 live users inside his world. And when he let them out again, they would awake in the real world with a new thought buried in their subconscious.

'Matthew Granger is in control,' he said clearly, his voice echoing off the quadrant of walls. 'Matthew Granger is in control.'

'If you believe that,' said a deep voice from behind him, 'then you don't understand the meaning of *control*.'

Granger turned, unwilling to believe that anyone could be inside his secret chamber. But his disbelief turned to shock when he saw the one avatar he thought he would never see again.

The red dragon.

Jonah watched the screens of the airborne Guardian command centre fill with error reports.

'Something's very wrong,' observed Torek.

At first hundreds, then thousands, and then hundreds of thousands of users were logging complaints. Their exit halos were not working.

'It's happening everywhere,' observed Jonah, scanning the messages coming from all over the Metasphere. 'People can't log off.'

'Give us eyes,' ordered Axel.

'Where?' asked Mallia.

'Anywhere,' said Sam.

Jonah tapped an error message from a flower-shaped avatar, a rose. It linked to the flower's in-world location, where Jonah spotted it banging its leaves against an exit halo that should have been glowing. The usually vacant inner circle looked like it had been painted black. It was completely opaque. 'He's trapped,' said Jonah.

He scanned another angry error message and tapped its avatar, peering into a lush jungle landscape. Frustrated avatars pounded on their unresponsive halos. Instead of offering a welcoming glow, the halos were dull and their holes closed off with a black circle.

'Somewhere else?' asked Sam.

Mallia pulled up a live feed from a sun-soaked beach, but the scene was the same. The defunct halos hovered in the digital air, sealed shut. The avatars were panicking, screaming with outrage and fright. Some dragged the halos to the ground, attempting to jump into them, wrongly believing that gravity might assist their escape. Others thrashed their digital bodies against the black barrier that kept them from the real world.

'They're all trapped,' Jonah remarked unnecessarily. 'Every one of them.'

'Granger lured them inside with his IPO and now he's trapped them,' said Axel. 'What's he up to?'

'He's gone too far this time,' growled Bradbury.

'There's over seven billion people in there,' said Sam. 'He's got almost three-quarters of the human population stuck inside.'

'Including half of our paratroopers,' said Bradbury.

Jonah looked to the forward cabin. The soldiers who'd logged on were still metatranced. 'But why?' asked Jonah. He didn't understand what Matthew Granger could hope to gain from trapping users in the Metasphere. 'It doesn't make any sense.'

Suddenly, the airship's loudspeaker crackled to life.

'This is Captain Zegar,' announced the voice. 'We're approaching the drop zone. We'll be directly over the mine complex in T-minus five.'

For a moment, amid the chaos and panic of the Metasphere, Jonah had almost forgotten the impending drop. The Guardians were due to parachute down to the Northern Corner in five minutes.

Jonah felt betrayed by Granger. He'd agreed to a truce while planning to tempt users online and to trap them. But Jonah also felt confused. He couldn't understand why Granger would want to lock the users in.

'This is why we fight, Jonah,' said Axel. 'Because every time we give Granger a break, he escalates this war. He's gone too far this time, and if we won't stop him, there's no one else to stand up to his tyranny.'

'You know he's right,' Sam said, putting her hand on Jonah's shoulder, looking him straight in the eye. 'It's time to fight.'

'Are the ground forces in place?' asked Axel.

'We can see them from here,' replied Bradbury. He

leaned over Mallia, took control of the computer and pulled up the live images from the camera under the airship's belly. Down below, hundreds of snowmobiles powered over the ice, racing towards the Northern Corner. 'They're on schedule. We can't let them down.'

'But half of the paratroopers are stuck in there,' said Jonah. The Guardians' forces were diminished before the fighting had even commenced. 'You can't go ahead with the strike.'

'We go to war with the army we've got, not the one we want. Everyone, fall out,' ordered Axel. 'Oxygen masks on, parachutes prepped, and weapons to the ready. It's time.'

Axel led the Guardians back into the jump room at the aft of the cabin. Jonah grabbed for Sam as she turned to follow her father.

'Please don't go,' he pleaded. 'Something about this isn't right.'

'I know,' she said. 'That's why we have to stop him. Now and forever.' Sam put her helmet on and tapped her right ear. 'You keep in touch from up here.' She gestured to the top of her helmet, where two tiny cameras were embedded in the hard plastic, one facing forward, the other back. 'And be my eyes in the back of my head.'

She squeezed Jonah's hand. He looked at Sam, but in her reflective visor, all Jonah could see was himself looking back. His worried eyes, the deep frown on his forehead. He looked anxious and afraid. He feared that he'd never see Sam again. He tried to rationalise that fear away. *She's been in battles before*, he told himself. But it wasn't enough comfort. She'd been in battles before, and she'd survived. Now, she should quit while she was ahead. While she was still alive.

As the armed Guardians filed out of the crew cabin and into the jump room, Jonah stood near the computer controls wishing they had all quit while they were ahead. When the last of the conscious Guardians left the cabin and sealed the door, a sense of dread gnawed at Jonah's soul. Something wasn't right, but the Guardians were too hungry for battle to see it.

He only hoped that he could spot it, from high above, before it was too late.

7

Granger examined the hulking digital dragon.

There was no mistaking its signature three horns on its snout, almost luminescent scales and massive wingspan.

'Jason Delacroix,' said Granger, speaking of the dead.

The dragon laughed, breathing out a stream of fire that circled around the room and vanished in a poof.

'For one who claims to be the world's smartest person, Matthew,' replied the dragon, 'you are a remarkably linear thinker.'

The voice was older than Granger's former pilot, and more arrogant. This wasn't Jason Delacroix. This was an imposter. But who was masquerading as Jonah's dead father?

'Who are you in there?' asked Granger, still reeling from the invasion of his supposedly secret chamber.

'I am the world's salvation,' the dragon replied in a calm, controlled voice. 'I am the father of Tomorrow's Children and I am here to save humanity.'

'From what? From me? Because my world is salvation, salvation from the real world—'

The dragon laughed again, filling the room with fire once more.

'I am relieved to see that the size of your ego, Matthew, has not been exaggerated. You believe yourself to be at the centre of your own web, while in fact, you are caught in mine.'

Granger spied his exit halo in the corner between two sloping walls, and noticed that it was still open. He'd programmed it that way, of course. While every halo in the Metasphere was locked, his, and his alone, would remain porous. Granger's spider form rose from the Imprint Chair, moving in front of his exit halo in case he needed a quick getaway. A part of him was tempted to dive straight through it, but he wasn't about to flee from this common hacker. He, after all, was Matthew Granger; he was in control.

'What do you want?' Granger asked. But the answer was obvious. They both looked at the Imprint Chair at the same time. It was the one device powerful enough to tell the world what to think.

'I simply want to save humanity,' the dragon repeated. 'From itself.'

The dragon pounced, faster than Granger had expected. Granger tried to seize the chair, but the dragon picked the spider up with its hind claws, ripping him away. Granger kicked and fought with all eight legs, but the dragon flapped his wings and suspended the spider in the air.

The dragon laughed. 'There is no use running to your mind-control chair. I've reprogrammed it so that only my avatar sequence commands it.'

'Put me down!' Granger spat.

The dragon obeyed, throwing him against a wall and smashing him into a sea of scenes filled with angry and scared avatars. Granger fell to the cold, stone ground. When he tried to move, all eight of his limbs were locked down; useless.

'Release me!' Granger shouted. He was held to the floor by some kind of immobilising code.

'And you are as demanding as your autobiography suggests,' said the dragon. 'But while you're used to doing the talking, today you will slump in that corner and listen. I want you to witness Tomorrow's rising.'

Granger decided to keep quiet. His protests were only giving the dragon more platforms to grandstand on. His exit halo was just across the room, but he couldn't move.

The dragon gestured to his invisible inventory space and activated an app that Granger recognised. A glowing red circle materialised on the ground. Granger knew the app because he had designed it. It was the Metasphere-wide broadcast system used to speak to everyone online at once. He'd used it twice recently. The first time was when he announced his escape from the California prison that had detained him for three years. The second time was when he announced his extractor virus as the Millennial solution to the scourge of the Uploaded. Now, this mysterious red dragon had control over his broadcaster and was about to address the entire virtual world.

Granger had dropped into the Imprint Chamber to tell the world that he was in control, but now it was obvious that he had lost control. For all of his scenario planning, all of his fail-safe backups, Matthew Granger was being outwitted by a ghost, a shell really, from his past.

He didn't know where this self-styled saviour came from, but for the first time in Granger's life – or more accurately the first time since the accident – Granger felt completely out of control. And it scared him.

The dragon stepped into the red circle, straightened his wings, and spoke to the billions of online users.

'People of the Metasphere, I offer the Earth the salvation it needs. But that salvation must come from your sacrifice.'

Jonah peered out of a cabin window to watch the paratroopers shrink as they fell to Earth.

Their silver parachutes opened as they glided down towards the ice-bound island, looking like candy wrappers floating on the wind. A pang of guilt shook Jonah's body. Here he was, safe in the sky, abstaining on principle, while Sam and the others were floating down to fight – and possibly die – for their cause.

'Who is that?' gasped Mallia from the bank of control screens.

Jonah thought the worst: that someone's chute had failed to open. He pulled himself from the window to look over Mallia's shoulders, hoping it wasn't Sam. But Mallia wasn't watching the live feeds of the paratroopers' helmet-mounted cameras, she was watching the Metasphere.

One avatar dominated the screen, an avatar Jonah thought he'd never see again but for in his dreams and in his memories: his father.

'Dad?' he said quietly, touching the screen.

A thousand questions raced through Jonah's mind. His father, or at least the Uploaded echo of the man he once was, should be thousands of miles above Earth, orbiting the planet in a satellite that Jonah had helped to launch. Jason Delacroix's final resting place was supposed to have been beyond the reaches of the atmosphere. Up there, safe from strife and conflict, soared a digital ecosystem where his father and countless others existed as one communal mind. And yet there he was. At once Jonah felt excited by the possibility of his father's return but also confused by how it could be possible.

It's impossible, he told himself.

Jonah had led his father and all of the Reborn out of their stolen, mortal bodies and back into the Metasphere. But in liberating the bodies that the

Reborn had occupied, Jonah had put the digital Uploaded at risk. And so he and Sam mounted a daring plan to extract them from Granger's clutches. Then something remarkable, miraculous even, had happened. The Uploaded had fused into one consciousness. Together, as a higher form of intelligence, Jonah knew there was nowhere safe for their kind on Earth. So along with some of the liberated users, pirates who used to be rocketeers, Jonah had launched the dead closer to Heaven.

He missed his father every single day, but took solace in knowing that he was up there, orbiting the planet in a satellite; that he was happy in his digital immortality.

Now, seeing the avatar again, Jonah felt betrayed by the universe.

How could his dad be back in the Metasphere?

But then the avatar spoke, and Jonah knew it was his father in looks alone. He felt overwhelmed by disappointment and relief. The two emotions quickly morphed into anger.

'People of the Metasphere, I offer the Earth the salvation it needs. But that salvation must come from your sacrifice.'

Jonah felt himself shuddering with outrage. Someone else was speaking through the vessel of his father's avatar.

Mallia randomly pulled up eight scenes from the

Metasphere. The red dragon was everywhere at once; a trick Jonah recalled Matthew Granger used to broadcast his spider-avatar self to the whole of the virtual world. The imposter hovered in the air, speaking to the entire online population.

'You hide in this world of make-believe while our real world, our one Earth, suffers. It is our only home and it is exhausted. And yet its plight is ignored by all of you who'd rather play pretend than heal the real. I am here to ensure our planet's cycle of life continues.'

His voice was low, calm and assured. It wasn't his father's voice – and yet something in the dragon's cadence was eerily familiar. Jonah swore he had heard it before, but he couldn't place it.

'I have control over your exit halos, and in forty-eight hours I will sever every halo, cutting your virtual self off from your real-world body. I am giving you this notice so that you may say your goodbyes and commune with your loved ones – and so that you may Upload yourself. Be reassured, I have full control over the Metasphere's source code and have reinstated the Uploading protocol. In fact, I have released a new app, the rapid Uploading pill.'

The dragon held up a small capsule that pulsed with a soft, turquoise glow.

'It needs no prescription and the effects are immediate. And final. There is no Island any more because there is no need for a specific place for the dead. In two days' time, the entire Metasphere will be taken off-line, and will be the sole domain of the dead. And with you, the seven billion people currently online, purged from the planet, the Earth will begin to repair itself.'

The dragon flapped his right wing, throwing a translucent digital clock into the corner of every Metasphere screen – a countdown. The number started at 48:00:00 and in a breath had clicked down to 47:59:59.

'It is my duty to save humanity from its past. For its future. It is my duty to make way for Tomorrow's Children.'

And then the dragon disappeared, leaving the Metasphere silent and stunned.

Jonah was unable to speak. In an instant, everything had changed. The crucible of conflict that had consumed the Millennials and Guardians had just been overturned by a mysterious man cloaked in Jonah's father's avatar. This man, whoever he was, had announced the annihilation of most of the human race.

8

In the pyramid chamber, Granger watched helplessly as the dragon declared genocide.

He was stuck, immobilised in one place, but his brain didn't stop turning. Granger organised his thoughts systematically as he'd trained himself to do. He broke down the threat into its core pieces: who, where, how. He assumed that the whole thing wasn't a hoax. The Metasphere, and the internet before it, had seen its share of horrifying hoaxes. But this was different.

The dragon stepped out of the red circle, lowered his neck, and taunted Granger. 'The countdown to salvation has begun.'

This is real, Granger told himself. He quickly calculated a list of options: he could offer this dragon money, find his RWL, hack the Metasphere code to banish the dragon, reprogram the Imprint Chamber back to his control, or conjure a more powerful deconstruction virus and simply destroy this offending avatar.

But Granger, still strapped into invisible shackles, didn't have a chance to act on any of his options.

'I am salvation,' the dragon said quietly, picking up

Granger's exit halo. The dragon held it in the air and the halo glowed, anticipating its owner. 'You and I have the only two functional exit halos, and because you have given me all of this—'

'I haven't given you anything, you stole—'

'Because you have given me all of this,' the dragon repeated, 'I will let you witness my salvation from the real world.'

The dragon slammed the halo over Granger. The portal between the two worlds enveloped him, plunging him into the temporary darkness between virtual and real life. A wave of nausea hit. Once the blackness faded, Granger opened his blurry eyes in the real world.

He blinked rapidly, refocusing his vision. Alexa wore goggles, which kept her long, black hair from straying in the wind. The Arctic gust assaulted his face and as his full sight returned, he realised he was hanging halfway out of the truck's door. The icy road sped by beneath him. His face was pummelled by shards of ice, shooting up from the steel-treaded tyres.

'Alexa, pull me back inside!' he shouted.

But the young Millennial woman, a protégée of Granger's since the Millennial Corporation had legally adopted her as a child, simply stretched her bright red lips. It wasn't a friendly smile. Granger recognised it as one of his own: a predator's grin.

'And now you know,' she said coolly.

'Pull me ba—'

Alexa leaned down over Granger. At first, he thought she was going to kiss him. He grimaced; it wasn't that she was unattractive, just that he'd never allowed himself to see his people as anything more than what they were: pieces on his chessboard. But he needn't have worried. She leaned in close to his face, the whipping wind and ice catching them both, and said, 'Now you know who is really in control; who has always been in control.'

'The Guardians?' asked Granger.

He realised now, too late, that Alexa was a mole. She was a double agent, a spy deeply embedded in his organisation. It was his chessboard, but somehow the Guardians had control over one of his pawns.

'Not even close,' she said. 'The Guardians are no more, and all of the Millennials who are not with us have been eliminated.'

'Impossible!' Granger shouted. 'I have offices all around the world and—'

'And we have people embedded in each of them,' she said, erasing her smile.

Alexa reached up under his parka to his lower back and twisted out his Direct Interface connection. He felt the plastic plug pop out of his flesh. He reacted quickly, reaching for the truck's doors, but Alexa grabbed both of his titanium legs and shoved him out of the moving truck.

The world turned upside down as Granger fell headfirst and bounced on the hard ice, his left shoulder bearing the brunt of the impact.

He rolled, toppling over himself as he slid off the main road into the dense snow banks, feeling the packed ice reverberate in his bones. Finally he managed to stretch his cyber-kinetic legs to stop his wild somersaults, and he sat up in the snow watching the convoy rumble south. He gave himself no time to recover, hoisting himself back onto the narrow ice road and making chase. His legs, attached to the stumps, allowed him to run three times as fast as an unenhanced man. He was the fastest man on two legs. But even at twenty miles per hour, Granger couldn't catch the convoy escaping at triple his speed.

But Granger knew the ice road was a temporary tether to the tundra further south. It was cracked and uneven, and so he figured the truck would have to slow, or stop at some point on the treacherous journey back to terra firma. He would keep running.

As Granger fought to see through the ice kicked up by the convoy's wheels, he noticed something spilling out of the back of the last truck. They looked like bowling balls, bouncing on the ice. He realised, almost too late, that the balls weren't spilling out, they were being thrown out. And they weren't balls.

They were bombs.

The explosions began to detonate with pops and

crackles. Soon, a wall of flames and smoke cut Granger off from the fleeing trucks. When he heard the loud crunching sound, he thought that the traitors had rolled out more bombs – bigger ones, perhaps. But then he understood: the deep, low crunch was something much more dangerous. The cracking of ice.

In front of Granger, a large fault line zigzagged in the road, cutting it in two and severing the icy link between island and mainland.

The ice before him fell away, creating a chasm of at least fifty feet of freezing water. He looked down into its depths. There was no way he could swim across; he'd die from hypothermia almost immediately. He was stuck on the island.

Granger thought quickly. His only hope was that there was a spare, functional snowmobile back at the mine. At high enough speed, and at constant trajectory, a snowmobile should be able to drive on water; but it was risky. His private plane was there, of course, if it was still intact. But there was nobody left to fly it.

He was a long way from the Northern Corner, however he calculated that he could get back there before morning. He was still in his blue, fur-lined hooded parka with fuel-cell-powered thermal bodysuit, but the temperature was dropping and he needed to get out of the cold before nightfall.

As he marched on the long, lonely road back to the

diamond mine, the long-time home of the Northern Corner, he knew everything had changed.

If what Alexa said was true, then everything he'd built, his Millennial organisation, a global movement for order in the face of chaos, had been stripped away. He couldn't fully fathom that possibility. He'd always felt like the all-knowing spider at the centre of his web of ambitions. Only now, he felt afraid and alone.

Of course, he wasn't completely alone. His thoughts turned to the life he'd been looking forward to creating after he'd won the MetaWars. He'd set his sights beyond war, beyond fighting for his rightful place atop the pyramid of human existence. There was someone, someone special, he'd met, befriended and romanced that he was hoping to share the spoils of war with.

Her name was Louise Thorne, she was a fellow captain of industry, and he'd built the digital fortress on Hawaii to tempt her to relocate her office to his island stronghold. She was the last purveyor of oil in the western world and Granger figured she could do that from just about anywhere.

He looked up to the grey sky. Granger was trying to imagine himself and Louise on a sun-soaked Hawaiian beach, controlling information and oil – the two dominant resources of both worlds – but he couldn't hold the fantasy in his mind.

Instead, he saw the sky filling with silver parachutes.

The Guardians.

He thought of Jonah and his misguided hopes of seeking peace. But the warriors raining from above signalled that there was no peace. There was only war.

9

Jonah watched the seven outbuildings of the diamond mine rush into view.

He was glued to Sam's live feed from her helmet camera. He toggled to her rear camera and looked at the airship, floating overhead but getting smaller. She was falling away from him.

He was safe in the sky while she was rushing down towards battle. The paratroopers, now two hundred and not four hundred, were the advance team. Their job was to secure the points of entry to the mine tunnels below where the servers were stored. Meanwhile the ground attack approached quickly from the east. Four hundred heavily armed Guardians on half as many snowmobiles flew over the iced-over lake directly below the airship. Jonah knew they'd land on the shore of the mine in a matter of minutes, storming through the openings that the paratroopers were tasked to create.

A rumble filled the sky, pulling Jonah's attention from Sam's cameras. Had a rocket struck the dirigible? No – the airship was still steady, still level. He was safe, for now.

Jonah rushed to the window to see a massive circle

of fire surround the diamond mine, creating a moat of icy water around the complex. The hard surface of the frozen lake cracked and disintegrated right in front of the approaching snowmobiles. The ground forces were plunging into the water.

Jonah ran back to the screen, pulling up the imagery from the camera underneath the cabin. He zoomed in and flinched at the sight – all of the Guardian snowmobiles swallowed up by Arctic water. Four hundred Guardians, the entire ground attack force, fallen into the freezing moat surrounding the Northern Corner.

Jonah swiped the screens to pull up the camera feeds from the ground forces. Water lapped onto the screens before descending into darkness. Unlike the paratroopers who were wearing airtight oxygen masks, the ground troops were only wearing goggles and facemasks under their helmets. Weighted down by Kevlar suits and ammunition, they didn't stand a chance against the cruelty of gravity. Jonah made the mistake of switching on the audio feed and his ears were barraged by hundreds of screams, gulps and desperate cries, all muted in a matter of moments as the Guardians drowned.

Jonah swiped the screen away and pulled up Sam's video feed.

'Sam,' Jonah called into the microphone, watching his best friend's point of view as she rapidly approached the mine from the sky, 'the ground force is gone! They're all gone!'

'Come again?' Sam said, touching down behind what looked like a radar tower. She was joined by three other paratroopers, all bigger than her.

'The ice surface of the lake exploded and they're in the water. They're gone, Sam. All of them.'

'We have to push on,' called Axel's voice over the radio. 'We're here now, we can't retreat.'

'Dad!' called Sam. 'Are you sure?'

'Axel, please don't!' shouted Jonah. 'It's a trap. The ground forces aren't coming. I said, they're gone! You're on your own down there.'

Jonah's worst fears were coming true. He'd failed to stop the conflict and now Sam was rushing into some kind of dangerous trap. He'd hoped that by staying aboard the airship, he might have convinced Sam to do the same. But maybe Mallia was right; maybe he was naive.

'I don't like this,' said Bradbury. 'The variables have changed.'

'Everything's changed,' urged Jonah. 'Axel, call off your attack. Please!'

'You've never been one of us, Jonah; I know you don't understand,' said Axel, ending the discussion. 'We push on!'

'Then watch over us, Jonah,' said Sam. On-screen, Sam's hand pushed open the steel door to the tower.

She was pressing on, and Jonah was helpless to stop her.

Sam didn't want to move forward, but she wouldn't let herself retreat.

She'd been a fighter most of her life, fighting for the Guardians at her father's side. Pushing through the metal door of the facility that housed the Northern Corner, the servers that powered a quarter of the Metasphere, her mind flashed to how far she'd come from blowing up apps servers and payment-processing facilities. She'd lived most of the past year on the front lines, taking on and defeating the Millennials in each battle. Now, she was close to the end. Their numbers might have been depleted, but once the Guardians secured this final Corner, they could give freedom to everyone. The Guardians would at last achieve their aim.

There might be billions of users trapped online because of Granger, but in Guardian hands, they would fix the glitch and finally offer the planet a free and open virtual world, a more perfect alternative to the decaying and violent real world that offered little but economic depression and emotional despair. This was her fight, and as much as she wanted to heed Jonah's warnings, she wasn't going to give up as she dragged the world across the freedom frontier.

* * *

Jonah saw what Sam saw. She was in position: on top of the mine with a sniper, to provide cover for the paratroopers on the ground.

'I'm in position on the radar tower,' Sam said over the radio. 'Dad, are we ready?'

'No, but you don't go to war when you're ready. You go when you have to. Everyone, listen up. We're undermanned and about to enter a dangerous bottleneck. But the prize is down there and it's worth pursuing. You all know that, now let's get this done.'

Had they still been on board the airship, Jonah suspected the troops would have whooped and hollered. But out here, in the cold, wind-swept surface of the mine, the only sounds from the forces were the quiet acknowledgement of Axel's order.

'Affirmative.'

As the Guardians below Sam cut their way through the sealed doors of the mining facility and disappeared underground, she was all alone.

'Jonah, are you watching me from up there?' she asked over the radio.

'Of course,' he replied. Jonah felt like her Guardian angel, but ultimately, ten thousand feet above, he was powerless to stop any harm from coming to her. But at least he could see things that she couldn't.

Jonah sat down beside Mallia and took control of the airship's camera, zooming in on Sam's position. She was alone, with no movement anywhere on the facility. He zoomed out, widening his view, and spotted a figure moving towards the buildings to the south of her position.

'Sam, you've got someone coming at your four o'clock.'

'Friendly or unfriendly?' she asked, her voice steady.

Jonah zoomed in to see who was approaching. From his high angle, this far away, he couldn't make out the face, but still there was no mistaking who it was. Jonah could place those gnarly dreadlocks anywhere.

'That's debatable,' he said. 'It's Jez.'

Jonah had never trusted Jez, even before he'd revealed himself as a double-agent. But he was the Guardians' advance recon man and he'd survived the ice collapse. What worried Jonah, however, wasn't his escape – for he should have been embedded on the island in advance of the snowmobile force – but the fact that he wasn't wearing a Guardian cold suit. Jez's outfit was black, not white.

'He's not in Guardian gear,' Jonah warned.

'Maybe he was blending in with the Millennials,' speculated Sam. 'He was supposed to get the early reconnaissance.'

'Something's wrong,' countered Jonah. 'I don't like this. Be careful.'

'I know you don't like him,' argued Sam, 'but

he's one of us.'

Jez had fought, killed and nearly died in service to the Guardians. He was a trusted and valued operative who'd earned his place near the top of the secret society's never-acknowledged but ever-present hierarchy.

Suddenly, another explosion lit the sky from below.

And then another, and then another. Jonah watched in horror as three of the mine buildings collapsed in on themselves immediately. The others were in flames. From up above, the orange flames and black smoke from the explosions reached into the sky and reflected off the grey clouds, creating a sickening light show.

Sam's tower was still upright, for now, and Jonah pulled up both her front and rear cameras to assess the immediate danger to her. All around her, the facility was cratering.

One building buckled as its corrugated metal exterior burned and melted in the flames. Another, a squat, square building with small windows, burst from the inside out, throwing furniture and what looked like beds across the charred grounds. *That must've been the miners' barracks*, Jonah thought.

'Sam, get out of there! It's all collapsing!'

'I can't,' she called back. 'The radar tower's bent in the middle; it's like the Leaning Tower of Pisa.'

Jonah didn't like the reference. Everyone knew what had happened to the Leaning Tower. It had

71

collapsed when Jonah was eight years old, killing a busload of tourists. He flipped the screen back to the overhead view and watched helplessly as Sam's tower wavered.

'Sam!' shouted Jonah. 'Your emergency chute, do you still have it on?'

'Ye-es,' she called back, her voice trembling – now clearly afraid and unsure.

'Pull the ripcord, throw it into the wind, and jump!'

Jonah stood back from the bank of screens. He spotted Jez trudging through the snow towards the burning buildings of the mine. Something was very wrong, and Sam was in trouble. If she caught the wind right, she'd be able to land in one piece. But something told Jonah that Jez poised an even greater threat than the toppling tower.

'Captain Zegar,' Jonah called on the cabin's intercom. 'Can you bring us back round to the drop zone?'

'In theory, but why would you want to jump into that chaos?'

'I've got my reasons,' Jonah said, though in truth he only had one reason. 'Please, I need to get down there.'

'That's suicide, kid,' said Mallia. 'Stay safe up here.'

'Thought I was the liability who had to go?' snapped Jonah.

Mallia huffed. 'Have it your way.'

Jonah sprinted back into the utility room and

assembled his cold suit. The Kevlar body armour was heavy and restrictive, but without it he knew he wouldn't survive the sub-zero temperatures at this altitude. He reached over his shoulder, twisted on his mini-oxygen tank, and snapped on his helmet. On his left wrist, he flipped open the fabric pouch on the sleeve above his left wrist and activated the camouflage. Once on the ground, the suit would react to the environment around him, giving him a chameleon-like chance of staying hidden from any Millennial snipers.

Jonah moved to the jump room and sealed the airtight door behind him. He stood at the doublewide door frame, freezing air blasting in, and readied himself to jump. Only then did he realise he had forgotten to pack a weapon.

Jonah didn't want to kill anyone, but he needed protection. He didn't want his principles to get him killed. The problem was, it was too late to turn back.

'You're back over the drop zone, kid,' came the call from Zegar over his helmet's radio link. 'It's now or never!'

It was now.

Jonah spotted a small red axe fastened to the wall, marked with the word: FIRE. He lifted it from its hook and clutched it tightly, facing the blade away from his chest. Jonah stood on the edge of the platform, where the platoons of paratroopers had jumped before him, looking down, surveying the awful landscape below. The diamond mine was aflame. Jonah noticed the massive pit mines to the north of the burning buildings and thought about aiming for them. They were safe from the fires, but looked too deep to be able to climb out of. He had to aim his landing just right because surrounding the entire complex was a circular moat of Arctic water.

He stepped off the platform and plummeted into the fires of Hell.

10

Sam unfurled her spare parachute and tried to catch the icy breeze.

As she held the tethers of her chute, desperate to fill it with wind before the tower collapsed, a flash of memory jolted her from her predicament. For a moment, she felt warm.

She was on a childhood beach holiday with her mother. Axel was off flying somewhere, as usual, and her mum had hired a weekend holiday cottage by the seaside for 'just us girls'. The tide was out and Sam was running on the beach, daring the waves to catch her. Her mum had surprised her with a new kite – a blue and yellow butterfly. Sam raced across the muddy, pebbled beach, holding the kite aloft.

Just catch the breeze, she told herself.

Her spare chute was smaller than her main one, but Jonah was right – it was big enough to slow her down if she had to jump from the tower. The radar tower rocked on its unhinged base. She didn't have long.

As soon as she felt the chute take the wind, she leapt into the air. She pulled the toggles and rose up for a moment, at the same time steering the parachute away from the crumbling concrete. And then she plummeted.

The parachute slowed her descent, but she was going to hit the ground faster than she'd like. She pulled the toggles again and gained lift just feet from the ground. As she hit the ground she immediately pushed her body into a roll; using gravity's momentum instead of resisting it. She rolled three times, keeping her body tight, before finally coming to rest in a tangle of tethers on the hard-packed snow.

She looked up. All around her, buildings were burning and collapsing. Sam skilfully sliced the ropes with her pocketknife and, once free, jumped up and ran towards the dented corrugated metal of the main lift shaft. It was the main attack portal for the Guardian paratroopers. She wanted to help as many people to safety as possible.

The door was blown back twelve feet from the frame, sizzling on the melting snow. Sam walked in slowly and stared into the darkness, clicking on her small torch to reveal the mangled metal of the elevator mechanism. The hoists had fallen down into the shaft.

'Is there anyone down there?' she shouted in desperation.

But silence shouted back.

She didn't linger, racing out and across to the smaller building that her father had entered. She knew it was an alternative access point to the tunnels below, but as she opened the door, her worst fears were confirmed.

The steel stairs had collapsed and rubble from the shaft had filled the cavity. If her father had somehow survived the cave-in, he was buried alive.

'Axel!' she called. 'Axel! Dad, are you down there?'

She tried to dig, pulling pieces of twisted metal and chunks of masonry off the pile, but it only revealed an ugly mash of concrete and steel. It was an impenetrable blockage. To clear the rubble required machines, not hands. There was nothing she could do, not right now. Sam turned to leave – maybe she could find another way in. But when she turned around into the fading daylight, a tattooed face stared back at her.

'Jez,' she said, startled and relieved. 'You're OK?'

He smirked, moving his tattoo ink around his face. 'That is the understatement of this age.'

'I need your help. Did anyone from the ground forces make it?' she asked. But even as she asked the question, she knew something was wrong. Jez stared at her with a predatory intensity in his eyes. She'd seen him scowl a hundred times before, but this time his sneer was smouldering with hatred.

'I've waited a long time for this day,' he said.

Sam felt for her pistol in her right pocket, but remembered too late that she'd moved it to accommodate the bulky rifle boxes. She was unarmed and caught in the doorway between Jez and the wreckage.

'What's going on, Jez?'

'A new era is upon us, Sam,' he said in a cool, detached voice. 'And there is no place in the new history for the Guardians—'

'Oh no,' she gasped. Jonah might have been paranoid, but he was right. 'You're back with the Millennials? I should've listened to—'

'—or the Millennials,' he concluded. 'Listened to whom?'

'Jonah,' she said. 'He knew that there was something wrong with you.'

'There is nothing wrong with me,' he said, pulling a gun from the holster behind his back. He pointed it at Sam, motioning her to kneel down. 'There is only what is wrong with the world. And I am part of the cure.'

Sam obeyed, kneeling on the cold floor, but now Jez pointed the gun at her forehead. Before she closed her eyes, anticipating the bullet, she saw something move in the distance, phantom-like in the snow. She put her face into her hands, stalling for time by pretending to cry, while peering through her fingers out into the icescape.

Even camouflaged, she recognised Jonah's uneven gait as he rushed, unseen by Jez, towards her. But she had to cover up his footsteps before they alerted her assassin.

'Ahhhhhh-wahhhhh,' she cried. In normal circumstances, she would never give Jez the satisfaction of tears, but this was far from a normal. 'Please-please-please don't, it's not fair,' she whimpered as loudly as she could. She wouldn't win a Tubey award, but her performance was doing its job. It was distracting Jez.

'Quit your whining, Kavanaugh,' he snarled. 'There's nobody left who cares.'

Sam took her face from her hands and looked at Jonah, holding a small red axe above Jez's head.

Jonah slammed it down and Sam smiled. 'Really?'

It was a last-second decision to rotate the handle in his hands as Jonah swung the axe. As he'd approached, adrenaline dominating his bloodstream, Jonah was convinced he'd slice through Jez's neck with the sharp blade. He had watched Jez point his gun at Sam, but she must've seen him because she started crying and screaming in a way that Sam would ordinarily mock. She wasn't a crier. She'd never give Jez the satisfaction, even when he was about to shoot her at close range.

She'd been buying him time.

Jonah had wanted to kill Jez. But it was then that he realised he had been plagued with guilt ever since he didn't kill Sam's attacker in Cuba. On that hot Havana night, a Millennial girl had targeted Sam and

Jonah hesitated. He finally shot her in the shoulder, stopping the Millennial from shooting Sam, but Jonah had felt like a failure.

This time, his whole body yearned to kill Jez. He wanted to see the bully's blood melt the snow beneath his feet. But he also knew that Jez might have answers to the madness going on there. And so, Jonah had twisted the handle.

Hit by the blunt edge, the Guardian traitor slumped to the ground, dazed but not dead.

Sam quickly snatched the gun from his tattooed hand, switched the safety on, slipped out its clip, and popped the waiting bullet from the chamber.

Jonah knelt down and pressed his right knee into Jez's lower back, just above where his DI socket was. He pressed the axe's sharp edge into the back of Jez's tattooed neck to keep him still. A thin red line joined the other decorations on the traitor's skin.

'I've only spared you for one reason,' Jonah said. 'So you can tell me: what is going on?'

'It's better that you don't know,' said Jez. 'Just join your girlfriend in crying.'

'As if. That was all an act – couldn't you tell?' Sam said calmly. 'Now use that head to talk or we'll cut it off.'

'There's been too much talk,' Jez grunted, spitting up blood. 'Now we wait for the new world that will come tomorrow.'

Jez reached up to his mouth, in a move Jonah thought was him wiping the blood that was trickling from his lips. But Sam reached out urgently, trying to swipe Jez's hand away.

'No!' Sam yelled in frustration as Jez shook and convulsed under Jonah's knee. His eyes rolled back in their sockets and a sick-smelling foam burst from his mouth.

'What's wrong with him?' asked Jonah, repulsed and confused.

'Cyanide,' Sam said as Jez's body fell limp.

'He's killed himself?' said Jonah, standing up from the corpse. 'Why?'

'So he wouldn't talk,' said Sam. 'The question is: what doesn't he want us to know?'

Before Jonah could guess at an answer, Sam stepped over Jez's body and towards him, her arms out for a hug. He held her shaking body tight, relieved that she was safe. He wanted to hold Sam in this embrace for as long as he could, but there were Guardians buried below and if they had any chance of rescuing them, he'd have to act quickly.

He pulled Sam gently by the hand, out into the open.

'My dad's down there,' said Sam.

'I know, we've got to get him out,' said Jonah, squeezing Sam's still-shaking hand. 'If we can.'

Jonah clicked on his radio and called the airship.

'Captain Zegar, it's Jonah. I'm here with Sam, but everyone else is trapped below, we need to—'

As he spoke, Jonah thought the bright light in the sky was the famed Northern Lights. But the loud boom that followed the flash and cut off his words told him it was not the aurora borealis. The explosion lit the dusk sky and the airship burst into flames.

Sam looked up, her jaw frozen open. Jonah saw the flames reflected in her green eyes. At first, the ship seemed to hang in the air. But the as the massive balloon contained within the aluminium struts burned and shrivelled away, the skeletal frame started falling fast.

It looked like the ribcage of one of the diseased cows that littered the British countryside. And it was getting bigger. The death cage was falling straight for them. Jonah grabbed Sam's hand hard and pulled her away.

They ran north across the charred snow, chasing their shadows formed by the fire above.

'Faster!' shouted Jonah. 'We've got to get clear!'

They raced towards a broken, orange barrier at the eastern edge of the mining facility. Jonah saw the diamond-shaped warning signs, but they were darkened by the shadow of the falling frame above them. Jonah could read the signs or jump to what he'd hoped was safety, but he couldn't do both.

Jonah flung himself awkwardly over the barrier.

As he landed, he looked down to see a vast, endless grey abyss the size of Manhattan. He stood at the edge of a massive hole in the Earth shaped by rock, gravel and sludge. He wondered if they could turn back.

He turned to see Sam vault the barrier with grace.

'Wait! Sam!' he warned.

'Jonah?' asked Sam, her vaulted momentum taking her forward and her footing already slipping.

'Grab on!' shouted Jonah, reaching his hand for Sam's.

It was too late to turn back.

Hand in hand, Jonah and Sam tumbled down the cliff. Rocks and gravel assaulted him from every angle as he flailed dangerously to the bottom. He lost his grip on Sam and tried to slow his descent, but there was no stopping his fall as the sky and the ground seemed to trade places in a sick stunt.

He tried to call for Sam once he'd hit the bottom, but he was too winded for any sound to come out. The rocky Earth smelled like rotting eggs and Jonah instinctively grabbed his nose with his left hand. It was a terrible mistake.

Jonah inhaled a mouthful of dust, throwing him into a coughing fit that paralysed his body and his mind.

Finally, after his muscles had been assaulted from all sides and his lungs abused from within, Jonah looked up.

He gaped at the rock face as tall as a skyscraper.
And then he passed out.

11

The sharp edges of Granger's titanium feet gripped the ice as he trekked north towards the mine facility.

The trucks carrying his micro-servers were miles south, rumbling to their rendezvous with the freight train. As Granger walked, the rhythmic crunching of ice beneath his metallic feet gave him time to think. He'd been unseated from within. Someone else, someone who occupied the dragon avatar of his former pilot and the father of his adversary, had planned and executed a coup within his kingdom.

Granger had built his organisation on a combination of loyalty and fear. He'd hand-picked all of his key operatives and followed a winning profile: pick disadvantaged yet brilliant kids and give them an escape from their miserable childhoods. He'd sent more kids to major universities on his Millennial scholarships than any government programme, and in doing so, had engineered his own recruitment procedure. He had access to the best, brightest and – importantly – the most loyal young minds. He'd scaled up the Millennial Corporation by leveraging these minds to iterate and improve his technology. But just as he felt on this windswept ice road, he reminded himself that even though he'd surrounded himself with people, he'd always been alone.

Of his Millennials, clearly some were traitors and he feared, if Alexa was to be believed, the rest were dead. Whoever wore the dragon was not taking prisoners.

Granger held up his hand to block the wind from his face and pushed on. At the mine he was hoping to find at least some of his people still standing. He needed them. The man who'd hijacked the red dragon had also hijacked his world, and Granger had been so focused on his war with the Guardians that he'd been blind to this new threat. But now he had a new purpose. He had to stop him.

When Jonah opened his eyes, it was morning. He didn't know if he'd broken any, or perhaps all, of his bones. Sam's body wrapped around him, keeping them both warm as he lay on the hard, gravel ground. He looked up at the impossibly high cliff, certain he was going to die down here.

He was north of nowhere, at the bottom of a massive pit in the wasteland of the Arctic. The attack on the Northern Corner was over before it began; a deadly trap that a lot of good Guardians had fallen into. Jonah felt hopeless until he heard the one voice that always gave him hope.

'Can you move?' asked Sam, moving off him to

give him some space. Jonah turned his head painfully to see her now lying crumpled beside him. He wasn't sure he could move the rest of his body, but moving his neck was a good start.

'Can you?' he asked.

'Yeah, but it hurts,' she replied, stumbling to her feet. 'A lot. But I suppose that's what falling three hundred feet will do to a girl.'

Looking up, Jonah took in the full scale of the pit from his precarious angle. He was surrounded on all sides by steep, sloping cliffs. He had fallen as far as a thirty-storey building.

'Don't move your neck!' Sam shouted. 'There might be spinal damage.'

Jonah's muscles and nerves shouted at him from every appendage. He couldn't tell if he felt nothing or everything.

Sam stood over him, inspecting him with a worried look. 'Try to wiggle your toes, and if you can, move your legs.'

Jonah didn't think he could do it.

Sam leaned over Jonah's face, blocking out the awful grey cliff walls.

'Concentrate,' she said softly.

Jonah closed his eyes, though he didn't want to stop looking at Sam, and focused his mind on his lower extremities.

He was relieved to feel the wiggle of his toes in his

boots. He shot open his eyes and asked, 'I didn't imagine that, did I?'

Sam shook her head and smiled.

Slowly and painfully, he lifted his feet off the ground, left and then right.

Jonah pulled his left knee in, followed by his right, and rolled over onto all fours. He took a moment to brace himself, then pushed himself up onto his knees. He felt like he might collapse, unable to hold himself in place, but he willed himself to stay up. Jonah reached out for Sam, steadying himself as he pulled himself to standing on his own battered but functional feet.

'We're stuck down here, aren't we?' Jonah asked.

'Better than burning alive up there,' Sam replied.

Jonah could see smoke rise from beyond the cliff. He considered a route up. 'It'll be a long climb.'

His resolve, his survival instinct, was returning. It had been knocked out of him by the fall, but Sam was right. He was alive, unlike Zegar, Mallia and at least two hundred metatranced Guardian soldiers who never saw their fiery death coming.

Had he stayed aboard the airship, he'd be dead and so would Sam. They might be at the bottom of an impossibly deep pit, but they were alive and they were together. If he wanted to stay that way, they'd have to climb.

'C'mon,' he said.

'What?' Sam mocked. 'You don't want to look for diamonds while we're down here?'

'A girl's best friend,' Jonah recalled from an advert or a song. He couldn't remember which.

'No,' said Sam, dusting Jonah off. 'That's you.' She grabbed his hand and gave it a squeeze. 'Now let's get out of this pit.'

Sam squared up to the sloping wall and searched for a hold. She grabbed at the edge of a football-sized rock and dangled herself off just inches from ground.

'Use these bigger boulders,' she said. 'They're sturdy.'

She clawed at the smaller rocks and the gravel and they slipped through her fingers. 'Don't reach for the small stuff.'

Jonah glanced down to see the pile of gravel and rocks collect by her feet. Her demonstration was successful. He didn't want to end up in a heap back at the bottom.

Sam pulled herself further up the wall. It wasn't vertical, but close to it. She carefully planted her feet on a rock, testing its strength before asking it to bear her weight. Then, she found a new boulder to grab. Once she was above Jonah, it was his turn to follow.

He kept to her left to stay clear of falling gravel. He matched her technique, securing footholds and steadying himself with his hands. Once he was several body heights above the ground, he made the mistake of looking down.

With no net, no harness, he was asking to be gravity's victim. He'd been in terrifying verticals before but something about the slow, deliberate pace of the climbing was scarier than the urgent zip-line across to the Freedom Tower or the improvised skateboard between wrecked office towers in Hong Kong. As Jonah wondered if his penchant for flying carried a death wish with heights, his arms started to get tired. He shook his right arm loose.

'Let your legs do the work,' she said. 'You're pushing yourself up with your legs, not pulling up by your arms.'

'Have you been rock-climbing before?' asked Jonah with a grimace, his face so close to the wall he could taste the chalky sulphur.

'Yes,' she said. 'No, wait. No, I haven't. But Andrea has.'

Andrea Brandon was the leader of the Uploaded resistance who had usurped Sam's body, hijacking it to be Reborn in the real world.

'Is she still in your head?' asked Jonah. As far as he knew, his was the only brain that could store two full avatars; two complete consciousnesses. But the Uploaded, once they'd usurped a live avatar, left their mark. They imprinted memories and emotions on their hosts that would live on forever.

'She's gone,' said Sam, lifting her foot expertly up the steep slope to find a new toehold. 'But it's like there's an echo of her inside me. It's different to memories, it's more like memories of memories. Like scenes from a holo-film, but one that I acted in. Or sequences from an RPG. Is it the same for you and Jason?'

As Sam spoke, Jonah watched Sam's positioning and copied her technique. He didn't have any rock-climbing experience, either experienced or imprinted, to draw on. He had to follow Sam's lead and learn it on the spot.

'For me, it's deeper than that,' Jonah said, gripping the latest handhold tightly. 'Sometimes I don't know where his memories stop and mine begin. They're all woven together, mixed up in my subconscious. It's like I have the full memories of two lifetimes.'

'Must make you feel old,' joked Sam.

Jonah knew she meant it in jest, but Jonah couldn't find it funny. His father had never got old – he was just forty-four when someone killed him.

Jonah had originally believed his father had been a Millennial supporter killed by the Guardians, who were already blamed by Granger for the attacks on the world's airports. But after Jonah joined the Guardians and realised the scope of Granger's ambitions and the ruthlessness of his methods, he had come to understand that the Millennials were responsible for his father's murder. But then Jason, while born again in a stolen body, shocked him with the revelation that someone else killed him, although he had refused to say who. Unlike Jez, whom he'd spared with the blunt side of the axe, Jonah had no doubt in his mind about what he'd do to the person who'd taken his father away from him.

For that person, whoever and wherever he was, Jonah was ready to kill.

12

Granger could hear voices.

Exhausted and dehydrated, approaching the charred wreckage of the diamond mine, he wondered if he was hearing the ghosts of the Guardians buried below or the spirits of his slaughtered Millennials. The skeletal remains of the airship slumped over the smouldering buildings, trapping them in a giant cage.

Granger thought of the Inuit people, the residents of this frozen wasteland, who believed in the spirits of people and animals. But he, his only faith in the certainty of ones and zeroes and the logic of science and code, scoffed at such naive beliefs.

And yet the voices that carried on the wind sounded real.

Granger turned from the burned-out facilities and walked towards their source. They seemed to float across the islands from beyond the barricaded area. He remembered the Inuit elders, who'd protested Granger's purchase of the mine, saying that the spirits of their ancestors roamed the ice. But Granger had dismissed the silly folklore as easily as he'd dismissed the Aboriginals in Australia who had claimed that their dead resided within Uluru.

Granger never understood why people were so insistent, arguing against all scientific evidence, in believing in the afterlife. As far as he was concerned, the only afterlife available was the one he'd provided the world: the Island of the Uploaded. He allowed millions of people to outlive their mortal bodies. The only ghosts were the ones he had created.

And yet the voices on the wind haunted him. They howled and echoed off the far side of the pit mine. Granger scaled the orange barricade, wondering if he'd been wrong about spirits all along, then looked down the side of the steep cliff and saw a ghost.

Jonah was nearly at the top of the cliff. He was so exhausted from hours of climbing that when he spotted a gloved hand reach down for his, he thought he was seeing things. The shock of the outstretched hand caused him to falter. He feared he'd tumble back to the bottom. He might not survive another fall.

Desperate, Jonah reached up.

'Jonah, don't!' Sam shouted. But Jonah had already grasped the gloved palm.

Jonah swung his legs over the edge, collapsing onto charred but firm ground. Two dirty steel feet stood in front of his weary eyes. He looked up to see their owner smiling down at him: Matthew Granger.

Now Jonah was convinced he was seeing things.

But he felt a tug as Sam grabbed at his legs,

pulling him back as she reached the summit.

Granger raised his arms in mock surrender. 'I'm not going to hurt you,' he said. 'Either of you.'

'Tell that to the Guardians you drowned on the ice,' Sam screamed as she stood up in front of her enemy. 'Tell that to the Guardians you burned alive up there! Tell that to the Guardians you buried in the tunnels. Tell that to my father. Oh, wait, you can't. He's dead. They're all dead!'

Jonah rose to his feet beside Sam. 'We don't know that,' he whispered.

'Along with all of the Millennials who didn't betray me,' said Granger calmly. 'Samantha, Jonah, someone has been playing us. Someone has been watching and waiting, probably for a long time, and now he has obliterated both factions.'

'What are you talking about?' asked Sam.

'We cannot afford to be enemies,' said Granger, 'because the MetaWars are over and we've all lost. There are only the three of us left. Us against the man behind today's massacre. A man who claims he wants to save the world.'

Jonah was confused and overwhelmed. 'Who?'

'Your father,' said Granger.

The words hung in the windy air. Jonah was prepared for lies – Granger had lied to him before, warped the truth to suit his own aims. Jonah instinctually looked up, to the darkening sky, before refocusing on Granger's bruised but cherubic face.

'But it's not my dad,' Jonah protested. 'My father is—'

He was about to say 'dead', but that was only half right.

'Of course, it was your father in scales only; his avatar somehow occupied by another man. I don't know how, and I certainly don't know who, but this man wears the red dragon – as you once did.'

'You have spoken to him? What does he want?' asked Sam.

'I don't know what his long game is,' admitted Granger, 'but he claims to want to save humanity.'

'From what?' asked Jonah.

'I asked him the same question, Jonah. You see; you and I aren't that different.'

'There's nothing *but* difference between you two!' spat Sam.

Granger grinned. 'Hit a nerve, have I? We're more similar than you care to see.'

'I'm not like you,' said Jonah. 'And I never will be.'

'And that's a great pity,' said Granger. 'You could learn so much from me.'

'Hardly,' scoffed Sam. 'Jonah's twice the man—'

Granger scowled at Sam. 'He's barely a—'

'Stop it!' shouted Jonah. 'Why should I believe you, Granger?'

'Because we want the same thing,' he said. 'We both want the war to end.'

Jonah knew the very nature of the war had changed.

'Whoever this guy is, with this threat he's ended the MetaWars and started a new one. I may not be like you and I certainly don't like you, but look around; it's just us three. And if we're all that's left, then we need to stop fighting and start surviving. If it's really just us three, we need to know who's running around in my father's skin, saying that he wants to save humanity from, from…'

'From what?' asked Sam.

'From itself,' said Granger.

13

Jonah searched the wreckage for a way into the tunnels below.

The seven buildings had been charred to rubble.

'He might be alive down there,' he urged. Jonah stepped carefully, trying not to dislodge the mangled walls, worried that he'd get trapped under debris.

But Sam was less careful, pulling at twisted steel beams and moving corrugated steel walls out of the way, desperately searching for a way down to her father. A sheet of mangled metal slipped from its place, sliding down the pile of wreckage like a grass-skier on a slope.

Jonah threw his aching body at Sam.

He knocked her out of the way just as the sheet metal sliced through the air.

'That could have cut you in two!' he shouted, angry with himself for letting Sam come so close to death.

But Sam stood up and resumed picking through the rubble.

'Be careful,' urged Jonah.

'We're wasting our time,' called Granger from the outskirts of the wreckage.

'If they're still alive,' said Sam, 'then they don't have much *time*!'

'Whoever did this knew the layout of the tunnels,' said Granger. 'They set the detonations to collapse them. I'm sorry, but anyone down there will have been crushed by rock and granite. It's too late for them, but it's not too late for us. It's up to us to stop the man behind this massacre, a man who's soon going to massacre everyone stuck online.'

Jonah caught up with Sam, who was growing increasingly frantic.

'Maybe we should let them rest in peace,' he said.

'What if it was *your* dad down there?!'

'I wouldn't stop digging,' Jonah said, feeling Sam's pain. 'You know that.'

'And that would be short-sighted,' Granger said. 'Because this phantom in your father's avatar is planning something much bigger and much more dangerous than collapsing a mine. And right now, the three of us are the only ones who can stop him.'

'We can't even get off this island!' shouted Sam.

'I have a plane,' said Granger, 'all I need is a pilot.'

'Show me,' said Jonah. He knew Granger was right, even though it would crush Sam to leave her father below. Most of the people on the planet were in danger, and if they didn't try to stop the red dragon from carrying out his plans, then who would?

'Jonah, please,' begged Sam. 'Please don't leave.'

'What would Axel want?' asked Jonah. 'It's not safe here. Would he want you to risk your life, digging in the debris? Or would he want you to try and save all of those people who can't save themselves? That's what he's always fought for, the freedom of strangers.'

Jonah saw Sam's eyes fill with tears. She shook her head, then knelt down and pressed her face to the dirty snow.

'Goodbye, Dad,' she whispered. 'If you're alive down there, please – hang in there. I'll come back for you.'

Jonah held his hand out for Sam, and guided her up. 'We both will,' he promised.

In silence, Jonah and Sam followed Granger around the wreckage to the icy airstrip to the north. Jonah spotted their aeronautical salvation silhouetted against the dusky-blue sky – a small plane with skis mounted on its wheels.

'Get on board, Sam,' Jonah ordered the shivering Sam. 'Stay warm.'

Granger and Sam boarded while Jonah circled the single propeller aeroplane, a Cessna 172, and began his pre-flight checks. He fell back on years of practice, his father's practice: checking the fuselage, flaps and wings. Jonah had never seen a plane on skis before, but Jason had. He'd flown into this facility many times during his time as Granger's private pilot – knew how to expertly take off and land with the skis instead of wheels.

Jonah climbed aboard the Cessna, a four-seater workhorse of a plane, and insisted that Sam sit with him in the cockpit. He started the engine and ran through his flight-deck checks.

'From back here,' said Granger, 'you look just like your father.'

'Except I'm alive,' snapped Jonah.

'Will it fly?' asked Sam, changing the subject.

'Yes, but the question is where to?' asked Jonah. He was uneasy about joining up with Granger but if they were going to find and stop the red dragon, he'd need even his enemy onside.

'Fort Mac,' said Granger.

'Where?'

'Fort McMurray, Alberta. It's five hundred miles due south of here. It's the closest town within range.'

'Isn't Yellowknife closer?' Jonah argued. He'd reviewed the maps of Canada on the long airship flight from Halifax to the drop zone. He thought America and Australia were big, but they had nothing on the sheer scale of this Northern nation.

'Yes, it's closer,' confirmed Granger. 'But I don't have any special friends in Yellowknife.'

'You have friends?' asked Sam sharply.

'Yes,' sighed Granger. 'And we're going to need her help if we're going to stop the dragon.'

Jonah and Sam shared a look. *Her?*

14

Jonah flew over a devastated wasteland.

After about three hundred miles, the pristine snowscape of the north gave way to barren, chewed-up landscape. It looked like an apple that an impatient toddler had taken a million tiny bites out of and left to rot.

Earth had been dug out, upturned and left in sooty piles. Between them, a network of dirt roads weaved, on which drove tiny yellow dump trucks hauling loads of black filth that occasionally skirted giant ponds of brown water.

'What happened here?' asked Jonah. He'd seen the vast desert of western Australia, the dust bowls of the American Midwest, and the dehydrated wasteland of Los Angeles, but he'd never seen as much natural destruction on such a mammoth scale. This was man-made, but bigger than anything he'd survived – including the bombing of Hong Kong.

'What do you think keeps us in the air?' asked Granger.

Surely he didn't need to explain the physics of lift and aerodynamics to Granger?

'Oil,' said Sam.

'Petrocarbons.' Granger nodded. 'And you're looking at the world's largest and last deposit. These are called the oil sands.'

Jonah spotted a cluster of lattice-like buildings below. Massive vertical cylinders puffed white smoke into the air, and Jonah gave the exhaust a wide berth.

'She digs up the ground and melts the bitumen to release the oil,' explained Granger. 'That's a processing facility below. That's where the magic happens.'

Jonah had a million questions about how oil came from sand, but the only question that bubbled up to the surface was, 'Who's *she*?'

'I suppose you could say she's my Sam,' Granger said.

'Be very careful what you say next,' warned Sam.

'Her name is Louise Thorne, but people here call her *The Baron*.'

'Um…' Jonah began, 'is she your girlfriend?'

'That's a childish term for a childish relationship. We are allies in spirit, Louise and I. We met at Davos and the connection was, well, I don't need to explain *connection* to you, Jonah.'

'OK, this is creeping me out,' said Sam. 'Can we not talk about Matthew Granger's love life? I swear I'm going to puke out of this plane!'

As Jonah rounded the billowing smoke, he caught a clear view of the city for the first time. Its towers glowed and stretched to the sky, a ring of green forest surrounded them, but that was the only greenery for as far as Jonah could see. Fort McMurray looked like an island oasis in a sea of sludge.

'That's her city,' Granger said, pointing. 'Louise runs SynCorp, the company that owns all of this. She's the last oil producer in the free world, and if we're going to get the resources we need to stop the dragon, we're going to need her help.'

'Let's hope she's happy to see you,' said Sam.

'It's been a while – too long,' said Granger. 'Other distractions have kept us apart.'

Sam scoffed. 'Wait a second, are you actually complaining that the Guardians kept you from seeing your girlfriend? Talk about childish.'

'The airport is to the south-east, Jonah,' said Granger, ignoring Sam.

'I see it,' he said. 'There's just one problem.'

'Which is?' asked Granger.

'The runway is made of tarmac, not ice.'

The radio crackled and a monotone voice filled the cockpit with a warning:

'*Single-engine craft, you are not cleared for SynCorp airspace. Redirect fifty miles to the east or you will be fired upon.*'

'Make that two problems,' Jonah said.

'Let me deal with the tower,' said Granger. 'You shake those skis off our feet.'

Jonah reluctantly handed Granger the radio-mic,

and he quickly demanded to speak to a superior. Jonah marvelled at the way Granger always got his way.

'What happens if we try to land with those skis on?' Sam asked.

'Could be fine...' Jonah began.

'Phew,' said Sam. 'I was worried—'

'Could be fatal,' he concluded. 'There's no such thing as a risk-free landing, but attempting a tarmac land with those things strapped onto the wheels is just asking to turn a smooth landing into something, well, much less smooth.'

'So how do we get them off?'

'We don't,' he said. Jonah knew there was only one way to decouple the skis from the wheels, manually – from the outside. And he wasn't letting Sam risk her life so that they could have a smooth landing. 'I do.'

'Jonah, you can't go out there in midair.'

'On the ground will be too late,' he said, then turning to Granger. 'Can you keep them from shooting us out of the sky?'

'They know me here,' he replied. 'We'll be clear to land.'

Jonah turned to Sam, looking her gravely in the eyes; hoping it wasn't the last time he'd see them.

'I need to you keep the plane steady, at this velocity, at this altitude,' he said. He trusted her in the cockpit. She'd taken some lessons from Axel, and had flown between Hong Kong and Los Angeles. If there was anyone he could rely on, it was Sam. 'I'll be right back.'

Jonah shimmied his way from the cockpit into the port side, rear seat next to Granger. He scanned the storage area behind the seat and found a line of rope. He was still wearing his paratrooper cold suit, with the in-built parachute harness. He asked Granger to thread the rope through the harness loops on his back.

'As soon as I open the door, I'm going to lean out and tie this onto the wing-strut,' he said. 'But I want you to hold onto my legs.'

'You really trust him?' shouted Sam from the front.

'What choice do I have?' Jonah called back.

'What choice indeed,' said Granger. 'But your trust is not misplaced. I've got you, Jonah.'

Jonah opened the port door and the howl of wind swept through the cabin. They were only at seven thousand feet, but the cold air made it feel like he'd opened the hatch at thirty thousand. Jonah slowly reached out and threaded the rope around the strut. He tied it carefully in a knot summoned from deep in his father's aeronautical memories. Once he felt secure, or as secure as leaning out of a moving aeroplane seven thousand feet above the ground could ever feel, Jonah leaned further down and unclipped the ski from the port wheel. The red plastic ski fell away and plummeted down to the sludge below.

'Pull me up,' Jonah called. Granger pulled his feet

further back into the cabin and Jonah slowly untied his knot on the strut and closed the door. The resulting quiet sounded like silence. Of course, the engine noise was still close to deafening, but at least he'd blocked out the outside world – for now.

Jonah traded seats with Granger, to the starboard side, and prepared to jettison the next ski. He opened the door and carefully slid out, tying the rope onto the starboard strut.

He inched his way down towards the wheel. As he reached to unclip the ski, the sky boomed and the plane lurched.

Jonah felt himself slip from Granger's grasp and plunge.

15

Jonah fell past the ski and dangled in midair.

He was suspended by the rope, which he hoped would hold. Ahead, a puff of black smoke warned the plane off its current path.

'I thought you said we were clear to land!' he screamed. But nobody could hear him above the engine noise and the rushing wind. A second crumple filled the air, followed by another spherical cloud of black smoke.

Anti-aircraft fire, Jonah recalled from his father's memories. In a flash, he saw through his father's eyes; at Axel beside him in the cockpit, flying over oil tankers in the Gulf. They were hunting a GuerreVert destroyer when the sky filled with the eco terrorist's anti-aircraft fire. Jason locked on the destroyer and deployed a guided missile. The boat exploded from the deck and sank in less than two minutes, clearing the way for the oil tanker to make the Gulf of Oman, and then onwards to its oil-thirsty destination.

Jonah reached for the rope, desperately trying to haul himself up. But he wasn't strong enough. He was already exhausted from his long climb up the pit mine, and the wind whipped and buffeted him. He hung only four feet below the ski, but it was four feet too far.

He still had the spare parachute intact. But to deploy it, he'd have to sever the ropes attached to his harness loops. He cursed himself for not having a knife on his body. As he considered his options, which weren't many, he felt his body being pulled upwards. He looked up to see Granger steadying himself by anchoring his metal legs in the doorframe, hoisting Jonah up with all of his strength.

He was already up a foot, maybe more. All Granger needed to do was give Jonah another two feet and he could grab for the ski, stand on it and step onto the strut.

With another unsteady hoist, Jonah rose. Finally, he was within clasping range of the ski. He reached up and over, grabbed the ski and hauled his exhausted body onto it. He crawled up, closer to the plane and wrapped his waist around the strut. This allowed him to bend down and release the catch, letting the ski drop to Earth.

Granger held the rope taut as Jonah made the frightening leap from the strut into the cabin. Granger caught him, placing Jonah on the seat as he closed the door.

'Thank you,' panted Jonah.

'I told you I've gotcha,' said Granger.

'You OK?' called Sam.

'I am now,' said Jonah. 'But why are they firing on us?'

Granger shook his head. He looked genuinely confused; baffled even.

'Maybe Granger never called his girlfriend back,' joked Sam. Jonah laughed, not because it was that funny, but because the tension had built up so high that his body automatically released it.

Jonah composed himself, caught his breath and jumped into the pilot's seat.

'I thought I'd lost you,' Sam said.

'You've got to do better than that to get rid of me,' Jonah said with a smile. He turned the plane to start his descent. He had full visibility of the airport, on the south-eastern corner of the oil city, but he hesitated before descending.

'Don't worry,' urged Granger. 'It was just warning shots. If they were shooting to kill, we'd already be on the ground. In pieces.'

Sam ignored Granger, placing her hand on Jonah's left knee. 'I don't want to get rid of you. Not ever.'

'OK, now you're creeping me out,' Granger huffed from behind the cockpit. Jonah chose to ignore it. He needed to focus on landing in what was clearly about to be hostile territory. He was already distracted enough by Sam, but it was a good kind of distraction.

Right then, Jonah wanted to be somewhere far away, somewhere real, with Sam. But instead, he was landing on an airstrip lined with high-end private jets, with his sworn enemy-turned-ally in the back, in an oil-rich city that seemed bent on killing them. The weird thing, Jonah realised, was that he was getting used to days like this.

The armed security vehicles didn't wait for Jonah to complete his taxiing. Two SUVs, with machine guns mounted on top, escorted the plane to a small terminal building separated from the rest of the airport. Jonah had no choice but to be guided by them.

The guards, wearing all-black body armour and sporting the yellow and blue SynCorp logo, surrounded the plane. 'Get out of the plane; hands on heads!'

At the rear of the group, Jonah followed Sam and Granger's lead by placing his hands on top of his head. He faced the two SUVs and six armed guards on the ground.

'State your names, affiliations and intention in Fort Mac!' said one of the guards in a metallic monotone.

'Matthew Granger, founder of the Millennial Corporation. I am a guest of Louise Thorne. Please tell the Baron that I'm here.'

'Sam, Samantha Kavanaugh. Guardian. I'm hoping someone here can help us get excavation equipment to the north.'

'Jonah Delacroix.'

'Affiliation and intention?' asked the guard, raising his weapon.

'My affiliation is with her. And my intention is to stay alive, long enough to stop whoever is pretending to be my father and threatening to kill most of humanity.'

The guard rolled his eyes. Another hulking guard walked forward, grabbed their hands in turn and pressed them onto a palm-reading tablet. He then held the datapad up to each of their faces and took a picture. The three captives could only wait as the guard studied the results and called over his superior.

He pointed to Granger first. 'He is who he says he is, and SynCorp has an alliance with the Millennial Corporation. He's cleared.'

The guard training his weapon on Granger lowered it and Granger nodded. But Jonah started to panic when the guard pointed at Jonah and Sam and shook his head.

'But these two are known associates of GuerreVert,' the man said gravely. Jonah's panic rose as all of the guards swung round in unison to train their guns at Jonah and Sam. 'And the penalty for affiliation is death.'

Suddenly, everything went dark as someone pulled a hood over Jonah's head.

16

Jonah paced in the tiny jail cell.

'How could he just abandon us like that?' he asked, turning around after just a few steps to pace the other way. The concrete box was no more than ten feet across. Jonah felt anxious and cooped up.

'He's Matthew Granger,' said Sam, sitting on the floor. 'What did you expect?'

'But he didn't have to pull me back into the plane,' Jonah said. 'He could have let me drop. Why did he bother to save me, only to give us up now?'

'Because if he'd dropped you,' Sam said, rising to place her hands on Jonah's shoulders, 'I would have thrown him out of the plane. Here, he gets rid of both of us at once.'

'Quit your gibberin', eh!' called a voice from the hallway. A pale, thin man in a black SynCorp uniform leaned close to the bars, but not too close. He held a baton in one hand and had a gun holstered to his hip. 'Yer givin' me a headache. If I was you, I'd be sayin' my last goodbyes before yer sent for processin'.'

'Processing?' asked Jonah. He didn't like the sound of that.

Since he'd joined the MetaWars, he'd learned too many clever words for killing. He'd learned that when someone wanted to kill another human being, and wanted to justify it to a higher purpose, they simply invented a new word for the deed. The word 'Uploading' was actually just another way of saying suicide. Matthew Granger had used the word 'purging' to mean ridding the Metasphere of the Uploaded. But 'processing' was a new one to Jonah.

'We got ourselves a Fort Mac way of dealin' with you eco-terrorist scum,' the man spat. 'We pile you in the dumpers with the sands and sendja for processin'. The heat that separates out the oil also removes them impurities – you.'

Jonah thought back to the little yellow dump trucks he'd seen from the sky.

'They're going to burn us alive,' Sam said with a shudder.

'Yer girlfriend's pretty smart,' he said, pushing his face closer, examining Sam with an unnerving, predatory look. 'An' pretty.'

Suddenly, Sam shot her hands through the bars and pulled the man's face into them with a thud. With his face squeezed between two bars, Sam dealt him a jab that broke his nose. The man went limp.

'Grab his keys!' she shouted to Jonah.

He could see Sam was struggling to hold the unconscious guard upright by his hair. Jonah jumped across and reached through the bars to unclip his keys from his belt.

'Got 'em!' Jonah confirmed.

'And his gun,' Sam ordered. 'Quick!'

Jonah pocketed the keys and grabbed the man's pistol from his holster. Sam released the guard and he slumped to the floor.

The gun was heavy in Jonah's hand. It reminded him of the gun he'd carried in Havana. He clutched it tight, worrying that if he handed it to Sam she might execute the slumped prison guard in her rage. Sam didn't need fancy words to justify killing. Sure, the guard was foul and disgusting, but Jonah didn't think he deserved to die.

Jonah stuck his hand through the bars with the keys and felt for the lock, fumbling in his haste and hoping he wouldn't drop them. He got lucky on his third attempt. The bars clanked open and he and Sam rushed into the corridor.

The hallway was long – Jonah and Sam passed a number of empty cells on each side – and ended at a windowless door; their only way out.

'Give me the gun,' asked Sam. But of course, she wasn't asking.

Jonah paused, the deadly weapon cold in his hands. He didn't really want it, but he didn't want to hand it over either.

'Look, I'm not going to shoot at will,' Sam reasoned.

'But we don't know who's on the other side of that door, and what they'll do to stop us from escaping.'

Jonah wanted to believe her. With a sense of relief, he gave Sam the gun. He had handed over the burden of killing, but felt responsible for giving her the power. Sam was raised by violence, and she seemingly had no problem taking a life. It scared Jonah sometimes, how quick she was to kill.

As Sam trained the gun, Jonah reached out for the door. But it had no keyhole and the handle wouldn't budge in his hands. He started to panic, pulling and tugging on the handle. Defeated, Jonah pressed his hands against the wall, slumping his body in disappointment. Suddenly, he heard a metallic click and the door swung itself ajar.

Both shocked and delighted, he looked at the key ring. Of course – there was a sensor embedded in it! He pushed the door open into a large, low-ceilinged, clinical office. At least a hundred uniformed men and women swiped at screens and tapped at datapads, taking no notice of their escaping prisoners. Jonah spotted the SynCorp logo on their shoulders.

This was some kind of command centre, and Jonah noticed banks of CCTV screens, monitoring everything from the city's walls to playgrounds where children played. The far side of the room was made of windows, facing the street. That was their exit.

One woman, Jonah noticed, was talking in a low

voice to a bloodhound avatar on a screen. The screen was perched atop a strange steel stand that looked like a human skeleton. He wondered if it was supposed to be art.

As they stepped tentatively into the office space, Sam hiding her firearm, Jonah couldn't believe their luck. Some of the office workers glanced their way, and yet nobody was stopping them from escaping their death penalty.

Jonah beckoned Sam and they continued towards the double doors that led outside. Halfway across the room, near the bizarre skeletal art installation, Matthew Granger stepped into their path.

'Looks like you don't need my help, after all,' Granger said with a smile. He was clean, shaved, and wearing a smart blue suit that made him look more like a statesman from digizine covers than a fugitive that had escaped a war zone.

Sam raised her stolen gun and pointed it at Granger's face.

In a flash, a shiny metallic arm reached out of nowhere and grabbed Sam's wrist.

'Ahhhh,' she howled in pain.

'Drop it,' ordered a voice.

As Sam released the gun, a metallic hand caught it. Jonah took in what had just happened. A steel robot had disarmed Sam. It was seven feet tall, skeletal with a humanoid shape, but instead of a head, it had a screen. On the screen was the bloodhound avatar Jonah had spotted earlier – and it was looking right at him. What Jonah had earlier thought was a monitor on a stand, was actually a stationary robot – albeit a skeletal one. And now the robot was armed.

'We were about to let you kids go,' growled the bloodhound avatar on the screen, 'since Mr Granger here is such a good friend of the Baron's. But if you misbehave again, it's back to detention.'

The bloodhound let out a loud chuckle. The SynCorp workers all laughed from their desks. It dawned on Jonah that the Fort Mac guards weren't at all worried about Jonah and Sam escaping – because they had a metallic member on their force.

'Ah, let 'em go, Charlie,' called a moustached man from the back, not even looking up from his datapad.

'Very well,' said the bloodhound, reaching out his metallic hand for Jonah to shake. Jonah tentatively reciprocated, hoping to avoid the type of hand-crushing that Sam had just received. He had no need to worry; Charlie's handshake was gentle, albeit cold and smooth. Although Jonah would bet it could crush his own hand if it wanted to.

'What is going on?' asked Jonah, looking down at his intact hand. 'What is that?'

'*Who* is that, you mean?' said the robot. 'My name was...is Charles Tewkesbury; Royal Canadian Mounted Police. Retired, so to speak.'

'You're the police?' asked Sam.

'We have our own law here in Fort Mac, ma'am,' said the bloodhound.

Jonah gaped at the robot, both in awe and in fear.

'You've never seen a ßeta?' asked Granger.

'Is that what that is?' asked Sam.

'*Who!*' repeated the bloodhound. 'I may be dead, but I'm still a real person. And on behalf of the security team, we apologise for the inconvenience of your incarceration. Welcome to Fort McMurray. Mr Granger explained the misunderstanding and you're free to go.'

'We are?' asked Jonah.

'He did?' said Sam.

'I believe the Baron herself has requested your presence at Maple Leaf Tower,' Charlie continued. 'Mustn't keep her waiting.'

'Thank you, all,' called Granger, waving to the uninterested security staff at their desks.

The robot had put its hand out to Sam, clearly waiting for her handshake.

'Don't be rude, Kavanaugh,' prompted Granger.

'It's OK, Sam,' said Jonah.

'Tell that to my wrist,' she said, finally extending her hand. The robot cupped her right hand in both of his shiny skeletal ones.

'I don't know my own strength sometimes,' he

said, gently shaking her hand up and down. 'Please forgive me.'

As soon as the robot let go of Sam's hand she gripped Jonah's arm. 'Can we please go?' she asked.

'This way,' said Granger, opening the door. 'Her office is just down the street.'

'I'm not going anywhere with you,' retorted Sam.

'Yes you are,' said Granger, 'because the Baron has the resources to send an excavation crew up to the mine to search for your father. But you'll have to ask nicely.'

Jonah stepped out onto an extensive promenade of skyscrapers. Driverless cars zipped up and down a wide road divided by manicured pine trees. All of the buildings sported the SynCorp logo and one building opposite, a three-storey brick building with a sixty-storey tower perched on top, boasted an old-fashioned painted wooden sign that read: FORT MCMURRAY – WE HAVE THE ENERGY!

'Pardon me,' said a voice.

Jonah turned to see another skeletal robot manoeuvre around him and continue to walk down the pavement. Jonah only caught a quick glance at its face-screen, but noticed it was a beaver. Around him were at least ten more robots, all towering a good foot or more over the human pedestrians as they glided along.

Granger pointed to a red-tinted glass triangular

building that rose into the sky, nearly touching the clouds at its peak. 'She's up there, and she needs us as much as you need her.' There was a barely suppressed panic in his voice that Jonah had never heard before.

As they walked, they passed another two robots – a meerkat and an octagon arguing about a hockey game.

'What are those robot things?' asked Sam.

'ßetas,' said Granger. ' *"You, only ßeta!"* ' Or at least that's the commercial. It's Offline Uploading. The newest trend with the rich and powerful. Why stay confined to the Metasphere in your afterlife when you can live forever in the real world?'

'Offline Uploading?' repeated Jonah, trying to comprehend the concept. He'd grown up with the idea of communing digitally with the dead, but to have them walking around in the real world was strangely unsettling. He thought of his father, and how just months ago he'd sent him off, secluded in a satellite for eternity. *What if*, he asked himself, *what if I had waited? Could my dad have inhabited a ßeta?*

'Manhattan's filled with them now, so I hear,' added Granger. 'Not that I'm welcome back because of you two.'

'You mean those are actual avatars on those screens?' asked Sam. 'Uploaded users walking among us?'

Two more robots passed by, their screens showing

a ladybird and a cat, gossiping and giggling as they strode down the street.

'For the Uploaded who has everything; everything except a flesh-and-blood body,' said Granger. 'The ßetas allow the Uploaded to live in the real world. They just launched a few weeks ago, but now that the dragon has made his ultimatum, I bet they'll be popping up everywhere.'

'An ultimatum assumes the possibility of an alternative outcome,' said Sam. 'From what Jonah's said, whoever is wearing Jason's avatar is only interested in one outcome – genocide.'

'It would appear that way, yes,' said Granger. He sounded composed and in control, but Jonah noticed his voice waver; betraying his smooth facade. 'Which is why Louise needs us. Her situation is precarious, and believe me when I tell you she has every incentive to help us discover that *alternative* outcome.'

17

Jonah stepped out of the lift into the reception area on the top floor of the Maple Leaf Tower.

The oak walls were decorated with paintings of industrial equipment: yellow dump trucks, giant diggers and a mass of pipes and towers that Jonah guessed was the 'processing' facility. Opposite the lift, the floor-to-ceiling windows revealed the endless stretch of upturned Earth beyond the other skyscrapers and high city walls. Jonah looked out and realised for the first time that they were in a fortified city. He wondered whether it was to keep people in or to keep people out. Either way, he couldn't shake the feeling that he was still a prisoner.

They were greeted by an overweight man, sweating from his brow, the buttons of his beige suit straining hard. 'She's in here,' he said with a twang that reminded Jonah of the nasty jail guard sixty storeys below.

The bulging man introduced himself as Karl Whittington, the COO – Chief Operating Officer – of SynCorp. He led Jonah, Sam and Granger to a pair of dark double doors.

'I know where she is, Whittington,' said Granger,

dismissively. 'I was here earlier.'

'Yes, of course,' said the man, wiping the sweat from his neck folds with his palm. 'You two were, um, close.'

'Still are,' shot Granger as he opened the door to a vast, oak-panelled office.

The first thing Jonah scanned for was an executive escape glider. He'd been in too many toppled tall buildings not to immediately formulate an exit strategy. Granger must've have noticed his paranoia, because he spoke to Jonah softly, with a reassuring voice. 'Don't worry, Jonah, Fort Mac is secure. That's why it took me so long to get you out of that cell. I'd apologise for that, but I suspect you two liked having a little alone time.'

'Matthew, darlin',' chimed a female voice that seemed to emanate from the walls all around them. 'Don't be a troublemaker, now.'

Granger walked over to a hospital bed behind a mahogany desk where a chair should have been. Granger sat down on the bed and stroked the blonde, wavy hair of a striking woman in her early forties. It shocked Jonah to see him behave so gently, so lovingly.

The woman's eyes were closed and Jonah noticed an Ethernet cable snaking from under her black suit.

'Jonah Delacroix, Samantha Kavanaugh, please meet Louise Thorne,' said Granger.

Jonah didn't know if this was Granger's idea of a

sick joke, but this woman was clearly in a deep metatrance. And if she was online, she was likely stuck there as the dragon's countdown ticked towards zero.

'Over here, lil' darlin's,' called the voice. Jonah turned to face a large screen illuminate on the inner wall. It was a window into the Metasphere, and staring back at the trio and the unconscious body was a wild pink rose.

'As you can see,' said the rose, 'I'm more here than there. Which presents something of a problem if that dragon is possible of doing what he threatens.'

The countdown on the top left of the screen clicked to 23:47:52. Less than a day.

'It's not a threat,' said Jonah. 'It's a statement of intent.'

'I think Jonah's right, my dear,' said Granger.

'Then how do we stop him?' she asked. The rose on the screen didn't angle to Granger; it was looking straight at Jonah.

'Me?' he asked.

'Matthew is the smartest man I know, so when he tells me that you, Jonah, are the most resilient, determined young man he has ever met, I take notice. And you, Samantha, from what Matthew has explained, and the hardship and terror you've caused him and his organisation, you are an unstoppable force of nature. It seems to me that I've got the perfect team right in front of me; not just to save my life, but to save the lives of everyone trapped inside here.'

Jonah looked at Granger, and then to Sam. A team? It seemed incomprehensible. But with the Guardians and the Millennials both gone, and the red dragon counting down to global genocide, he didn't feel like he had much choice. But he didn't like it.

Sam spoke first, shifting her focus between the comatose body on the bed and the lively rose on the screen. 'Granger says you can help us excavate the mine; there might be people trapped under there. My father is down there.'

'If I get out of here,' the rose said, 'I will send a drilling team.'

'Why not now?!' urged Sam.

'Because that's not how I negotiate.'

'Then how do we get you out?' asked Jonah.

Granger spoke first.

'There is a train between Banff and Vancouver, and the servers were scheduled to be loaded onto that train. I'm assuming that whoever hijacked them from me still needs to transport them. If I can get a force together to take that train—'

'I have offices in both of those places, people I can trust,' said Louise. Jonah thought she sounded like she was boasting.

'Good,' continued Granger. 'We might just have a chance to access the Metasphere code at the source level – unlock the halos manually or disable the

Impr—' Jonah noticed Granger pause ever so slightly before continuing, 'The improvements the dragon hopes to make.'

'Murdering nearly everyone isn't exactly an improvement, Matthew,' snapped the rose. 'It's bad for business.'

'To him it is,' explained Jonah. 'He believes that killing most of humanity will serve his goal. He reminds me of you, Granger. He's playing the long game.'

Sam interjected, 'But there's no justification for killing that many—'

'There's never justification for killing,' said Jonah. 'Full stop. Don't you guys see, that's why we're in this mess; because people with the means to kill find their own justification for murder.' He looked at Granger, and added, 'To build a better world,' and then to Louise. 'To deter eco-terrorists.'

Lastly, he looked to Sam and finally voiced his disdain for her killer instinct. 'To stop dictatorship. Or just because it's the only life you've ever known. It's still not right. So if we're going to beat this guy, we can't think like killers.'

'Like what, then, Jonah?' asked Sam.

'Like saviours,' he replied.

But before Jonah and his 'team' could begin planning to save humanity, the red dragon appeared on screen.

18

Jonah watched as his father's avatar, the one he once wore, broadcast himself to the Metasphere again – appearing everywhere at once. Louise thrashed at her captor with her thorns, but he was just a projection – immune to any attack.

The dragon spoke in the same calm, calculating manner as before, but this time he outlined a new proposition aimed at the world's wealthy.

'For those with the means to afford it,' he said, 'I am offering a way out. I have set up an auction for two thousand exit halos to be unlocked. The top two thousand bidders will find their halos will glow for them once again. They will simply dive through and wake up in the real world. The auction is now open. To bid, just follow the short cut at the bottom of your screen. I wish you luck, but luck is expensive. My advice is to bid high.'

With that, the dragon disappeared again.

'Matthew?' asked Louise. Her voice was trembling, terrified. 'What do you think I should do?'

'Louise,' he said, looking back at her rose avatar on the screen. 'You are one of the wealthiest people on the planet. As much as it goes against every instinct in my body to do business with this madman, I think you should do exactly as he suggests – bid high.'

'Very well,' she said, 'I'll make the necessary arrangements with the board and with the bank.' She disappeared from the screen, leaving Jonah and his team alone with her metatranced body.

'This is about money,' mused Granger.

'What?' asked Jonah. 'What do you mean?'

'This auction, the ransom proceeds from the top two thousand bidders, will make him the richest person on the planet.'

'But what choice does she have?' asked Sam.

'She doesn't,' sighed Granger. 'He's one step ahead of us, ahead of everybody.'

'So how do we catch up?' asked Jonah.

'We don't know anything about him,' said Sam.

'We know one thing,' said Jonah. 'We know he's in a stolen avatar. He had to get it from somewhere.'

'There's a black market trade on avatar code,' confessed Granger. 'When I was in control, it was almost non-existent, but since you…since the Guardians took over most of my world, the black market has exploded.'

'Maybe,' conceded Sam, 'but Jason's avatar would have been copied over three years ago, before Heathrow, before—'

'But whoever copied it must've kept it and then sold it,' declared Jonah, recalling his father's instructions to trust a man called Sal Vator, a man that Jonah had brought the dehydrated and homeless Lakers to. What if the man Jonah's father had trusted was no better than a petty crook, fencing someone his ID once he was dead?

'I think we should contact Sal Vator,' said Jonah. 'He made the backup copy of my dad's avatar. The trail might start with him.'

'It's a long shot,' said Granger.

'It's worth a shot,' said Sam, nodding to Jonah in support.

Granger shook his head. 'Far better we try to secure the servers; try to extract the data. At least we know where they are.'

'I know where Sal Vator is,' said Jonah. 'He's in a commune in the Rocky Mountains. Not that far from here, actually.'

'But what about Axel?' asked Sam.

Louise returned to the screen. 'As soon as I wake up in my body,' she said, 'I'll deploy a crew.'

'The first thing you do!' insisted Sam.

'The first thing,' repeated Louise.

'Have you placed your bid?' asked Granger.

'My entire share portfolio in SynCorp. I can only hope it's enough.'

The screen flashed with a pop-up, announcing the end of the auction.

Jonah spotted Granger actually holding his breath.

'As we say in the oil business,' Louise began, 'this is when we find out if we've got a gusher.'

On-screen, the rose clicked on the pop-up, revealing a long list of names and corresponding avatars. As she scrolled from the bottom to the top, Jonah recognised a few names on the list, including Luke Wexler, who must have been unlucky enough to have been online at the time of the halo closure, and the King of England. Jonah wondered if he used public funds to pay his ransom bid. Finally, the rose found her own name at position number six.

'Oh, thank God,' she said.

Granger exhaled, returned to her side, and clasped her limp hands. 'It's going to be all right,' he whispered assumingly. 'You're getting out.'

'Five billion dollars poorer,' she laughed, breathing a big sigh of relief. 'Look,' she said, 'it's glowing.'

'I'm here waiting for you, Louise,' said Granger softly. 'On the other side of that halo.'

Her exit halo glowed as she hovered towards it. Louise didn't waste any time; the rose dived straight in, disappearing from the screen. Her exit halo faded away behind her as she safely left the confines of the Metasphere.

Her body twitched and Granger held her shoulders gently as she shuddered and opened her eyes. She opened her mouth to speak, but no words came out.

'Water!' Granger barked. 'Jonah, please; get her some water.'

Jonah fetched the lemon-water pitcher from the sideboard and poured a tall glass of clear water. His mind was still spinning with the mystery of his father's avatar, and as he thought of the Lakers, he remembered their waterless existence in parched Los Angeles. All around Fort McMurray, the sludge pools looked filled with rancid water, but here, sixty storeys up in an executive suite, clean water was at the ready.

Jonah thought of the lucky two thousand people who'd successfully paid for their own ransom, releasing them from certain death, and fumed at the injustice of a world where the rich thrived while the poor could not survive.

But as much as he resented Louise Thorne for buying her salvation, he still brought the water to her.

Granger placed the glass on Louise's lips and allowed her to sip at her own pace; slowly at first, then gasping at the water, her thirst seemingly unquenchable.

She spat up some of it, and embarrassingly tried to wipe the liquid off her blouse, but Granger helped her wipe it.

'It's OK, my dear,' he said. 'I'll buy you a new one.'

Finally sated, Louise sat up on the bed and gingerly placed her feet on the floor. She was clearly weak, but determined to stand. Jonah didn't know how long she'd been in-world, but guessed that she wasn't used to long metatrances. She had a distant, faraway look in her eyes. The readjustment to the real world could be disorienting, but Jonah worried that something else was wrong with Louise Thorne.

She stepped unevenly but managed to pull a chair over to her desk. She sat down behind the desk as if she was about to convene a meeting.

'Same old Louise,' Granger chuckled with a nervous laugh. 'Always ready to get back to work.'

But Louise didn't smile back. She didn't seem to show any expression. She had a haunted, vacant look on her face. Jonah recognised it, but in the moment that he associated it with the look on his mother's face before she pushed him out of the City Tower, Louise was already opening her desk drawer. He knew it now; it was the look of resignation.

But before he could say anything, Louise took out a gun, pressed it against her right temple and pulled the trigger.

19

Matthew Granger's world shattered in slow motion.

He heard the gunshot and watched as Louise's head flew back. The window behind her blew apart as Louise's dead body slumped forward, slamming onto her desk. It happened instantly, but Granger saw her suicide play out over minutes and not seconds.

He loved Louise, planned to spend the rest of his life with her. And suddenly now she was gone. Granger couldn't understand why. She had won the auction, saved herself by buying her freedom. And yet she had taken her own life. It defied all logic.

Granger feared it was pride that had trumped logic. Louise had pledged her entire fortune to escape the Metasphere and he wondered if she was too proud to be poor again. Louise had come from very little to become the most powerful woman in the world and often joked that she'd 'never go back'. Was her suicide the awful punchline to that unfunny joke?

His world had been ripped away. He'd lost his company earlier but now he'd lost his future. Once he'd won back the Metasphere with his Imprint Command, Granger had planned to live with Louise in Hawaii. She'd been urging him for years to stop 'while he was ahead', but he refused. There was always more to do, more improvements to make. When he was arrested and imprisoned, she waited for him. But Granger's focus turned to winning back his creation. He knew she didn't understand. He couldn't stop until his world was in his hands; until it was perfect. The Imprint Chamber was his chance to turn the tide, and end the battle for control forever. He'd promised Louise that as soon as the world knew that Matthew Granger was in control, he'd stop and they'd start their life together.

But in one shot, it was all gone.

Jonah flinched as the window behind Louise Thorne smashed open.

The fatal bullet must have gone straight through her head. Louise's body landed with a thud on her desk, rapidly marinating the unfinished paperwork in blood. So much blood.

'Louise, no,' Granger sobbed, rushing to her dead body. 'Why? Why did you do that? You were free.'

Jonah shuddered in shock. He'd seen plenty of death, too much death, but he'd never seen anyone take their own life. He didn't understand. He looked to Sam for answers, but also to avoid looking at Louise's burst skull. In his peripheral vision, Jonah saw Granger brush her hair from her neck and feel desperately, unsuccessfully, for a pulse.

Sam was also looking elsewhere, and Jonah saw her eyes suddenly widen. Jonah turned to see what had caught her eye.

In the glass tower opposite, a window smashed open. Shards of glass showered the streets below and Jonah saw a black desk chair hurtle down to the ground.

'What's going—'

But before he could finish his thought, a man in a suit stood at the open window. He spotted Jonah and nodded. And then he jumped.

Jonah gasped as the man plummeted to the street. No parachute opened. No executive escape glider wings snapped into place. The man just fell as far and as fast as gravity would allow.

Jonah pulled back his gaze before the man hit the pavement. He'd just witnessed one suicide; he didn't need to see another.

Suddenly, the double doors opened and two armed guards, wearing reflective black helmets and black body armour, burst in. They must have heard the gunshot and stormed into Louise Thorne's executive suite in search of the shooter.

Jonah and Sam both raised their hands, but Granger wouldn't leave the body of his girlfriend. The gun was lying in Louise's pooled blood on the desk, right beside Granger.

'Hands in the air!' shouted one of the guards, pointing his gun at Granger.

'I don't understand,' whimpered Granger to Louise's lifeless body. 'Why?'

'Granger,' called Jonah, urgently. 'Put your hands up!'

'What don't you understand?' shouted the other guard. 'Hands up, away from your weapon?'

'My...w-w-weapon?' stuttered Granger, clearly in a state of shock. There were tears streaming down his face, which bore a blank, dazed expression.

Karl Whittington strode in between the two armed guards. He looked at Granger with disgust and spat, 'Pretty despicable, even for you!'

Jonah realised the situation looked bad for all of them, but especially for Granger, who was almost literally holding the smoking gun.

'Um, sir,' Jonah uttered, keeping his hands on his head to show that he meant no threat. 'This isn't what it looks like. Ms Thorne logged off and she, um, she just...' As Jonah struggled to say it, he understood how unbelievable it would sound. But he said it anyway: 'She just shot herself.'

'Shot herself?' mocked the obese executive. 'Right after she transferred five billion meta-dollars worth of SynCorp shares into a secret numbered account?' He glared at Granger. 'Did you know she thought you came here to propose to her? But instead you came here to rob her. You robbed her and then murdered her!'

'He didn't,' defended Sam. 'She bid in the dragon's auction and as soon as she logged off, she just…she just shot herself.'

Four more armed guards filed into the room. They trained their stubby semi-automatics on Jonah, Sam and Granger while the first two handcuffed them behind their backs.

'Please, you don't understand,' said Jonah. 'We didn't do anything.'

'You say she just logged off and shot herself,' Karl said.

'Yes, exactly,' said Jonah.

'I know how it sounds,' said Sam. 'She was going to help find my dad. But then she—'

'You did nothing to stop her,' concluded Karl. 'Either you murdered my sister or you stood by and did nothing while she—'

'It's not like that,' explained Granger, as the guards thrust the three prisoners into the lift.

His sister. Jonah knew this meant trouble.

'Either way, I'm sentencing you three to death – by processin'.'

The lift doors closed – they were in another prison of sorts. The four faceless guards stood at the corners. When Jonah looked at them, he saw only death-row prisoners reflected back.'

'I *was* going to propose,' Granger said blankly. 'Right after I'd got out of jail. She would finally drop her ex-husband's name and become a Granger. But then the Guardians mobilised and I got so caught up in defending *what* was mine, I ignored *who* was mine.'

Jonah's ears popped. It was the first time he'd seen Matthew Granger as a real human being, and not as a corporate icon or a manipulative monster. He was a sad man who'd let his ambition blind his affection, and despite all of the horrible things he'd done to the world, Jonah pitied him.

The doors whooshed open and they were marched out onto the street. A security platoon had blocked off the pavement opposite and erected a screen to stop rubberneckers from spying on the squished body.

Two men in suits passed by, clutching expensive white paper cups, the status symbol of the rich and privileged. As they passed by, sipping on their coffee, Jonah overheard them snigger at the suicide:

'—coulda Uploaded instead of jumping.'

'Ha! Shoulda gone ßeta, that's what I woulda done if I had his cash.'

As Jonah tried to understand why two people in Fort McMurray would spontaneously commit suicide, a low rumbling sound interrupted his thoughts. A convoy of three yellow dump trucks drove towards them, dominating the street. Jonah recognised them as the toy-sized trucks he'd seen from the Cessna. But these trucks weren't tiny; they were the size of mansions. The guards moved their captives towards the last truck. Of course. It was here to collect them for *processin'*.

20

The black sludge tried to pull Jonah under.

The guards had forced the trio into the massive dumper filled with sludge. The tar sands were black and viscous. Jonah's cold suit, which he had not taken off since arriving in Fort Mac, was so black he could have passed for a SynCorp guard; which wouldn't have been a bad plan if he weren't suffocating in the sticky contents of the truck. And then there was the cold. The freezing air against his face was biting and fierce.

'Try to keep still, Jonah,' Sam called. 'Lie on your back.'

Jonah tried to float, but felt himself being pulled under. 'I'm sorry about Louise, Sam. For Axel.'

'Me too,' she said.

'Spread your arms and legs,' Granger contradicted Sam, 'like you're making snow angels!'

'What's that?' asked Jonah. The first time he'd seen snow was just yesterday, soaring over the snow-dusted tundra of the Canadian north. He spread out his arms and legs like Granger had instructed, keeping himself above the sludge. It was a small mercy, a temporary reprieve, since they were on their way to be executed at extreme temperatures.

'Seriously?' laughed Granger. 'You're that young you don't know snow angels?'

'Is it a rock band?' asked Sam.

'When I was a little boy, before my parents...before the accident, we'd drive up to Lake Tahoe at Christmas. They put me into ski school but I was terrified by the idea of throwing myself down a mountain on two planks of plexi-glass. So I'd stay by the school chalet, build snowmen. You do know what those are, don't you?'

'Sure, from the book,' said Jonah.

'My mum used to read that one to me too,' said Sam.

Jonah felt a tingle on his left-hand fingers. Frostbite, already? But then he looked over and saw that it was Sam, touching her fingertips to his. They shared a smile that was half reassurance and half resignation.

'Kids,' groaned Granger, before continuing. 'I'd stay at the chalet and my favourite thing was making snow angels in the pristine powder. I'd lie down, like this, and whisk my arms and legs around, creating the most beautiful imprints in the snow.'

'We've been to Lake Tahoe,' Jonah said. 'Sam and I. It was beautiful and filled with fresh—'

'Imprints!' Granger shouted suddenly. 'Imprints! That's what he's done!'

'What?' asked Jonah, tensing his body and immediately slipping back down into the sludge.

'Louise's suicide,' Granger said. 'It wasn't her idea. You saw her avatar before she dived through her halo. She was excited, relieved to get back to the real world.'

Jonah willed himself to relax. He focused on slowing his breathing and spreading his arms and legs wide to survive the pull of the tar.

'I don't understand,' said Sam. 'Why would she kill herself, then?'

'She didn't kill herself,' stated Granger. 'She was murdered.'

Jonah didn't want to protest, it didn't seem sensitive. But he'd seen Louise coldly and calmly pull the gun out of her own desk drawer, point it at her skull, and pull the trigger. The bloody scene stained Jonah's memory. He had seen it with his own two eyes. There was no doubt in his mind that it was suicide and not homicide.

'She was murdered by an idea,' said Granger. 'An idea imprinted onto her consciousness. An idea conjured by someone and projected onto her brain through her own exit halo.'

Jonah recalled the man across the street, the man who'd jumped to his death at the same time as Louise Thorne ended her life. Then Jonah realised he hadn't seen everything. What if he was a high bidder as well?

Fort Mac was filled with oil-rich billionaires. What if he was in the top bidders and dived through his exit halo at the same time?

'But that's like mind control,' said Jonah, doubting his conclusion. 'How could anyone control someone's mind?'

'The user must pass through the exit halo every time he or she moves in and out of the Metasphere. It's a central piece of programming code and is part of the Direct Interface link. It literally accesses and activates the subconscious to conjure the avatar. Diving back through simply closes the loop, and in that moment, whoever controls the central programming code could imprint a thought into the user's subconscious.'

'How do you know so much about this?' asked Sam with suspicion.

'Because I built it,' Granger boasted. 'I created the Imprint Chamber, a mechanism where one person could tell the world what to think.'

'And you're the one person?' accused Sam.

'Her brother was right,' realised Jonah. 'You murdered her.' Granger really was a monster.

'No!' countered Granger. 'I built the chamber. But the dragon, he hijacked it from me. He turned it into a weapon.'

'And what were you going to use it for?' asked Sam. 'Tell people to plant flowers?!'

'Peace,' said Granger. 'An end to this MetaWar. I was going to use the Imprint Chamber to finally ensure peace; peace through control.'

'Thought control,' corrected Jonah.

And then everything went black.

21

Jonah was drowning in the black sludge.

He tumbled and turned in the darkness; not knowing which way was up. It was no good trying to float any more. The bitter black sand filled his nose and mouth, slowly suffocating him. He tried to grip through the stickiness for Sam, but only felt the thick sludge slipping through his freezing fingers.

He had been expecting some type of signal, perhaps the jolt of the truck stopping, before it dumped them into whatever cauldron awaited. But the end came without warning. At least he'd suffocate before burning alive. Jonah closed his eyes – the tar stung and burned his pupils – and waited for death's grip to close. He had been fighting for so long, trying to make things right with the world, with his father, and with Sam. And now, it was all over. There was no hope of Uploading. There was no immortality awaiting him, online or off-line, only the nothingness that surrounded him as he exhausted his final breath. In that last moment, Jonah only wished he could find Sam's hand in the mud. He wanted to hold it, to touch her one last time, to tell her that he loved her.

But as suddenly as the darkness had come, he hit

the hard ground with a thump. Death's grip had loosened. He knew he was on the ground, and he knew which way was up. All he could see was a small mountain of tar sands pouring over him. He rose on his two unsteady legs, relieved that he could put his head above the black avalanche. He spat out the slime clogging his mouth and inhaled a life-saving breath. He was alive. He knew something had not gone to his executioner's plans. Jonah drew in another large breath and looked around, scanning for Sam.

He was outside, somewhere in the wasteland between Fort Mac and the processing plant. The dump truck lay on its side, burning. Its giant tyres were still spinning, but the truck was stationary. Smoke billowed all around, and several small fires burned on the road. The truck at the front of the convoy had gone off the road and lay grille first in the large ditch between the road and the churned earth.

A roadside bomb, Jonah concluded. *It must have upturned the trucks and spilled them, and the sludge, onto the road to the processing facility.*

Jonah didn't know if it was a lucky escape or another form of death waiting to take him.

The middle truck looked unscathed but it wasn't moving. Its driver opened the door and surveyed the wreckage of the other two trucks. Suddenly, he slumped backwards and then slid down from the doorway. He hit the road and didn't get up. Blood oozed from the bullet hole in his forehead.

Jonah looked around for a sniper, but didn't see anyone, including Sam. He quickly scanned the spilled dirt, searching for her. He finally spotted her feet protruding from the pile of sludge.

He trudged through the tar and grabbed onto Sam's ankles, pulling frantically until her blackened body was uncovered. He dragged her onto the softest part of the rocky roadside he could find, hoping not to trigger any undetonated land mines.

Her face was covered in tar, but she was alive. Uncovered from the noxious pile, Sam spat out a mouthful of sludge and let out a groan. Her green eyes against her black face could have made her look like a monster. But to Jonah, she was beautiful. She caught her breath and inhaled loudly.

'Easy now,' said Jonah. She was hyperventilating; but she was alive. 'You're safe now.'

Jonah turned her over into the recovery position, gently placing his hands on her shoulders.

'I'm here for you.'

She slowed her breathing and reached up to hold his hand.

Jonah almost cried with relief, but he didn't. He focused on tending to Sam instead. He kneeled down to her level and wiped the side of her mouth, cleaning it as best as he could despite his own filthy hands. She propped herself up on her knees and flung her arms around him, resting her head on his shoulder.

And then she sobbed.

She didn't say anything, and neither did Jonah. They just held each other beside the burning truck, thankful to be alive, and to be together.

'Is this what life is like with you two?'

Granger. Jonah turned to see him rising from the tar. He stepped over the mess, his titanium legs shimmering in the low afternoon light, but his upper body just as filthy as Jonah's.

'You kind of get used to it,' said Sam, her breathing returning to normal.

'But it takes a while,' added Jonah, reluctantly separating himself from Sam.

It was then that Jonah spotted their black-clad driver hoisting himself out of the cab. His reflective helmet was smashed, revealing his confused and angry face.

'You prisoners,' he called, 'don't move a—'

The air above Jonah's head whistled for a split second and the man's helmet cracked. The force of the bullet propelled the driver backwards and his body disappeared behind the wrecked cab.

Jonah pushed Sam to the ground instinctively, taking cover from whatever sniper lurked on the horizon. That's when he heard the laughing on the wind.

'What did you think, *mes amis*?' chuckled a voice in

a thick French accent. Jonah turned to see a red-cheeked man rise from the scarred earth, slipping a sniper's rifle over his back. He was dressed in a black jumpsuit but didn't sport the SynCorp logo on his chest. As he turned to straighten the rifle over his shoulder, Jonah noticed a green and black flag patched on his left arm. 'Did you think your Frère Jacques was sleeping? Ha! Ha! Ha!'

'Sam,' Jonah whispered. 'He's GuerreVert.'

'Then he's either here to save us or kill us,' said Sam.

22

Jonah held Sam tight.

They'd survived the sludge and escaped an explosive ambush, but Jonah didn't know if the approaching, chuckling sniper meant to finish them off. GuerreVert was the ruthless, international eco-terrorist group that the Fort Mac police had accused Jonah and Sam of being 'known associates' of.

'The morning bells are ringing,' the gunman sang, approaching the wrecked truck and spilled sands.

Jonah had never liked the GuerreVert. They had been allies of convenience, but then their European leader, Delphine, set Jonah and Sam up to be killed when they borrowed one of their planes in Sydney. Was this sniper here to finish the job?

'A friend of yours?' Granger asked Jonah.

'Not exactly,' said Jonah.

'More like a brother, *mon frère*,' said the man. 'My name is Jacques, and we have a friend in common.'

'Did Delphine send you to kill us?' asked Sam.

'*Mais non!*' Jacques laughed. 'She was delighted to hear you were in the Fort McMurray. Your presence, together with over half of their carbon-contributing population stuck inside the Metasphere, creates the perfect diversion; the perfect conditions for our plans.'

Was GuerreVert behind the red dragon? It made sense, they were eco-warriors, with no qualms about killing innocent people. Perhaps they'd escalated their war. Perhaps they'd decided that the only way to save the Earth was to eliminate humanity.

'What plans?' asked Jonah.

'To burn Fort McMurray like it burns the Earth,' he said with maniacal glee.

It was the first time Jonah had looked into the distance. Several miles away, the gleaming glass towers of Fort Mac were exploding. Among the skyscrapers, Jonah spotted the red-tinted Maple Leaf Tower. It was engulfed in flames. The entire city was burning.

Jonah swung around at a loud boom behind them. What next? He realised it came from the processing plant at the end of the long road, which now shuddered and sent out a mushroom cloud of black smoke into the sky. The mark of a bomb – or several, Jonah thought glumly.

'It has begun,' Jacques said with a smile. 'The city walls are locked, and the polluters will pay for their crimes. And to you, we say *merci*.'

Fort Mac had been a walled city-state, a secure oasis of gleaming glass amid the near infinite expanse of upturned landscape. But now, Jonah realised, it was a prison for its people.

'All those people!' Jonah protested. 'There are innocent people in there, whatever you believe about what they do here!'

'Everyone in there is complicit in burning the Earth,' Jacques said, his smile disappearing for the first time. 'And with the gates locked by GuerreVert, they will know what it feels like to be burned.'

'You're insane,' said Jonah.

'*Non*,' said Jacques. 'I'm hungry, and I think a popcorn would go well with the campfire, *non?*'

Jacques stared at the burning city, miming eating popcorn. He continued the repeated movement as he turned to look at the exploding processing facility to the north. He was transfixed. Jonah decided there was no point trying to reason with this insanity. Jacques, and those like him, were beyond reason. But that didn't mean he had to stand in the middle of nowhere and watch a city burn and people die.

'Sam, Granger; we have to get those people out.'

'Those people sentenced us to death,' reminded Granger.

'Even them,' said Jonah. 'We have to give them a way out, a way to save themselves.'

'Louise surrounded the city with fifty-foot concrete walls to keep people out,' said Granger. 'And we don't have a key. Your girlfriend Delphine is using their own security against them.'

'She's not his girlfriend!' said Sam. 'I am. And

154

who says we need a key?'

'Really?' said Jonah, at once surprised by Sam's use of the word 'girlfriend' and inspired by her resourcefulness. They had exactly what they needed to bust down the city gates right in front of them. They had a dump truck the size of a mansion.

'We're going to smash our way in,' said Sam.

'With what?' mocked Granger. 'Your fists?'

'No,' said Jonah, pointing to the middle dump truck. 'With that!'

He and Sam walked to the truck. Jonah stepped over its dead driver's body and climbed the ladder up to the cab. Twenty feet up, he swung himself inside. The engine was still running and Jonah surveyed the surprisingly simple controls: gas, clutch and brakes. He took the wheel as Sam joined from the other side, seating herself beside Jonah.

But Granger stood outside.

'Get in!' Jonah called. 'Like it or not; we're a team now.'

Matthew Granger, Jonah's deadly adversary for so many months, climbed aboard and completed the trio.

A team, thought Jonah. *A team with Matthew Granger*.

Channelling Jason's memories of driving RAF trucks around base, Jonah turned the vehicle around to face the burning city and accelerated as fast as the giant machine would allow.

There might have been over seven billion users trapped in the online death chamber that the Metasphere had become, but there were at least a million lives about to be burned to death right in front of him. He'd see to the Metasphere, starting with hunting down the man who copied his father's avatar, as soon as he'd given the trapped residents of Fort McMurray a chance to escape their fiery fate.

They might have sentenced him to death, but Jonah Delacroix did not want to become the type of monster that took pleasure in revenge. He wanted to stop the cycle of violence that was consuming both worlds. And he'd start with one desperate act of compassion. He'd start by smashing down the city's gates.

He'd start by acting like a saviour.

23

Jonah's airbag smashed him in the face as the truck's grille slammed through the iron gates at eighty-two miles per hour.

He'd been wearing his seat belt, of course, and Jonah slammed on the brakes as soon as he'd penetrated the gates successfully. He pushed the white airbag down – it was covered in blood from his nose – then threw the truck into reverse, opening up the escape route for the city's desperate citizens.

The mangled metal fell from its hinges, lying on the ground like a warped welcome mat. At first he thought he'd have to honk, holler or shout to alert the residents, but they found it on their own. Tens followed by hundreds and then thousands of frightened men, women and children bled through the incision he'd created. Desperate and afraid, the newly homeless families spilled out onto the great sludgy expanse beyond the city's walls.

Peering behind the walls, Jonah saw Fort McMurray burning from the ground up. The fires climbed the tall buildings as the skyscrapers shed their glass facades. It reminded him of the shards of ice that fell from the rocket that Howie and the pirates had launched; the rocket that launched his father's avatar into space. Those beautiful, crystalline flecks of ice were formed because the rocket heated so quickly that the air around it condensed into ice and fell away from the fuselage as it rose to the heavens.

The visual parallel was frightening to Jonah. As the glass panels fell away from their burning buildings, he shuddered at how two events, one beautiful and the other destructive, could look so similar. Maybe, he wondered, that was how people like Delphine and the red dragon saw the world; with no distinction between beauty and destruction.

The red dragon had used words like 'salvation' and promised to create a better world. Matthew Granger used to speak like that. He used to justify his actions by promising a better world for regular people. Even the Guardians spoke the same language as the murderous madmen and women who tried to shape the world to their vision through death and violence. The Guardians trumpeted freedom, but as one of them, Jonah had taken the lives of more Millennials than he could ever attempt to count.

Granger interrupted his thoughts. 'For those of them that have planes,' he said, 'there's going to be a mad dash to the airstrip.'

He was right.

Jonah had never seen so many private planes in one place before as the Fort McMurray Airport.

It made sense: a city that burned the Earth around it to make oil hardly had to worry about fuel shortages. Jonah felt a fresh sense of panic. If they were going to get to Sal Vator, over the border in British Columbia, they would need their plane. The certainly couldn't risk any of the fleeing Fort Mac residents stealing it.

Jonah backed the truck up, leaning on the horn to warn the fleeing crowd swarming all around. He put the massive dump truck into gear and drove onto the ring road that encircled the city's walls. On the service road to the airport, his lumbering truck was passed by impatient motorcycles and speeding SUVs. Granger was right; those that could were planning to get airborne.

As he approached the airfield, with the city burning in his side-view mirrors, Jonah yearned to know if there was a way to stop it all. Was there a way for people to live in the reality that existed, instead of seeking to shape reality to their vision?

If people just lived for real, Jonah wondered, could the world be saved? But then he asked himself: was the world worth saving?

'We don't have much time,' said Granger, again interrupting Jonah's vexing thoughts.

'We have to stop the dragon, stop the genocide,' said Jonah.

'We need to find him first,' argued Sam.

'But if we can't,' suggested Granger, 'we need a fail-safe.'

'What are you thinking?' asked Jonah.

'What I told you in Louise's office is true,' he explained. 'The program that controls the Imprint Chamber is loaded onto the servers that are bound for that train. And it's on the move. If it's not already, it'll be loaded onto the train and heading for Vancouver. My plan was to move it by ship to my base in Hawaii, where I'd transmit from the Imprint Chamber and—'

'Be in control over the entire online world,' snapped Sam.

'Bring order to chaos,' countered Granger. 'But the dragon's already used the chamber, and he might use it again. I think he's still going to move those servers somewhere, and the Vancouver port is his only option. Don't you see? Those servers contain the Imprint Chamber and the locking mechanism for the halos. If they go down, the defaults switch on and everyone can get out. But those servers are out in the open, on the tracks, for as long as it takes them to move the boxes from Banff to Vancouver. After that, they could go anywhere. And if that happens before his deadline runs out, everyone trapped inside, all seven billion, are as good as dead. If we can't find the dragon in time to stop him, there's only one choice left – our fail-safe.'

Jonah knew what he meant, but he couldn't fathom the choice. Granger meant to destroy the servers.

'But that's a quarter of the Metasphere,' said Jonah. 'Almost two billion users are in there,' said Jonah. 'They'll all die.'

'Two's a smaller number than seven, Jonah,' said Sam. 'That's the maths.'

'We sacrifice two billion people to save the rest, to save the five billion that won't stand a chance if we can't find and stop the dragon.'

'Then why didn't you tell us about this before?' asked Jonah. 'We could have flown to Vancouver instead of Fort McMurray.'

'I came for Louise. I feared she was in danger because of her, well, her connection to me. But I had no idea she was trapped in the Metasphere. No idea that after buying her freedom she'd—' Granger winced, swallowing his words.

'But now that she's dead,' started Sam, 'you don't mind sacrificing the rest of the people stuck in those servers.'

'Now that she's dead,' said Granger, 'I'll strap on a bomb and sacrifice myself if I have to.'

For a moment, silence filled the cab as the airstrip came into view.

'I'm going to get to Vancouver and prepare to blow up that train,' declared Granger. 'It's our only fail-safe. That gives you eighteen hours to find the dragon and stop him.'

'You don't think we'll find him?'

'I don't honestly know,' said Granger. 'But I do know that blowing up that train will save more than five billion people. It's the only certainty we've got.'

'And sacrificing two billion people is the price of that freedom,' said Jonah.

'I hope it doesn't come to that,' said Granger. 'But you need to track down that copied avatar and see if the breadcrumbs lead home.'

At the mention of food, Jonah's stomach groaned. But he had no choice but to ignore his hunger and exhaustion and press ahead.

'The avatar is the only lead we have,' he said. 'We'll start with the source; with the person who copied my father's avatar in the first place.'

'Sal Vator,' said Sam. 'At Quesnel Lake.'

'Then this is where we split,' said Granger. 'You two take the plane and I'll bribe a pilot to take me to Vancouver. I still have secret funds and even in this chaos, money talks.'

Jonah brought the dump truck to a halt behind the rows of private jets and prop planes.

'Then this is goodbye?' said Jonah.

'This is good luck,' said Granger. 'We'll all need it.'

They jumped out of the truck and Granger reached out his hand. Jonah thought he was going to shake it, but instead he placed a small glass square in his palm.

'It's an 8G communicator,' said Granger. 'Use it to stay in touch.'

'I thought those were illegal,' said Sam. 'Radiation and all that?'

'One day won't kill you,' said Granger.

Jonah thought about the day he'd already had and what might lie ahead. It hit him that there was a very good chance that this day *would* kill him.

As Jonah took the square and clipped it on the zip of his Kevlar jacket, Granger threw his arms around him. Jonah shuddered. His first instinct was that the man was going to snap his neck. But Granger simply squeezed Jonah's torso in a long embrace. Jonah didn't know what to do, but he responded by gently patting Granger's back.

Matthew Granger pulled away and looked at Jonah.

'Find him if you can,' Granger said softly. 'For Louise.'

'For everybody,' Jonah replied, turning to join Sam in running towards their aeroplane.

It was time to hunt the dragon.

24

Jonah soared the Cessna high above Quesnel Lake, the fresh water below sparkling in the setting sun.

'It's just as beautiful as last time,' said Sam.

'But more dangerous,' replied Jonah. 'This time we're flying with wheels, not pontoons.'

In theory, Jonah could put down in the water with the wheels down – his father had done it before – but it was an option only when no others existed. And it would wreck the wheels, making another take-off impossible. Instead, Jonah pulled the plane up, over the sloping hills that protected the Y-shaped lake, and searched for a stretch of road close enough to be of use and straight enough to be safe.

'We don't catch a break, do we?' asked Sam.

Jonah almost laughed. He was exhausted, covered in tar, and his face stained with dried blood. And he was sickened that he had just made a deal with Granger to kill off two billion people.

'No, we don't,' he replied. 'But we keep going.'

Jonah scanned the horizon, searching for a suitable landing strip. He'd need at least a mile of straight, wide road, ideally two, to land on. But straight and wide were not synonymous with the mountain roads.

So Jonah widened his search, flying further from their destination in the hopes of catching that break.

'What is it?' asked Sam.

'What's what?'

'Well, you've never really been a Guardian—'

'How could you say…' said Jonah, not finishing his thought.

'Not *really*,' she said. 'And yet you never, ever stop. So what propels you forward?'

Jonah thought about the question. He'd been lurching from one crisis after another since he'd first met Sam.

That night he'd risked his last meta-dollars on a skate-race around the Clapham Common bus-burb. He'd bet his meagre savings on the chance to win enough money to eat proper food, drink clean water and maybe even move out of the slum. But he hadn't wanted those things for himself. Jonah didn't care for Pro-Meal pouches, but he didn't mind too much. He was used to them. Water was always a concern, but wasn't it for everyone? And as for the bus-burb, he knew his mother was ashamed and embarrassed to live that way, but it didn't matter to him where he lived in the real world, so long as he had Metasphere access.

He'd risked it all for her. His mother, Miriam Delacroix, was widowed by forces outside her control and then murdered by a war she had no part in. When

Sam asked him what drove him, his first instinct was to say *survival*. But that was only partly true. Jonah wanted to survive long enough to stop this MetaWar, to stop the endless cycle of fighting and to push people, as many people as he could, over the threshold of enlightenment. He wanted to drag humanity, kicking and screaming if necessary, across the freedom frontier.

In a world where everyone lived for real, his mum would still be alive.

'I can't ever get her back,' Jonah said. 'But maybe I can stop other people from losing their parents.'

'Do you think Axel is still alive?' asked Sam. 'I don't know if I should hold on or let go. I just don't know.'

She'd lost her mother long ago, and Jonah knew there was a very real risk that Axel hadn't survived the cave-ins at the mine.

'We're going to find out,' Jonah promised. 'But the Axel I know would want us to press ahead, save as many people as we can.'

'He would,' said Sam quietly. She turned and looked out of the window, pensively, finally shouting, 'There! What about that one? Right between those two smaller lakes.'

Jonah examined the road from the sky. Sam was right; it was a long stretch of straight road nestled between two oblong lakes, about six or seven miles from the south-western shore of Quesnel Lake. On the opposite side of the mountain ridge, facing the stem of the Y-shape, was where the commune sat. That was where Jonah hoped to find answers to his questions about his father's avatar.

Matthew Granger stood outside at the Vancouver outpost of the Millennial Corporation. The company's logo, the stylised 'M' with the lone eye watching from the loop, hovered over the glass doors of the six-storey building. The Vancouver office was his first international outpost, home to bright young coders pulling twenty-four-hour hackathons to make the Metasphere great. In those early days, he had people around him who shared his vision, shared his passion. Like him, they wanted to give people an escape from the cruelties of everyday life. They were united in purpose, and determined to create a place better than the real world could ever hope to be. Granger had personally hired everyone in the office, ensuring each of them were as dedicated as he was. Over time, the Vancouver office grew its own identity and its own culture; a mix of laid-back coolness and world-saving earnestness. And he was proud of the place it had become.

As Granger pressed his face into the retina scanner at the doors, the glass doors swung open for him automatically. Once inside, Granger found the reception area deserted. He scanned his face again to access the open-plan offices at the rear of the ground floor, the centre of the coders' hive. That's when he saw the blood.

The fresh corpses of his people slumped at their computers and lay lifeless on the floor, partly hidden behind desks and under tables. It was obvious they had been hiding for their lives from an ambush and been massacred. Blood and brain matter decorated the white walls like a sickening Jackson Pollock canvas.

But on the far wall, the decoration was much more specific. Scrawled in the blood of his people, the murderers had left a message: TOMORROW IS COMING.

Granger immediately scanned the room, looking for any lurking gunmen. Convinced he was alone, he locked himself in his corner office. Granger kept an office in every one of his buildings around the world. Inside each one, he had access to both local and global CCTV footage – live and archived – so he could keep a close watch on his entire organisation. *Not close enough*, he thought. Somehow he'd been sabotaged from within.

He waved his hand across a bank of ten flat-screen monitors behind his metallic desk and pulled up the CCTV surveillance app.

On the map of the world, he tapped the Millennial logo hovering above the city of Chicago. The screens showed the same gruesome scene. Young programmers slumped over their desks and sprawled on the floor. Granger quickly tapped the looped 'M' icon above Paris to witness the identical carnage. One wall was covered in red graffiti: *DemAin aRriVe*.

It was the same story across the globe. Moscow, Seoul, Mumbai, Shanghai, Sao Paulo and Tokyo. Every Millennial office in Granger's portfolio had been attacked.

But how?

Granger flew his fingers over the screens, returning to the footage from Vancouver. Scrolling backwards in time, he searched the video feed for his answer.

The dead coders seemed to miraculously spring to life as Granger rewound over the moment of their death. He saw the employees rise from their deaths to panic and then resume work as normal...

Granger hit the parallel dashes of the pause icon, and then pressed play. He'd been expecting the killers to walk through the door. Instead, something much more terrifying unfolded. In an instant, four of his own people, people he had hired and welcomed into the fold of the Millennial family, stood up from their computers with machine guns and opened fire. They were attacked from within.

But there was something different about the shooters. All four of them, two men and two women, were wearing identical brown robes. Granger was used to coders wearing the oddest of clothes, and he never cared what someone wore to work so long as their code was ironclad, but these four murderers looked more like monks than assassins.

As his employees slumped to their desks he turned away. Unlike the video feed, he couldn't go backwards in time; there was no use dwelling on the deaths he could not prevent. His only focus, he decided, had to be to stop the larger massacre awaiting the human race.

Granger reached under his desk and felt for the smooth square of glass. It was a secret palm scanner and he placed his palm upright against it.

He heard a triple click and stood back as the desk moved two feet forward, revealing a secret trapdoor concealed by the desk's footwell.

Granger slid open the trapdoor and lowered himself into the hidden bunker below, into his personal arsenal.

Matthew Granger was a man who liked to be prepared, and since he'd built his fortunes on the fact that the world was falling apart, he'd built arsenals into every Millennial office around the globe. The lights flickered on with a wave of his hand, revealing shelves of food and medical equipment on the left side and racks of guns, ammunition and explosives on the right. If he was going to blow the train before the dragon's countdown ended, he'd need all the C-4 he could carry.

25

Sam's entire body ached.

She and Jonah had been hiking for hours up a steep incline through dense forest. She was filthy, covered in tar, and cold. The mountain air was cooling and the dusk sky was darkening. If they didn't make it over the ridge by nightfall, they risked getting lost in the vast woods.

The forest chirped and buzzed with natural sounds that sounded unnatural to Sam. Unseen animals, birds and insects seemed to surround her. She'd camped in the New Forest when she was a child, but the scale of British Columbia dwarfed anything she'd seen before. Compared to her small and crowded island, this land was immense and filled with wildlife. There was nothing British about it. The forest seemed endless, and she was surprised there were this many trees still standing. Most of the UK's forest had been razed for fuel, replaced with fenced-off farmland or fenced-in tenements.

Finally, by the time she and Jonah reached the summit, they had a clear view down to the moonlit lake. She noticed a few torches burning by the shore, but no other sign of inhabitants.

'Do you think she'll remember me?' asked Sam. She was thinking of Kit, the girl who helped Sam and Jonah escape from Los Angeles. She was the younger sister of the gang's leader, and she betrayed her brother to help Sam, Jonah and most of the gang flee the parched wasteland of Santa Monica.

'How could she forget?' said Jonah. 'You're probably the first person in a long time who truly listened to her. And you got her out of there, brought her to his beautiful place. She'll be glad to see you.'

Jonah knew just what to say. She loved him in a way that she had never known before. He had a purity of purpose that she loved, but that she also envied. His resolve was noble, while hers was tinged with darkness tainted with violence. It sometimes made her feel like a bad person, made her feel unworthy of their close bond, because he was so good and she had so much anger still circulating inside her. But he swept all of that away by reminding her of the good she'd done.

She had listened to Kit. She'd listened to Kit in a way that few people had ever listened to her, in the way that her mother used to when she was a child, but that Axel was never capable of. She listened to Kit because she saw herself in the young girl. She saw a girl filled with anger and drive and ingenuity, and she knew that in the wrong hands, those were the ingredients for a life dedicated to violence and hatred.

Sam knew that if she'd left Kit in Los Angeles, she

would have become a more dangerous version of herself. But she was able to see the good in Kit, like Jonah saw the good in her.

'I'm looking forward to seeing her too,' Sam replied.

Sam navigated the dark on the slope down. She stayed close to Jonah, her best friend, her only true friend, taking in the unfamiliar sounds of the strange forest. The evening breeze rustled the pine needles overhead. Somewhere in the distance, perhaps across the lake, she thought she heard a wolf howl. Sticks broke under her feet and occasionally she swept up dried needles with her shoes. The gentle noises filled the cool night. They carefully stepped down the mountain, staying close, until one sound stopped her cold. She reached out for Jonah, holding him back, as she heard the all-too-familiar double click of a handgun being primed.

Someone was preparing to shoot.

26

A flash of white light blinded Jonah.

'Jonah? Sam?' called a girlish voice from the darkness. A girl with a torch trained on his face. Jonah recognised it immediately, but Sam was first to speak.

'Kit?' she said, shielding her eyes from the light. 'Is that you?'

'I almost shot you,' the girl's shaky voice replied.

The figure, mostly in shadow, wore a dark cloak tied like a robe. Its hood covered her face with a mesh mask. She could see out, but Jonah could not see in.

'I'd never forgive myself,' she said.

'It *is* you, Kit,' replied Sam.

The figure lowered her torch and stepped through the forest to greet them. Kit pulled the mesh mask over her head, resting the hood behind her flowing hair. This girl looked much healthier than the dehydrated, desperate girl they'd rescued from LA, her bright complexion reflecting the full moon above. She also looked much more grown up, standing tall.

Kit safetied the gun, dropped it in a deep pocket of her robe, and enveloped Sam in a hug.

'I can't believe you're here,' she said. 'But I'm not sure you should be.'

Kit withdrew from Sam and Jonah reached out his hand to shake her hand. But Kit threw open her arms and wrapped Jonah in a tight squeeze, either oblivious to, or unconcerned about, his filthy condition.

'You know,' she said. 'I thought it was your voices, but figured my imagination was playing tricks on me. Then when I saw you two, covered in black camouflage from head to toe, I guessed you must be attacking from one of the ranches over the ridge.'

'It's not camouflage,' said Sam.

'But we did come from over the ridge,' Jonah said.

'In that plane?' Kit asked. 'We saw it circle overhead. It spooked the elders. They put us all on watch.'

'Sister Kit! Sister Kit!' rang a voice through the trees.

'Brother Tony!' she called back. 'Over here. Follow my voice, it will guide you. It will give you the path.'

Jonah recognised the name, but something troubled him. Tony was the real name of Jackson, the leader of the Lakers gang that Jonah helped to overthrow and betray. At the last minute, when his defectors threatened to throw him out of the aeroplane, Jonah had stood up for him. Jonah had insisted that no one was going to kill him, or anyone else, while he was piloting their escape plane. In the end, Jackson turned his back on gang life and decided to join the defectors in their new life in the Canadian mountains.

But it wasn't the anticipation of meeting Jonah's former captor that troubled him; it was the way that Kit was speaking.

Jonah had noticed it with the two adults he'd met at the dock when he'd led the Lakers kids to their new home. The scene flashed in his head, reminding him of the last time he'd come to Quesnel Lake:

Jonah crested a ridge of British Columbia's Rocky Mountains and spotted the Y-shaped Quesnel Lake below. He circled the plane above the lake and brought them down gently in the stem of the Y.

It wasn't long, of course, before the gunboats found and surrounded them. The locals were as wise to water theft as were the owners of Lake Tahoe.

The three boats herded Jonah's plane to a small pier, where armed men and women, dressed in long, brown robes were waiting. They signalled to Jonah to come out of the plane.

'Stay inside,' pleaded Sam, gripping Jonah's arm.

'It'll be OK,' said Jonah, as he stepped out of the cockpit, through the hatch and onto the bobbing pier. 'My name is Jonah Delacroix, and I'm looking for Sal Vator.'

One of the women laughed. 'Aren't we all!'

The others joined in her laughter and Jonah forced a grin.

'We disturb no one up here,' said a man with long, braided hair. 'Why do you disturb us?'

'He helped my father once, and now I need his help. We're carrying, um, water refugees, children mostly, from—'

'And are you not a child?' asked the man.

'I'm just trying to help,' said Jonah. 'And I'm hoping you will too.'

'I am not the salvator,' said the man. 'I am merely a servant. But we know the name Delacroix here. He is a friend to our community, and helped us when we needed it. You can tell him that we will honour our friendship by helping out his child.'

'Thank you,' said Jonah. 'But I'm not a child, really, I'm...'

'We are all tomorrow's children,' said the woman, pointing to the pier. 'And if your charges will work the land to earn their keep, live at one with the land, then we will welcome them here.' She looked past Jonah to the plane and asked, 'Will you join us?'

Jonah turned to see Kit standing at the hatch. She jumped onto the pier and stood bravely beside Jonah.

'We've come from Los Angeles,' she began. 'And Jonah has helped us escape. We just want to survive.'

The man with the braided hair knelt down to look Kit in the eyes. 'You have a brave spirit, my child,' he said softly.

He rose to address the other robed men and women. 'We will welcome these newcomers. These children will take lessons alongside our children. They will farm

and nurture the land alongside our children. And they
will be one with our way of life. So it is said.'

The others bowed their heads, and repeated his words.
'So it is said.'

'Thank you,' said Jonah.

'You are a Delacroix,' said the man. 'And you are their
saviour. And we will honour that.'

'Thank you,' said Jonah. 'My father was right about
you and your people.'

'I would ask you to stay with us as well,' said the man.
'But I know you are still walking your path.'

'Jonah, my saviour,' said Jackson, now Tony, stepping
from the darkness and removing his mask. 'Have you
come to join us?'

Jonah gave a slight shake of his head. 'We're here
to see Sal Vator. I have something very important to
ask him, and not a lot of time.'

Tony looked around, his eyes darting about, and
pulled Jonah into a quick embrace. He whispered into
his ear in a rushed, panicking voice, 'Things are not as
they seem here, Jonah. Have you come to save us
again?'

Tony quickly pulled back, resuming his previous
composure, as if he were acting in a holo-film.

'We have endless time here in the mountains; for
we wait for the new era to begin,' Tony said cryptically.
'Do we not, Sister Kit?'

But if Tony was acting, Jonah wondered who, and where, the audience was.

'We do, Brother Tony. We are Tomorrow's Children.'

27

Jonah was uneasy about meeting the man who'd copied, and likely stolen, his father's avatar. But he was his best chance left to save humanity.

He stepped through the hanging animal skins that covered the doorway to the long, low wooden building. A burly man in a brown cloak rose from the ground where he'd been sitting beside one of two fires in the room.

'The pied piper has returned,' he said, pulling back his hood. The man had long white hair and a matching beard, making him look like a woodland Father Christmas. He smiled a wide, welcoming grin.

'Sal Vator?' asked Jonah.

The man walked towards Jonah and opened his arms.

'And you are the only son of Jason Delacroix. Your face has aged, and you carry yourself like a man, but I see you as the child your father sought to protect.'

'You knew my father, you helped him copy his avatar,' Jonah said, getting straight to the point and not yet walking into Sal's offered embrace.

But Sal stepped forward and clutched both Jonah

and Sam in his arms. He was stronger than he looked and held them tight.

'We do not speak of such things here,' he whispered in Jonah's ear. 'Those days are behind me, like a distant yesterday.'

Jonah felt his grip loosen and he stepped back nervously, pulling at Sam's hand, but Kit and Tony were blocking the doorway.

'We speak only of Tomorrow here, don't we, children?'

Tomorrow. Children.

'Yes, Father,' Tony and Kit answered in unison.

Tomorrow's Children.

The term haunted Jonah. But it wasn't until he'd heard Sal Vator use the words that he realised he recognised his voice. They'd never met, but suddenly it all clicked into horrifying place. He'd first heard the phrase 'Tomorrow's Children' when he'd dropped off the Lakers. One of the commune members, a woman, had uttered it. And then Tony had said it on the lakeside of the ridge. But that wasn't the full connection. Jonah had heard the phrase when the red dragon had threatened to kill the seven billion users stuck inside the Metasphere.

Sal Vator was the red dragon.

And Jonah and Sam had just stepped into his den.

'And Tomorrow is a day anew,' Sal continued. 'Tomorrow you will rise, cleaned from the filth that poisons your skin, and purged of the sins of the world that you carry with you. I can smell them on you.'

'It's the oil sands,' said Jonah, stalling for time, not knowing how to signal to Sam that they had to get out of there. They weren't safe – far from it. 'We've just come from Fort McMurray.'

'One of the worst offenders,' Sal said. 'They cut the trees and remove the topsoil to dig up the ground underneath only to boil it. I'm sure you witnessed the destruction all around that sinful city.'

'We did,' said Sam, still oblivious to the threat. 'It was awful.'

'Here we live in harmony with the natural world. We worship her. We are her humble servants, disciplining ourselves to reject the hubris of man that thinks he can win dominion over the natural. We are nature's allies here, and she can always use two more. Which is why I am so pleased that you have returned to join us; to live in harmony.'

'We have?' asked Sam, looking at Jonah.

'Yes,' confirmed Jonah, realising that Sal Vator probably didn't know Jonah had worked out his alter ego. Sal Vator, Jonah reckoned, was so consumed by his own ideas that he simply thought that he and Sam were wayward teenagers returning to a place of beauty they once discovered. Jonah decided to play to Sal's ego. 'We've seen the destruction out there. We've seen what happens when people abuse nature; just look at us. We're covered in the blood of the Earth. After what we witnessed at Fort Mac, Sam and I…'

Jonah reached out and grabbed Sam's hand. He wanted everyone to see that he and Sam were inseparable.

'Sam and I thought about the kind of place we wanted to live,' continued Jonah. 'And we remembered how your people opened their arms and their lives to Kit and to Tony, and to all the children we flew here. You welcomed them into your community. We hoped that perhaps you would welcome us as well.'

Jonah didn't like to lie, but he figured his best chance of stopping the genocide was to get close to Sal, to discover where he hid the halo controls and hack them if he could. He just hoped his performance would persuade Sal to take them in.

As the robed leader grinned as wide as a Cheshire cat, Jonah got his answer.

'You are both welcome here,' the man said, gripping them both in a tight embrace for a second time. 'You are my children now.'

28

Jonah saw the shoreline sparkle through the trees.

He and Sam followed Sal by the hand down the gentle slope towards the lake. The man gripped Jonah's hand with a tight, leathery grip that wasn't painful but was strong – to show Jonah that he had no intention of letting him go. He walked tall, clearly proud of his newest recruits; or as Jonah felt, his newest captives.

As they'd left the longhouse, Sam had shot Jonah a concerned look, asking Jonah *'What are you doing?'* with her eyes.

He had not wanted to arouse any suspicion, so he quickly mouthed, *'Trust me.'*

Sam rolled her eyes, but nodded slightly in agreement.

Kit and Tony walked in front, lighting the way with their torches. Jonah could hear the muffled garble of excited voices down below as Kit and Tony reached the shore. Jonah saw the full moon reflecting in the twinkling lake's gentle waves and spotted a dozen silhouettes standing in the near darkness. The owners of the voices, waiting by the pebbly beach, all seemed to speak at once.

'He's here?'

'Jonah?'

'—they've returned!'

'And Sam?!'

'—Father, is that really them?'

Jonah looked around at the faces stepping from the shadows. He recognised Kareem, Shaq and half a dozen others. Even in the moonlight, covered by the same brown cloaks that Kit and Tony wore, he could tell they looked healthy and well fed. Unlike the last time he'd seen them, their skin was smooth and flushed; they had plenty of fresh water to drink.

'Your Deliverer has returned,' stated Sal. 'Brother Jonah and Sister Sam have come to join us.'

The Lakers cheers and whooped. For a moment, it reminded Jonah of the rowdy enthusiasm they displayed when Jonah had first returned from Lake Tahoe with tanks full of fresh water. It gave him hope. While they might have been indoctrinated into Sal's cult, under their cloaks they were still excitable teenagers.

Sal finally released Jonah and Sam's hands. The Lakers rushed the newcomers, embracing and hugging them despite the filth that covered them. Shaq ruffled Jonah's hair and Kareem tenderly kissed Sam's forehead. Then Jonah felt his feet lift from the ground as Kareem picked him up in a bear hug.

'It's good to see you guys,' Jonah said through

squeezed breath. Kareem released him and Jonah planted his feet back on the soft ground.

'You look a lot healthier than when we brought you here,' said Sam.

'Can you believe it?!' squealed Kit. 'We actually live beside this lake. The water's so clean you can just walk right into it and take a drink. And sometimes, you know what? I do. Just because I can!'

'But what's happened to you two?' asked Kareem. 'You look a whole lot worse than when we last saw ya.'

Jonah put his arm around Sam, and pulled her close. 'We've been through a lot,' he said.

'Ha!' shouted Tony, pointing at the two of them. 'I knew it! Didn't I call it? And you denied it, Jonah! Sam *is* your girlfriend!'

Jonah smiled. He remembered protesting the fact the last time he stood on this shore.

'You're right, Tony,' Jonah said. 'You're right,' he repeated, meaning Tony was right about Jonah and Sam's intentions at Quesnel Lake. Tony locked eyes with Jonah; held his gaze. He understood. Jonah just hoped he could count on the former gang leader to help when the time came.

'Let us welcome Brother Jonah and Sister Sam into our community with the Ritual.'

Sal Vator led them in procession along the pebbled shoreline until they came to a clearing with a large steel-bottomed wooden tub. It was on stilts, about ten feet off the ground. Underneath, a fire roared.

Jonah looked at Sam nervously. They'd narrowly escaped an execution by 'processing', and now, as he looked at the steam rising from the tank, he feared they were about to be boiled alive.

29

Jonah surveyed the steps leading up to the boiling cauldron and then back to the darkness of the line of trees, eyeing an escape.

'Do not be afraid, Brother Jonah,' said Kit, as she and the Lakers gathered around the cauldron. She must've have sensed Jonah's panicked hesitation. 'We've all taken the bath.'

The *bath*?

Jonah allowed himself to relax, ever so slightly. After everything he'd been through with Sam, and knowing the Sal Vator was the red dragon, he'd jumped to the conclusion that he wanted to kill them.

'It's the first step in the Ritual,' added Tony.

'The first step to a new beginning,' declared Sal Vator. 'You are both covered in the filth of the man-made world. Here, we seek to return you to a more natural state. Please, ascend the steps, remove your clothes and we will burn them in the fire below.'

Jonah was relieved not to be climbing to a boiling cauldron but to a steaming bath instead; but now a new fear rose within him: taking his clothes off in front of the group, in front of Sam.

'Excuse me?' snapped Sam. 'Take our clothes off?

Burn them?'

'Modesty is not a function of the natural world,' said Sal, 'but if it makes you more comfortable, you may leave your undergarments on. But your outer clothing is contaminated. Here, we wear the sacred robes. It is our way.'

'It is said,' said Tony in a monotone. Jonah caught Tony glance his way and shoot him an encouraging wink. Tony was play-acting too.

Jonah reached the top of the steps and stood on the small platform. He noticed two brown cloaks pegged to an adjacent pine tree. He thought back to being aboard the *Marin Avenger*, when Matthew Granger asked him to remove his wet clothes and put on the Millennial uniform to stay dry.

You'll catch your death, Granger had said.

Jonah realised there were great similarities between Granger's ship and Sal Vator's Quesnel Lake commune. Both had charismatic leaders who demanded loyalty and respect. Both asked their followers to shed the clothing that gave them outward individuality. And both demanded their followers wear a uniform to demonstrate their belonging and their loyalty.

If Jonah was going to keep up the act and infiltrate Sal Vator's operation in time to save the users stuck online, he'd have to continue to play along. He unzipped his sludge-smeared Kevlar suit and peeled it from his weary body. He removed his inner thermals and took off the long-sleeved grey T-shirt that hugged his skinny, pale torso.

He tried not to look at Sam as she stripped to her underwear beside him, but he'd never seen a girl undress before and couldn't help catching a glimpse of Sam's athletic body in the moonlight. Before he could dart his eyes away, Sam caught him looking.

She shot him a smile, and rolled her eyes. She raised one leg over the rim of the tub and then another. She sat on the edge and slowly lowered herself in. The steaming water covered her body up to her shoulders.

'It actually feels really nice, Jonah,' she said, leaning her head back and dipping her red hair into the water.

Jonah followed her lead, stepping over the rim and immersing himself. She was right, the hot water felt incredible. Jonah couldn't remember the last time he had taken a bath.

He scooped up some water and rubbed his face, trying to remove the grime from his skin. As he scrubbed his palms against his cheeks, removing the sticky tar, it felt like peeling off a part of his life he was happy to leave in the past. Everything about Fort McMurray haunted him, from the endless tracts of dug-up earth around it to the skyscrapers burning within its own walls.

'Is that not better, my children?' called Sal. 'Is that not a more natural state?'

A black, sooty smoke rose all around the tub – Sal must have tossed their clothes on the fire. The night air smelled foul as the synthetic fabrics burned below. But the smoke also gave Jonah and Sam a brief moment of privacy.

'Are you OK?' mouthed Jonah.

'What are we doing here?' asked Sam in a low whisper. 'Joining his crazy cult?'

The black smoke was fading away, the shoreline regaining its natural, wooded scent. Their smokescreen was gone. Jonah pushed himself to Sam, whispering into her ear.

'Sam, Sal Vator is the red dragon. He's behind the lock-in in the Metasphere. He's behind the suicides and he's planning the genocide. As long as he thinks we're no threat, we can find out how he's keeping everyone trapped in the Metasphere and stop him.'

'And then we kill him,' she replied.

Before Jonah could respond, before he could plead with her not to jump to the violent extreme, he felt the entire tub tilt, and then the rush of water, as he and Sam were emptied into the cold, dark lake below.

The near-freezing water of Quesnel Lake shocked Jonah. He panted for breath and searched the dark water for Sam.

'Sam!' he called.

She rose from the lake, drenched and disoriented, but quickly stood in the waist-deep water.

On shore, the Lakers cheered. Only then did Jonah notice that the tub's stilts were on hinges. Two of the Lakers, Kareem and Shaq, slowly pulled it back, resting it upright.

'You are cleansed!' called Sal Vator. 'And ready to be enrobed.'

Jonah and Sam stepped back onto shore, the pebbles hard and slippery beneath their feet. Kit wrapped Sam in a large, brown cloak, and Tony did the same for Jonah.

'You are one of us now,' said Tony as he helped Jonah to slip his wet arms through the sleeves. He tied the soft belt around Jonah's waist and pulled up the hood. Jonah stepped into the soft leather sandals that were laid out for his feet.

'And we welcome you gladly,' said Sal.

'Thank you, we're glad to be welcomed,' said Jonah, hoping his act was still convincing.

'And now to your bunkhouse,' ordered Sal. 'The sun will soon rise over that ridge, and with it rises *Tomorrow*, my children.'

30

Jonah heard the bunkhouse door lock from the outside.

He was under no illusions; he was a prisoner again. Jonah, Sam and thirty of Sal's 'children' were locked inside their log-cabin dormitory. He turned from the door to survey the kids – aged from eight to eighteen, he guessed – cloaked in identical brown robes and perched at the bottom edges of their identical single beds. Jonah walked the length of the prison, thinking about what to do next.

'He locks you in each night?' Jonah asked the group. 'Are there other adults here?'

Slowly, once they knew their 'father' was gone, the kids collected in the middle of the room.

'He's good to us,' said Tony. 'He and the elders provide food, shelter and only ask that we work the land in return, which we're happy to do.'

'Did you know,' chirped Kit, 'that if you put seeds in the ground here, you can grow food?'

Jonah caught Sam offering the girl a sad grin.

'He doesn't mistreat us,' Tony continued. 'He doesn't hit us, doesn't touch us except for his hugs, so don't go thinkin' there's anything weird or perverted going on here; cuz there ain't.'

It was strange to hear Tony speaking like Jackson again, but Jonah guessed that he, and the other children, were expected to speak a certain way in front of Sal Vator.

'He's a good man,' added Kit. 'But he isn't who he pretends to be.'

'We know,' said Jonah. 'That's why we're here.'

'Something terrible is happening out there,' said Sam, 'beyond this valley. And we think Sal Vator is behind it. We need to know everything that you know about what's going on here.'

'And then we need to know if we can count on you to help stop him,' added Jonah.

'We could tell you,' said Kareem.

'Or we could show you,' said Shaq.

'How? We're locked in,' said Jonah.

Kit answered cryptically at first, explaining that when the Lakers arrived, the first project Sal set for them was to build this bunkhouse. 'It was great,' she said, 'all of us working together, alongside the Quesnel kids who were already here, building our own home. It really brought us all together, like a family.'

'Which was probably the idea,' added Tony. 'But I used to be a gang leader and I saw that's what Sal Vator was too. All of us here, we're just his gang. "Cept this ain't no street gang. Somethin' else is goin' down, and whatever it is, it happens in the mountain.'

'*On* the mountain?' asked Sam.

'No,' said Kit. '*In* the mountain. Inside of it. Sal Vator says that he's turned his back on computers and techy stuff and all that, but we saw it one night when we snuck out. The mountain is hollowed out and it's filled with computers and with…' Kit looked around nervously, clearly unsure about finishing her thought.

'We need to know, Kit,' Sam said, putting her hand gently on the girl's shoulder.

'Inside the mountain, where it's hollow, it's filled with computers and…skeletons.'

Jonah heart rate suddenly rocketed – he felt it pounding in his chest. He'd been worried earlier about being killed by Sal Vator, only to be lulled into a sense of security by the cleansing ritual. He immediately looked at the rafters, searching the roof and walls for signs of gas lines. He remembered his teacher, Mr Ping, discussing the gas chambers used in the Syrian civil war. When British soldiers finally went in, they found piles of skeletons buried outside the death rooms.

'Shiny skeletons, like metal,' Kit clarified. 'There's thousands of them – with black shiny screens where heads should be.'

'ßetas,' gasped Jonah, at once relieved and confused. 'Why would Sal Vator have a stash of ßetas?'

Tony shrugged his shoulders. 'We know somethin's strange,' he said, 'but we don't know what exactly.'

'We need to see all of this,' said Sam. 'We need to get out of this cabin.'

Tony motioned to the kids to clear away from the bed he was standing beside, moved the bed and pulled up the small rug that ran underneath it. He tugged at a floorboard, revealing a handle, and pulled up the trapdoor.

'When we built this bunkhouse, we gave ourselves a way out,' he said with a proud smile.

'Always leave yourself a back door,' Jonah whispered to himself, echoing Granger's mantra.

'The tunnel below runs 'bout seventy feet up the hill,' Tony explained. 'It's not a lot, but it's enough to get outta here.'

Jonah was happy to have them as their guide, but at the same time he worried about getting them into more trouble that they had signed up for. They seemed willing enough, but Jonah was very wary of what Sal Vator might be capable of.

'Ladies first.' Jonah smiled, gesturing to Sam to go ahead.

'How very gentlemanly of you,' Sam said, lowering herself into the darkness. 'Here we go again.' She grimaced and dropped down into the black hole.

Jonah followed closely behind. 'It's the least I could do since I've seen you half naked.'

'Almost fully naked!' corrected Sam. 'And you

certainly took a good long look,' she said with a smile in her voice.

Jonah suddenly felt very nervous. 'You were right beside me,' he said defensively. 'What was I supposed to—'

Sam laughed.

She kicked up dirt into Jonah's face with her heels. 'Boys.'

'Is that what I get for being gentlemanly?' asked Jonah, wiping the soft dirt from his cheeks, crawling behind Sam on all fours in the pitch-black darkness.

'No, that's what you get for staring,' said Sam.

Jonah couldn't see her expression, but he was pretty sure she was smiling. It felt good to be able to tease her, and to take a teasing. They'd been so focused on fighting to stay alive ever since Sam jumped out of the airship that they'd barely had any chance to catch their breath, let alone catch a laugh.

'Not that there was much to see,' Jonah lied playfully.

'Uh huh,' said Sam.

The strange thing was that it didn't feel strange. Here he was in the dark, buried beneath a mountain, crawling to almost certain death if he was discovered; and yet Jonah felt like he was on a first date.

They crawled in single file through the dirt and darkness. Up ahead, a dappled light marked their target. Sam held back a large bush, allowing the moonlight to illuminate the opening.

Jonah crawled through the mouth of the tunnel and joined Sam in the fresh night air.

Kit and Tony followed them out of the tunnel.

'You guys either really love each other or really hate each other,' said Kit, dusting herself off.

'It kind of depends on the hour,' said Sam.

'Well, it's sweet and funny to hear you talk,' said Kit. 'But mostly funny.'

'This way,' beckoned Tony, quietly calling them along the hillside. 'There's an opening around this corner, but stay low; the elders come out at night.'

'What about weapons?' asked Sam. 'You two were armed when you found us in the forest. We're going to need those guns.'

'There's an armoury down by the lake,' whispered Tony.

'Can you access it?' demanded Sam.

'I'm not supposed to know the combo, but I do,' he said. 'Do you think—'

'We don't know what to think just yet,' interjected Jonah. 'Let's find out what's going on inside and then form a plan. If we're caught with weapons, people will start shooting.'

Jonah noticed Sam shaking her head. 'Then let's not get caught.'

The foursome snuck through the evergreens, walking amid the dappled, silver light of the moon until they saw a soft-blue glow emanating from a cave-like opening in the mountainside.

As Jonah carefully rounded the corner, he was struck by how much technology was buried inside the mountain. The opening was deceptively small, only ten feet wide, but the chamber inside was cavernous.

The immense interior reminded Jonah of the inside of Uluru in Australia; hollowed out and filled with technology. But unlike Ayers Rock, this mountain lair was filled with stacks of silent ßeta robots. They hung on racks, at least twenty on each, and Jonah did a quick scan to count them. He lost count at one hundred racks, and that was only the ones that were stacked sixty or so feet above them on one wall. Jonah had never excelled at maths, but he forced his brain to quickly tally the population of sleeping ßetas.

There were over six thousand robots hanging inside this mountain. Whatever Sal Vator was up to, it was much bigger than killing off the seven billion people who were trapped online. Whatever he was planning, it had something to do with the real world.

31

Jonah quietly stepped into the high-tech cavern, looking for answers.

The hollowed-out mountain chamber was several storeys tall with a shiny, polished concrete floor. The pale rock of the mountain formed the walls, lit by pale blue floodlights bolted into the granite. As he stepped silently across the room, towards a large array of computers and flat-screens, Jonah caught his shadow move against the ancient rock.

With the racks of ßetas behind him, Jonah noticed that the chamber tapered into a long corridor that led deeper into the mountain.

He didn't want to admit it, but the lifeless robots, hanging on racks, spooked him. They looked like marionette puppets just waiting for someone to control their strings. Jonah's mind flashed to a day at the seaside with his parents, where they'd watched a puppet show on the Brighton pier. The other children in the audience were mesmerised by the seemingly autonomous puppets. But Jonah was unsettled by their masters, these unseen puppeteers pulling the strings of the wooden marionettes. To him, it was frightening to think that the hidden masters could make the puppets say and do anything they pleased.

'What do you suppose they're for?' asked Jonah.

'Nothing good,' Sam replied. 'Shhhh. Do you hear that?'

Ahead, down the corridor, he could hear the muffled sounds of adult voices.

'That's the elders,' said Kit. 'They come and go, but when they meet with Sal, they stay in here.'

'C'mon,' Jonah urged. 'Let's find out what's really going on.'

They proceeded down the dimly lit corridor, penetrating deeper inside the mountain. The voices got louder and Jonah could here Sal speaking softly and seriously:

'—The world is almost ours,' he said. 'And your faith in a better tomorrow will be rewarded.'

'And no one suspects zee final purge?' asked a woman with a familiar French accent. It was Delphine.

'How could they?' responded a man in a nasal voice that Jonah knew but couldn't place. 'The programming code is buried into the ßetas' OS. The protocol is dormant until it is time. Dormant and undetectable.'

'There are three billion people on this planet who are not online,' said Sal. 'They believe that through serendipity or through divine intervention they are safe. Some feel lucky. Some feel a great sense of validation in their choice not to enter the Metasphere. Some feel chosen, blessed even. But all feel safe because they are not trapped behind a once-golden halo. But they are not lucky, they are not blessed, and nowhere is safe. The ßetas will see to that.'

'And we will start anew,' said a man's voice in an ever-so-slight Chinese accent. It sounded like Mr Chang, but Jonah knew that was impossible. The young titan had been crushed when Hong Kong fell.

Jonah knelt down and pushed his head around the steel doorframe. He looked into another cave, smaller than the main chamber and carved out to appear like a dining room. Four people were seated for a candle-lit dinner. A ßeta robot, with a snail-shaped avatar on its screen-head, served steaming vegetables onto their plates while another, a cobra snake, filled their goblets with blood-red wine. Jonah took it all in; but as much as he believed what he was seeing, he couldn't believe who he was seeing.

Delphine sat with her back to Jonah, but he recognised her as she brought the bulbous glass to her lips and drank. She wore the same brown cloak as Sal and the others, but there was no mistaking her short, black hair and ruby lips.

To her right sat a ghost, to Jonah at least; a man Jonah thought had perished in the fires of Hong Kong. Mr Chang smiled at the others, wearing an impeccable grey suit under his brown cloak.

Opposite the Chinese billionaire sat a man with a long, mournful face; a man Jonah knew to be a

Millennial turned Guardian, but who now appeared to be neither. It was Erel Dias. Jonah couldn't comprehend it all. Delphine, Mr Chang and Erel Dias dined with Sal Vator inside a mountain and congratulated themselves on a new world they planned to create.

They clinked their glasses together. Sal raised a toast: 'To the second great flood. This time,' he added, 'we chose not to wait for God.'

The elders nodded and drank, sipping their crimson wine, while seven billion people panicked for their lives online and another three billion were oblivious to whatever terror was to come.

Jonah recalled the stories from the Bible about Noah, a man God had instructed to build a great Ark. Noah collected two of every animal, plus his family and loyal friends, and floated on the murderous waters that God sent to purge the Earth of evil. Sal Vator seemed to see himself as a modern-day Noah. And unless Jonah stopped him, he would succeed in bringing about a second great flood: a deluge of blood.

Suddenly, Jonah felt himself rising into the air. The cobra ßeta had hold of him from above and yanked him into the dining room.

'What's this? An additional guest?' mused Sal Vator, unflustered. 'But there is no more room at my table.'

Mr Chang rose and bowed. 'Master Delacroix.'

Jonah didn't know if Sam and the two Lakers had been caught, but he didn't look back to check. He didn't want to give away that he wasn't alone.

The robot held Jonah tightly in an upright position, Jonah fighting for breath in its grip.

Sal's guests looked shocked to see him.

'What an unexpected *surprise*,' whispered Mr Chang.

'You're telling me,' said Jonah, wheezing.

'I thought you were lost in the Northern Corner,' said Erel Dias. Jonah couldn't tell if the brilliant Brazilian bio-programmer was relieved or disappointed.

'Or at zee Fort McMurray?' suggested Delphine. 'Where you met my comrade, *non*?'

Jonah scanned their faces, which oscillated between surprise and curiosity, and decided to play for time. He might have been caught, but his mission was the same; he was here to understand what Sal was up to and how to stop him.

So he decided to lie.

32

Sam led Kit and Tony back down the corridor and out through the main cavern where the lifeless robots hung.

'C'mon, we have to get the others,' she commanded, leading them back to the bunkhouse.

'Are you sure we should just leave him in there?' asked Kit.

'No,' said Sam. 'But Jonah's smart and he'll stall for time, giving us a chance to regroup and return, armed and ready.'

As Sam raced through the forest, her heart felt that she'd betrayed Jonah by leaving him behind, but her head told her she was doing the right thing. It would be harder to explain what they were doing in the cavern as a foursome, but on his own, Jonah stood a chance of concocting a convincing story.

But she only half believed her hopeful delusion. Sam cursed herself for allowing Jonah to push forward unarmed. It was the one thing they disagreed on, their only division. Sam had learned the hard way to walk softly and carry a loaded gun. Whereas Jonah still clung to a naive sense of mind over matter. She was convinced that unless she watched out over him, protected him with deadly force, it would get him killed.

'Will they help us?' asked Sam, rushing through the woods with Tony.

'I'm still the Jackson,' Tony boasted. 'And Jonah's still our saviour.'

'Jonah and *you*,' added Kit.

They reached the locked bunkhouse and Tony tapped rhythmically on the wooden door.

'You guys, it's me. Jonah's been caught – it's time to fall out,' he said with an urgent whisper.

'We'll meet you at the end of the tunnel,' came a voice from inside.

Sam thought back to her journey through the long tunnel, and quickly scanned the forest around her. She spotted a pile of firewood in the next clearing. She ran to it and found the axe she was hoping would be there.

'Stand back,' she called to Tony, as she raced towards the door, swinging the axe at the large bronze padlock.

It smashed off easily with the brunt of Sam's swing. 'That tunnel will take too long,' she explained, opening the door to face the captives inside. 'We need to get to Jonah now. He's not a great liar.'

Kit led Sam, with the axe still in her hand, to the concrete bunker that housed the guns. The armoury, which was built into the side of the mountain, was triple locked with more padlocks, which only slowed

Sam down long enough to formulate a plan in her head. The grey interior was massive, opening up into a smaller carbon copy of the ßetas' cavern. Sam scanned the weaponry and slung a stub-nosed semi-automatic around her shoulder and pocketed two grenades. Kit chose a handgun while Tony reached for a rifle. Once the whole group had armed themselves they assembled in the clearing outside, Sam striding out to give orders to the group.

That's when they turned their guns on her.

Time and time again, Jonah acted on impulse without thinking through the consequences of his actions. Matthew Granger had chastised him for not playing the long game, not thinking ahead. So Jonah decided to channel Granger's mantra as he hung helpless in the air, gripped by a silver robot that he knew could rip him apart. Jonah tried the long game. He told Sal Vator what he believed the man wanted to hear.

'I don't just want to join you here at Quesnel Lake,' Jonah began, still breathless. 'I want to join your larger quest; your larger goal.'

'And you know of our purpose?' asked Sal, but not really asking at all. He waved to the ßeta to put Jonah down. As the robot released its grip, Jonah flexed his lungs, filling them with air.

'Is that why you snuck in here?' asked Sal. 'To join our cause?'

'They wouldn't understand,' said Jonah. 'They are just children. They don't see the big picture; they don't see what I've seen since I got pulled into the MetaWars. I used to live on a bus, and attended one of your schools, Mr Chang, but then everything changed. I learned how people were fighting over the Metasphere, but nobody was fighting for the real world. Delphine, your GuerreVert network was fighting the symptoms, but not the cause. Doctor Dias, you switched from Millennial to Guardian and I guess you found out the same thing that I did: that both were the losing side of a futile war. I've lost both of my parents to this conflict, and since there are no winners, there can only be losers. The only way to save humanity, is to destroy it.'

'I cannot tell you how happy this makes me,' said Sal. 'I have been following your progression, your growth, since you were a little boy. When your father first came to me, he was concerned that something terrible would happen to him.'

'You helped him,' said Jonah, hoping to stoke Sal's ego. 'As only you could. But how?'

'I provided him an insurance policy against his death; I copied his avatar without Uploading him. In return, he gave me access to the Millennial organisation, believing I was a sympathiser to his true Guardian leanings. But my plan has always been broader than that short-sighted skirmish.'

Jonah thought back to his father's suggestions of contacting Sal Vator. Jonah had always assumed it was in case Jonah needed help. But now he wondered if Jason had suspicions and wanted Jonah to investigate the mysterious monk. Jonah wanted to learn all that he could to find a way to stop Sal's war on humanity.

'You played the long game,' said Jonah. 'The very long game.'

'I helped both sides escalate their war to the point of running down their troops and depleting their resources. Both sides posed a grave threat to my purpose. Organised and united, they could have stopped me. But divided and in conflict, they let me slip silently between them, planning a future that neither could fathom. And since I have your father to thank for helping me to get started, it is only fitting that his only son joins me at the dawn of this new tomorrow.'

'I'm ready,' lied Jonah. 'You said it yourself. I came here covered in the filth of the man-made world. It's time we changed the course of the planet, forever.'

Sal reached for the bottle of red wine and poured it into a spare goblet. He lifted it up for Jonah to take. The dark red liquid reminded Jonah of the blood of so many people who'd died in the MetaWars. He held the glass, but was he ready to drink with the man who was planning the extinction of all but a handful of the human race?

His hand trembled, waiting for Sal's signal to drink.

'But I believe your father discovered my purpose and unlike you, did not approve,' Sal said. 'And that's why I killed him.'

33

Sam thought about running.

She quickly calculated her chances of survival: zero. So she decided to talk.

'Jackson, I know—'

'He's not the Jackson, no more,' spat Kobe. 'I am. And we've got a good thing goin' here.'

Sam noticed for the first time that Tony and Kit were unarmed. They'd stuck their necks out for Jonah and Sam and now theirs were on the block just like Sam's.

'You guys,' said Sam softly, not wanting to make anyone jumpy. 'I know what Sal Vator means to you all.'

'You have no idea,' said Kobe, pushing his pistol closer to her face.

'I know you feel like a community here,' she added.

'Like a family,' called one of the younger kids who Sam didn't recognise – a Quesnel Lake 'native' who'd never been a Laker.

'Adam's right,' said Shaq. 'We are a family, and we have to protect one another.'

'You're right,' said Sam. 'You're part of a family, but it's a much bigger one than you think. You're part of a family of everyone on this planet and the man who calls himself your father is planning to kill them all off.'

'Some family,' scoffed Kareem. 'Where were they when we were dehydratin' to death in the LA desert?'

Kobe nodded. 'Yeah.'

'And where were they when my mother was dying of a treatable disease?' asked Sam, trying to reason with them. 'Where were they when my father was being crushed to death under rock and granite in the frozen north? Where were they when Jonah's dad burned to death when the airports went up in flames? And where were they when his mother pushed him out of a window to save his life, only to die when the building collapsed around her?'

'See, she agrees with you,' stated Kit, her eyes widening at Kareem.

'There's a part of me that does,' Sam said. 'There's a big part of me that's been all around the world and seen the very worst of what humanity has to offer. My mother was a religious woman. She wore a cross around her neck and prayed every night, and when she was dying, she believed that God was taking her to Heaven. So I know my Bible, and I know the Book of Genesis. And I know that your *father*, Sal Vator, thinks he's the new Noah. But we can't let him extinguish the wickedness of man. It's not up to him.'

'But you just said—' urged Kobe.

'There's just too much good,' Sam continued. 'And you know who I'm talking about.'

'Jonah,' said Kit.

'I don't know if it was chance, coincidence, God's hand, or just dumb luck that landed Jonah and I on your shores that morning, but he saved you and brought you here to the one place he believed you'd be safe and happy. And, Tony, when your gang wanted to toss you out at ten thousand feet without a parachute, was there one person who stood your ground?'

'Jonah,' said Tony quietly, looking down. 'He did.'

'He saw the good in you, just like he sees the good in everyone. And if he was willing to save you, we need to save him. And if he sees the good in everyone beyond this valley, even all of those people who've turned their backs on us, then we have to too. It's that simple and we don't have much time.'

'She's right,' said Tony. 'The first time Jonah came here, he saved us all, especially me. This time, he's come back, but to save everyone else. And Sam's right; we have to help him.'

'But Father will protect us,' said Kobe with a confused, torn look on his face.

'This is the one place no harm will come to us,' added Shaq.

'He's not your father,' said Sam. 'He's a monster. And I bet your real parents would want us to stop him. I know mine would.'

Jonah had so far kept himself calm and composed as he'd lied to Sal Vator. But now, he was trembling with hatred and fury.

'Y-you?' he stuttered, feeling so tightly wound, like a spring about to explode. 'You killed him?'

'I wish I could tell you that he was an innocent bystander,' Sal said coolly. 'But nobody who stands by while the world slowly dies can be innocent.'

Jonah hurled the glass of red wine at his father's murderer. The goblet smashed into Sal's face. Wine and blood trickled down his checks. But Sal simply smiled. He looked like a deranged, washed-out clown. As the red cocktail dripped towards his mouth, Sal licked his upper lip.

The blood-and-wine-soaked grin enraged Jonah. The spring sprung. Jonah lunged to strike Sal. But before he could land a punch the cobra-screened robot grabbed Jonah by his shoulders and hauled him into the air.

'Now tell me what you're really doing here, orphan!' commanded Sal.

'I'm here to stop you,' said Jonah, wincing through the pain of the robot's metallic fingers pressing into his flesh. 'Even if it kills me.'

'It probably will,' promised Sal. 'Your father tried, and you know what happened to him.'

Jonah thrashed to get loose, but the ßeta's grip was too tight. Sal laughed and Jonah caught a glimpse of the dinner guests, awkwardly looking down and away. They wouldn't, or couldn't, face him.

Sal stepped forward and swung. Sal's fist slammed into Jonah's cheekbone. For a dizzy moment, Jonah thought he might black out. But Sal pressed his face right into Jonah's and whispered, 'You are *yesterday's* child, and there is no place for you in my tomorrow. I could kill you now, or wait to deploy the ßetas. I'll give you the benefit of choice.'

'Did you give my father that choice?' Jonah spat.

'I gave him the choice to join me here, and he refused. I told him I wanted to build a better world; a world not concerned with who owns what on a bunch of computer servers. But he thought I was just hiding out in the mountains. He didn't understand that it's not enough to wait for Tomorrow, you have to create it. You have to pull the sun into the sky to shine on the new era.'

'It doesn't have to come with death,' said Jonah. 'You can show some mercy.'

'We've pushed this planet to its breaking point and it's fighting back. As a species we face a long, painful road to extinction at the hands of plagues, storms, starvation and dehydration. So much suffering to come.'

'You're a sick monster if you can't show mercy,' sobbed Jonah as the robot's steel fingers dug into his skin, suspending him in the air.

'Don't you see, Jonah? I am showing mercy! The people locked in the Metasphere will die a painless death. They have the chance to Upload themselves. I've secured enough server power here to house them all. I am offering those not on my Ark the lifeboat of digital immortality. You would offer them the certainty of suffering. Who's the sick monster, Jonah?'

'But what about the off-liners?'

'I've programmed the ßetas to be quick and efficient. When they cleanse the Earth they will take no joy in killing. They won't be like humans, who taunt and torture. No, they will put no emotion into the exercise. And when it's all done, they will clean up the bodies, return them to the Earth and repair the planet.'

'While you stay safe in this valley?'

'This is the Ark,' said Sal. 'And like Noah, I am but a servant.'

'Awfully convenient,' said Jonah. 'You survive while the rest of humanity dies.'

'We will start anew,' said Sal. 'We are *Tomorrow's* Children.'

'Then you'll have to do it without us,' called a voice from behind Jonah. He swung his head and saw Tony and Sam leading all of the kids into the dining-room cave.

Jonah gulped in relief when he saw they were heavily armed. Every single one of his 'children' trained their gun on Sal Vator.

34

Jonah watched the look of defeat and disappointment crawl across Sal's bloodied face.

'Looks like your Ark's emptying out,' Jonah said.

Sal stared down the barrel of Sam's approaching gun, calm, unblinking.

'It's over, Sal,' Sam said. For just an instant, she glanced over at the table, where the three stunned diners sat. Jonah saw her look of recognition and then confusion. But Sal saw it too. In that instant, he swung Sam's gun from his face and jumped up into the air, kicking it out of her hands.

Jonah was still gripped by the robot, unable to help as Sal threw Sam to the floor.

Sal pulled a gun from inside his robe and aimed it at Sam, stopping the Quesnel kids from advancing. Without taking his aim off Sam, Sal crossed the room and headed for a second doorway behind the dining table.

'Father!' shouted Kit, distracting Sal Vator for an instant. But it was long enough.

'I'm not your—'

A single shot silenced the room.

Jonah looked to see Kit holding the gun, trembling

in the aftershock of its discharge.

'Nobody moves,' called Kobe, as the platoon trained their guns on the other three elders at the table.

Suddenly, the ßeta robot dropped Jonah. He fell to the cold, concrete floor with a painful thump. He lay beside Sam, looking up at the steel skeleton of the ßeta, which had immediately charged to Sal's side, administering first aid.

'Are you OK?' Sam asked, reaching out for Jonah's hand.

'I am if you are,' he replied, grasping her hand. Jonah rose painfully to his knees, helping her up. He suspected her pride was more injured than her body; knew she'd be feeling stupid for getting distracted.

'No more shooting!' called Jonah. 'We need Sal alive. Only he has the codes to unlock the exit halos. If he dies, everyone online dies too.'

Jonah rushed to Sal, slumped over on the far side of the room. The blood was already soaking through his brown cloak. His wound was just above his waist and Jonah worried that he might bleed out on the grey concrete before revealing how to stop the impending genocide. As the wounded man gave a sputtering, laboured laugh, Jonah realised that was exactly what Sal Vator intended to do.

'It's not important if I survive,' he said, fresh blood bubbling from his mouth. 'It's only important that my children survive.'

'We're not your children,' said Kit.

'And we never were,' added Tony.

'No, you're right,' coughed Sal. 'You're Tomorrow's Children. And Tomorrow begins today.'

Sal closed his eyes as his head slumped. Blood trickled from his mouth, but a much larger pool of crimson spread out from his cloak.

'Sam,' called Jonah desperately. 'We can't let him die.'

'Dias!' shouted Sam. 'Get over here!'

Dr Erel Dias slowly rose from his seat, clearly terrified by the gang of armed children aiming their weapons at the remaining adults. He knelt down beside Jonah and Sam at Sal's body.

'He is alive, but barely,' Dias confirmed.

'Then we only have once choice,' said Jonah. 'We have to Upload him.'

'We can't force a user to Upload,' protested Sam. 'The software doesn't work that way.'

Jonah looked Erel Dias in the eye and said, 'Then someone who values their life will have to hack it.'

He rushed over to the dining table and pulled off the white linen cloth. Food, plates and cutlery smashed to the floor as Jonah revealed the wooden tabletop underneath. Jonah flipped the table onto its side and pulled one of the table legs out. Sam joined him on the other side and yanked out two legs as Jonah removed the fourth one. She seemed to know exactly what

Jonah was doing, constructing a makeshift stretcher.

In sync, they flipped the tabletop over and carried it to Sal's slumped body.

'Give us a hand,' called Jonah to the Lakers, still with their weapons aimed at Sal's stunned conspirators. Kareem and Kobe disappeared into the rear doorway, which Jonah noticed was a kitchen, and returned with long tablecloths that they used to tie up Mr Chang and Delphine at gunpoint. Once the prisoners were being secured, Tony, Shaq and Kit lowered their guns and joined Jonah and Sam at the deconstructed table on the floor, helping to pull Sal Vator's bloodied body onto it. 'And lift,' Jonah commanded.

Sal rose into the air as his 'children' carried him out of the room towards the computer banks in the main cavern to save his afterlife. Jonah's only focus was to preserve Sal Vator's stolen avatar, which held the bio-kinetic key to unlocking the Metasphere's exit halos.

They placed the makeshift stretcher in front of the row of servers Jonah searched the desk drawers, finding an Ethernet and adaptor pack. He tore open the DI adaptor with his teeth and carefully placed it at the end of a snaking cable coming from a terminal.

'Plug it in,' Jonah asked Sam.

'Are you sure this is a good idea?' she asked. 'Perhaps we just let him die?'

'Granger said that the code to unlock the halos is

embedded within his avatar,' said Jonah. 'If he dies, so does that code.'

'And you, Dias?' asked Sam. 'Can you Upload him?'

'To save the saviour,' he said. 'I will do it.'

'If you save humanity from this sick monster,' said Jonah, 'then *you* will be the saviour.'

Dias tapped the screen and opened a line of computer code. Jonah watched as Dias logged into his personal inventory space and launched a hacking program that filled the screen. The Brazilian man, whom Jonah had once looked up to as a genius bio-hacker, quickly found the source code to the Dias Protocol, the program he had created to extract an Uploaded usurper from its host. Jonah watched as he deftly altered the program, reversing it to force a live user to Upload. Jonah hated this man for his true allegiances, and yet he couldn't not respect his brilliance. In a matter of minutes, Erel Dias completed the hack and visualised the new program on screen as a bear trap.

'Place this icon near Sal's avatar when he appears in the Metasphere,' explained Dias, 'and it will pull him into the Uploading program.'

'It'll force him to commit suicide?' confirmed Sam.

'It will make him immortal,' countered Dias.

Jonah tugged off Sal's robe, now heavy with blood.

Underneath, the soon-to-be-fresh corpse wore brown canvas shorts and a crisp brown, cotton T-shirt.

Jonah lifted up the bloodied shirt from Sal's lower back. The gunshot wound was close to Sal's Direct Interface port, and at first Jonah feared that it had damaged the opening. But as Jonah wiped away as much blood as he could with his hand, revealing the opening in the base of Sal's spine, he relaxed ever so slightly. The port was still there and it looked undamaged. Jonah inserted the adaptor into the small plastic ring that waited in the base of Sal's spine. He twisted the adaptor clockwise until it clicked twice. Sal Vator's body shook slightly; the connection was made. The man's body might have been dying, but his mind was already projecting itself into the virtual world.

'Point of Origin?' asked Sam, now leaning over the control bank.

It didn't matter where he went, and the first coordinates to pop up in Jonah's mind were for Venus Park, the ornate park space outside the vacant remains of his family gift shop. He called out the eight digits to Sam, shuddering as he remembered the day he had entered the Metasphere in Venus Park, glided amid the lovers who congregated there, and discovered the copy of his father's dragon avatar in the secret cellar of the gift shop.

The park space appeared on the terminal's screen;

it looked very different from the happy place in Jonah's memories. It was night-time, and hundreds of avatars were holding a vigil by candlelight. The gatherers looked mournful and resigned. They were turning round to say final farewells to family and friends before reaching their hands to their mouths and swallowing a glowing blue capsule; the suicide pill. For some, it was already too late.

In a blur of red pixels, Sal materialised as the dragon. He looked around at the dark, unfamiliar environment and spread his wings to fly away.

'Now!' shouted Jonah.

Erel Dias slid the bear-trap icon from one screen to the next. The jaws of the trap opened below the dragon, bathing him in a soft, white light. The glow enveloped the escaping avatar and like a hurricane wind dragged him into the mouth of the afterlife. The dragon disappeared and the jaws snapped shut.

Sal Vator's physical body began thrashing around as his mind Uploaded to the Metasphere, and Jonah was careful to hold the DI in place.

'You've got him,' said Sam to Jonah. 'But what are you going to do with him?'

Jonah couldn't bring himself to tell Sam what he was thinking. He knew she would try to stop him. If Sal Vator's immortal avatar was the key to unlocking the exit halos, then Jonah would have to fuse himself with the madman's consciousness.

Jonah was going to let Sal Vator usurp him. He was going to allow Sal's ghost to take over his mind, and then turn the tables on him. He would have to take control over his usurper in order to access the controls to the exit halos. The only problem was, those controls were on a secret server, travelling by rail, bound for the port city of Vancouver.

'Sam,' Jonah said. 'We have a train to catch.'

35

Matthew Granger's titanium feet clanked rhythmically on the wooden railway ties as he hiked along the empty line.

He had cleaned the Vancouver office's secret armoury of all of its explosives, hired a helicopter with his secret stash of meta-dollars, and was now walking east along the railway through the mountains that overshadowed him. The rail line soared over a deep gorge above a raging river called Stoney Creek, just west of the British Columbia border with Alberta. Sal Vator's deadline would expire in less than two hours. Granger would set the explosives on the sturdy steel trestle bridge that spanned the gorge and blow up the freight train as it trundled past. He would destroy his Northern Corner servers before Sal Vator's deadline, before they reached the city.

He was distraught at the massacre of his own people and numbed by the prospect of destroying the Metasphere, and yet he felt relieved by his own paranoia. He was a man who liked to be prepared and thus he'd secretly stashed equipment, food and weapons in every Millennial office around the world. He saw early on which way the winds of the future were blowing, and he vowed to be prepared for the downfall of the real world. But as prepared as he was, he came to the lonely realisation that it was all a facade.

His organisation had been infiltrated from within. Traitors had spent years, decades even, in his ranks and seemingly at his command. But secretly they were serving another master. Granger chided himself for being so blind, so unaware of what was really going on around him. Ever since he broke out of jail, he'd been plagued by the relentless advances of the terrorist Guardian network. The insurgents, claiming to fight for freedom, consumed his attention and distracted him from the greater threat rising from within. The two sides, his Millennials and the rag-tag Guardians, ground each other down in a MetaWar that had no winners.

He'd once lectured Jonah Delacroix, the boy he'd hoped would join his side and become his heir, on the merits of patience and perspective. But walking alone on the tracks, without any organisation behind him, Granger had to face the harsh truth. It was he who had been dangerously short-sighted.

The red dragon, the mysterious man who had hijacked his code and his Imprint Chamber, had been pitting the two sides against each other while standing back and waiting; waiting for a very long time. The dragon has been playing the long game; not a MetaWar, but a war of attrition.

But Granger was determined to see the dragon fail – and this was the cost. He vowed he would not be outwitted by this man. He refused to become a footnote in history.

As he trekked eastwards, with a backpack of C-4 slung over both shoulders, he arrived at the bridge. It stretched hundreds of metres across the Stoney Creek gorge. Down below, the white water raged, snaking its way through the mountains, making its mark on geological history. But up here, on this manmade viaduct, the train carrying his servers would soon pass. And when Matthew Granger destroyed the bridge, he would leave his own mark on history.

Still in their brown robes, Jonah and Sam hiked the steep hill abutting Quesnel Lake to return to the sky.

Jonah had watched Sal Vator's body die. He wanted to be sure. Jonah then returned to the dining room to ensure that the other two elders, Delphine and Mr Chang, were secure. They, along with Dias, would answer for their crimes, but first Jonah had to free the online hostages. He didn't want to waste any more time by changing clothes, even though he felt ridiculous traipsing up the mountain in what amounted to a thick dressing gown with a hood.

They'd said goodbye to Kit and the others. Jonah hoped the children of Quesnel Lake could survive on their own. Tony and Kit had stepped up, proved themselves to be leaders, and Jonah told himself that they would reconstruct everything that was good about Sal Vator's commune without any of the negatives. He told himself that, but he wasn't sure if he believed it.

As soon as they reached their aeroplane, Jonah carried out his pre-flight checks and joined Sam in the cockpit. She had taken a satellite-linked datapad from Sal Vator's control centre and opened up the map that showed the rail lines snaking west through the Canadian Rockies to Vancouver on the coast.

Jonah felt Sam shudder beside him.

'What is it?' Jonah asked.

Sam held up the datapad for him but he didn't look at the screen because Sam was crying.

'He is alive,' she said. Jonah looked down at the screen to see a message from an avatar with the body of a lion and the head of an eagle.

DARLING SAM – BODY TRAPPED IN MINE TUNNEL. MIND TRAPPED IN METASPHERE. CONSIDERING UPLOADING MYSELF BEFORE IT'S TOO LATE. I'M SORRY. FOR EVERYTHING.

I LOVE YOU.

– DAD.

At once, Jonah was relieved that Sam's dad had survived the terrible explosions at the mine, but also terrified that she might lose him again if they failed their mission.

'He must've logged on to contact me,' said Sam. 'And now he's stuck.'

'What's Sal's countdown at now?' asked Jonah.

Sam held up the datapad, showing a vast cornfield, where thousands of avatars were congregating in a trampled-down crop circle. The clock blinked: 01:52:38.

It wasn't long. And Jonah knew that if Sal Vator's deadline passed without freeing the hostages, then Axel's mind and body would be separated permanently.

'We're going to open those halos so he can get out. You message him that. You tell him not to Upload. We're coming for him!'

She started tapping a reply, but stopped herself. 'But what if it's no use?' she sobbed. 'What if his body is so badly damaged that Uploading is his best chance? My mum never Uploaded—'

Jonah reached out and held Sam's hand. He knew how sad, how angry she was that her mother never joined the Uploaded 'club' – as she'd once called it. That she had no post-mortal connection to her mum. Without speaking, he wanted her to know that he remembered.

'—and every day I wish she had. I don't want to spend the rest of my life wishing that about Axel too.'

'Sam, I promise you I'm going to do everything I can to get your dad back to you,' he said. He knew how horrible it was to be without both parents, and he didn't want Sam to live through the grief he'd endured in losing his father. But he didn't want to tell her how far he was willing to go to save the users trapped online; how far he was willing to go to make good on his promise to Sam.

Jonah watched as Sam finished her message back to Axel. A moment later, a pop-up chimed up on the screen:

OK. KIDDO. HOLDING TIGHT, CROSSING MY PROBABLY VERY COLD FINGERS.

Axel was trapped in two places, but they'd first have to release his mind before they could even attempt to free his body.

'Now,' said Jonah. 'Let's find that train.'

Jonah taxied back onto the straight road and started up the plane's single propeller. He glanced at the fuel tank gauge – less than a quarter full – but he knew their journey was going to be short and it was going to be one-way.

As they took the plane to the sky, Jonah and Sam soared over the long stem of the Y-shaped Quesnel Lake. Jonah looked down, considering the path not taken. He could have hidden out in the mountains, together with Sam, and waited while the world started anew. But Jonah had seen too many people justify their violence with grand world visions. If he chose hiding over fighting, then he was no better than Sal Vator. Some time ago, perhaps when Jonah was still a bus-dwelling student at the Chang Academy, he might've believed that fighting for freedom was someone else's job, someone else's responsibility. But that was a long time ago and Jonah was a different person now. It was up to Jonah and Sam, and hopefully not to Matthew Granger, to stop the genocide of the human race.

As Jonah levelled off at his low cruising altitude, his mind turned to their newfound ally.

'I think it's time to check in with Granger,' he said to Sam.

She held the square, shiny communicator in her hand, pressing her thumb to the glass plate.

'Granger, it's Sam and Jonah. Do you copy?'

'You're still alive,' said Granger in a metallic tinny voice that filled the cabin.

'We found the dragon,' said Sam. 'And *he's* not. Not any more.'

'But you need him alive,' gasped Granger. 'He's locked the halos with his own bio-metric code, contained in his avatar. If he's dead, then everyone's stuck inside.'

'I thought of that,' explained Jonah. 'So we Uploaded him and then trapped his avatar.'

'Still does us no good,' complained Granger's voice,

dripping with disappointment. 'You can't force an Uploaded avatar to…'

For a long moment, the only sound in the cabin was the whirl of the propeller. Granger spoke again, 'Oh, Jonah, no, no. Please, no. You're acting on instinct alone again.'

'What's he talking about, Jonah?'

'Sam, um, well…' began Jonah, searching for the words to explain his plan. But Granger beat him to it.

'Your boyfriend is going to be bait. He's going to let the dragon usurp his avatar in the hope that maybe, just maybe, he can then take control of the beast. It's madness – you have to talk him out of it!'

'It's the only thing that makes sense,' said Jonah calmly, 'in a world full of madness.'

'Samantha,' urged Granger. 'Don't let Jonah sacrifice himself for people he doesn't know. I'm the fail-safe now. I'm going to blow up the mainline bridge over Stoney Creek before that countdown hits zero. That's in less than two hours.'

Jonah looked at Sam, convincing her with his eyes. 'You know I have to try.'

Sam shook her head.

'Sam,' said Jonah. 'Axel would've logged on through the Northern Corner servers. His mind is on that train.'

'It's not fair,' she said.

'Never is,' said Jonah. 'Never was.'

'Then I'm with you,' she said.

'Granger,' said Jonah. 'Blow up the train if you have to; if we fail. But there is someone I know among the seven billion trapped online, Sam's dad. And I promised her I'd get him out.'

'I'm messaging you a short cut to the pyramid that contains the Imprint Chamber,' Granger said. 'If you're foolish enough let that man usurp you; you'll need it.'

'Thank you,' said Jonah.

'Don't thank me,' Granger replied.

Jonah took his hand off the steering column and pressed his thumb down over the glass square, ending the conversation with Granger.

He kept his sights on the horizon as he crested the plane over the mountain and headed the plane south-west. 'We have to find that train and get online to unlock the halos before it reaches that gorge.'

Sam pulled up the interactive map application and scanned the live satellite feed for any trains on the line. Jonah watched her zoom in on the map, highlighting a train inching its way across the screen. When she zoomed out, she held up the datapad for Jonah to see. He wanted to keep his eyes facing front as he weaved through the craggy Rocky Mountains, but he took a quick glance without moving his head. He spotted where Sam had placed a pulsing red pin: a bridge spanning Stoney Creek at somewhere called

Rogers Pass. The train icon was almost upon it.

'We've got less than two hours,' Sam sighed.

'I hope that's enough time to save the world,' said Jonah.

36

Jonah followed the tracks through the mountains.

The thin parallel lines weaved through passes and hugged the shores of lakes so blue and clear that they looked unreal, almost virtual. From the sky, he chased the tracks, hoping for a glimpse of the train. As he banked left he emerged into a narrow valley and saw it – the long, black freight train snaking through the mountains. Twenty box cars, housing the microservers that powered the Northern Corner, were sandwiched between a hulky green locomotive in front and an open, flat car taking up the rear. The last car in the convoy, the flatbed, housed an industrial contraption that looked like a cross between a crane and a digger's arm. Jonah figured it would be used to shift the containers off the train in Vancouver.

Suddenly, the train was gone again; swallowed up by a tunnel in the mountainside, leaving Jonah and Sam flying straight into the mountain's peak.

'Pull up!' shouted Sam.

Jonah was a breath ahead of her. He pulled back hard on the steering column, gaining altitude; but not fast enough.

'I can't clear it,' he shouted, blood rising to his head

as he strained to avoid the fast-approaching cliff.

He pressed his foot down on his left rudder pedal, banking the plane hard to starboard. The Cessna tilted to the right at such a steep angle that Jonah was almost directly above Sam. Jonah could see the cragged lines etched into the fierce mountain and the small pine trees nested in their roots – they were so close that one of these hardy trees could easily clip his wing or wheels.

But the mountain peak angled away the higher Jonah climbed, and he got the turning radius he needed. The plane came within just feet of scraping the mountainside, but it was enough. Jonah levelled the Cessna and banked portside, resuming his original course as if the one hundred million year old mountain had never been in his path.

Jonah suddenly felt very small and insignificant circling the massive rock that measured its age in geological time. The mountain was oblivious to the toils and struggles of humanity. It didn't care about Guardians or Millennials or Tomorrow's Children. It had no affiliation or association. It simply towered above it all. Jonah soared in the air at its altitude; though hardly its equal. The mountain would be standing long after Jonah was gone. The mountain might not have cared what happened to the humanity around it, but Jonah did. His future might have been short when measured in geological time, but it was his future; and Sam's future. And that was worth fighting for.

After clearing the mountain, Jonah and Sam were silent in relief. They flew over a large valley and Jonah re-spotted the train chugging forth below. The far end of the valley was book-ended by another steep mountain. Jonah guessed they had less than nine miles to board the train before losing it again through another tunnel. This was their chance, but it didn't change the fact that Jonah and Sam were in the air while the train was rolling forward on the ground. They were going to have to jump.

Jonah brought himself over the train, preparing to match its speed and trajectory.

'Jonah, we don't have any parachutes,' said Sam. 'I really hope you're not planning on landing this plane on top of that train.'

'The thought did cross my mind,' he confessed. 'But very briefly.'

'Then how do we get from up here to down there?'

'There's towing cable in the back,' said Jonah. 'So we're going to use your favourite mode of transport; we're going to zip-line.'

Jonah thought back to the rooftop in Manhattan, when he and Sam had zipped across to the Freedom Tower to rescue Jonah's father from Granger. It was a dangerous, exhilarating way to travel. Amid the chaos of the attack, something quite unexpected had happened: it was the first time Sam had kissed Jonah.

'You've got to be kidding me,' said Sam.

But Jonah was deadly serious. Their only option was to latch the tow rope onto the train while holding the plane at a constant speed and heading – and then they'd zip down the line onto the moving train.

'There should be wheel chocks back there, Sam,' Jonah said. 'Find them, and tie the rope to one of them. We can use it as a fishing hook.'

Shaking her head, Sam crawled into the aft of the cabin and found the pair of wheel stoppers, big rubber wedges that ordinarily would keep the plane's wheels locked in place when grounded. The two wedges were tied together with a two-foot length of yellow and black nylon rope. Sam tied the tow rope around the nylon connector rope, creating her 'hook'. Jonah brought the plane directly above the rear of the train and descended, using all his dad's experience and skill to do so.

'Tie the other side to the strut and I'll lower us enough for you to catch the stopper onto the crane arm at the back.'

'Fishing for freight trains, eh?' Sam said. 'When you said "We've got a train to catch", I didn't think you were being literal!'

Jonah matched the velocity and trajectory of the train as best he could, holding the aircraft just two hundred metres above the rolling stock. Sam opened the door and leaned out, dangling the wheel chocks below, swinging them until they slipped through the crane-arm and caught like a grappling hook.

'It's in,' said Sam.

At least that bit was easy, Jonah thought. He looked ahead at the next mountain range. It was getting bigger. Of course, they were rushing towards it at seventy-seven miles per hour. Their window to jump was rapidly closing. Jonah climbed the plane slightly, allowing the rope to pull taut between the Cessna and the train. Then he engaged the autopilot and rushed to join Sam in the cabin.

'You go first,' he said. 'I want to make sure you're safe before I zip.'

She grabbed Jonah with both hands around his jaw bones and pulled him close. She pressed her lips against his in a forceful, passionate kiss that took Jonah by such surprise he didn't know whether to close his eyes or not. But before he'd made the decision she pulled away and turned her attention to the sleeves of her cloak, pushing them up to protect her hands from rope burn.

'You just make sure you're safe,' she said. 'I'll see you on board.'

'Save me a seat,' Jonah joked, his lips still sizzling.

Sam launched herself onto the rope and rapidly slid down the taut line. Jonah watched her steady herself on the rear car and then jump across to the penultimate car, ready to open the rear door to the last of the twenty carriages containing the servers.

Jonah took one large inhalation of mountain air and swung his legs out of the plane. He grabbed onto the line, covering his palms with the sleeves of his cloak as Sam had done, and jumped. His arms burned as they held him, zipping quickly down, rushing towards the contorted steel arm of the lifter and swinging his legs up onto the zip to slow himself in the final metres of his descent. He hugged the cold steel frame of the arm and scrambled down to join Sam. The rail ties and gravel rushed past beneath Jonah's feet as he stood at the edge of the rear car, facing Sam. He tried to calm himself from the adrenaline rush of the jump, but his heart was racing.

They were divided by less than three feet, the world furiously rushing by beneath them. Jonah felt at once so close yet so separated from Sam; the girl he loved with all of his heart. He jumped over the couplers and landed in Sam's arms on the other side.

'You made it,' she said.

'So did you,' Jonah replied.

A shadow was cast over them – the Cessna soaring overhead, like a kite on a string. And then darkness consumed them. They'd been swallowed by another tunnel. Instantly, a wave of fiery heat brushed across Jonah's body. He covered Sam as best he could, protecting her from the blast. The tethered plane must have slammed into the mountainside and exploded on impact.

There was no turning back.

37

The tunnel had curved, the train leaving behind any hint of daylight and powering forth into the darkness. The immediate danger of fire or debris was gone, replaced by the near-deafening noise of the train filling the tunnel.

Jonah couldn't see anything, but he held Sam in his arms. He could tell she was speaking, although he couldn't hear her voice, but could feel her soft breath against his ear. It didn't matter that he couldn't hear her. They both seemed to be thinking the same thing. Jonah found her lips in the darkness and pressed.

He held Sam as tightly as he could, never wanting to let go. He said, 'I love you,' hoping she could tell he was thinking it too, knowing she couldn't hear him. Travelling through the base of the mountain, in the darkness, he wished he could slow time to a geological pace. He'd never felt so close to Sam before and didn't want the feeling to change. But the train was trundling rapidly forward, and he and Sam had a job to do.

The tunnel was growing lighter and suddenly they burst into daytime again. Jonah squinted and blinked his eyes while they adjusted to the painful onslaught of sunlight.

Sam was looking at him, smiling.

'Hi,' he said, nervously.

'Hi,' she said.

'We made it,' Jonah said.

'It's not over yet,' Sam said, angling herself towards the door to the train.

'No,' sighed Jonah. 'It's just beginning. Do you think anyone on board heard us?'

'I'd be surprised if they didn't,' she said. 'But this train is stupidly loud. You didn't hear me, did you?'

Jonah shook his head. 'And you couldn't hear me.'

For a moment, bathed in daylight, he just looked at her. Sam's red hair flapped uncontrollably in the breeze as they rushed through another mountain pass.

'Those containers don't have windows,' said Sam. 'We may still have the advantage of stealth.'

'It's possible,' agreed Jonah. *But not probable*, was what he was thinking.

To their right, the tracks were carved into the stony mountain. Above them, the tree-covered slope rose up to the heavens. Jonah had never seen so many trees. They were woven into the mountainside so perfectly that they looked more like carpet than vegetation. To their left, a long turquoise lake hugged the tracks. Jonah found himself distracted, wondering how so much fresh water sat unprotected, when the entire US South West had dried up.

'We have to stop doing things like this,' Sam said.

'I'm ready to stop when you are,' he joked. He knew that the real danger lay behind the door that clearly neither of them wanted to open. The real danger would come when he logged into the Metasphere, into a world where his halo would be locked; into a world where he was planning on a dangerous gamble with the world's most dangerous man. 'But first we have something to do.'

'We always seem to have something to do, Jonah,' she said. 'Do you think we seek out trouble, or does trouble find us?'

'A bit of both, I suppose,' he said. Jonah wanted to kiss Sam again, in the daylight, and tell her that he loved her so that she could hear it. But he knew if he did he wouldn't want to stop. He wouldn't press on into the danger and uncertainly of his mission. And he didn't want to let Sam down. He'd made a promise to her. And he loved her too much to not fulfil his promise.

Finally, Jonah opened the door outwards to the windowless car, careful not to lose his footing on the narrow platform. A whoosh of metallic-smelling air breezed past his nose, and he suppressed a sneeze. Inside, the narrow corridor was lined on both sides with stacks of micro-servers and lit by a line of small circular lights in the ceiling. Fortunately, there was not a person in sight.

He reached back for Sam and guided her inside the

high-tech carriage. Sam pulled the door closed, blocking out the rush of wind and the repeating roll of the train's wheels. The exterior world was silenced. He could hear the familiar spinning of hard drives and the whirl of computer fans, but they were completely cut off from the noise of the outside world. Jonah breathed a bit easier, hoping that their arrival might have gone undetected.

Jonah held his hands up, and ran them along the parallel wall of servers. He gently touched the smooth grey surfaces of the computers. They hummed with life, two billion people trapped inside. He couldn't see them, but he believed that he could feel them. Jonah was searching for a Direct Interface portal because he was going to join them.

He found the DI cable and a stash of adaptors. Jonah snapped the adaptor on the top of the Ethernet cord and reached around to find the hole in his lower back. He'd done this thousands of times before, but this time, as he prepared to glide the cool adaptor into his warm flesh, he knew this could be the last.

He knelt on the cold floor, preparing to enter the metatrance. He felt Sam slide down on the floor beside him.

'Watch over me, Sam?' he asked, resting his head in her lap.

'In every way I can,' she said. Sam had tethered her stolen datapad to the servers. She'd be watching over his physical body and watching over his online avatar at the same time.

Jonah tapped his familiar Point of Origin coordinates into Sam's datapad: Venus Park. He pushed the cold adaptor into the plastic ring in his back and shivered. Sam gently stroked his hair to reassure him, making him feel safe and secure. It was an illusion, of course – he was neither safe nor secure – but it felt real enough to prompt him to twist the adaptor.

Click.

The DI adaptor found the first groove in the plastic ring. Jonah twisted it further.

Click.

Jonah looked up at Sam one last time. Her hair fell onto her face and he reached up and brushed it away, tucking it back behind her ears. He stared into her eyes until everything went dark.

The real world slipped away and Jonah found himself in a pitch-black netherworld between real and virtual. But his senses quickly came back as the bright, digital landscape of the Metasphere pixelated all around him. He felt sick and disoriented as his brain acclimatised to the rush of digital information flooding his mind. The nausea quickly passed. Jonah's brain was used to this transition.

Venus Park was packed with avatars. They were praying and chanting. A large, translucent countdown clock hung over the park, counting down at 00:33:17; just thirty-three minutes until Sal Vator's virus would cut off the entire Metasphere, leaving the avatars' real-world bodies to die.

One avatar, a llama, led the makeshift congregation. He spoke with a soft cadence that reminded Jonah of a lullaby.

'And so, my brothers and sisters, we wait not for the end,' the llama leader said, 'but take our first step together into a new immortal form.'

Jonah was still shaking off the last of his nausea and reacted too slowly to the meaning of the words. The entire group, at least three hundred avatars, all held an identical glowing blue pill in their hands, claws and paws. At the instruction of the llama, they swallowed it.

Jonah froze. An eerie silence swept over Venus Park as the avatars enacted their mass suicide. He wanted to shout to them, tell them not to give up yet; but it was too late.

Jonah had risked his life to come back into the Metasphere to save these people, but he wondered how many other gatherings across the virtual world were preparing to Upload. How many people, hopeless and distraught, were taking their own lives?

'Sam!?' he called. 'Did you see that?'

A pop-up window opened to Jonah's left and Sam's face, filled with tears, looked back at him.

'I wish I hadn't,' she said. 'But it's happening throughout the Metasphere. They've lost hope.'

Jonah knew he was the hope they needed.

He opened his inventory space and found the short cut that Granger had messaged to him. He tapped on the glowing arrow and it transformed into a door. Stepping through it would take Jonah to a secret place contained on the Northern Corner servers; the Imprint Chamber.

'Sam, copy this short cut for your dad and any other supporters he can organise,' said Jonah. 'I'm going in, but I might need help on the other side.'

38

A blast of dry, hot air hit Jonah as soon as he stepped into the endless desert.

He stood on an infinite sandy ground under a boundless blue sky. The unending landscape was dominated by one giant pyramid. Jonah walked towards it, dwarfed by its bulk.

The immense scale of the pyramid reminded Jonah of the mammoth grey prison that Matthew Granger had constructed to house his Uploaded prisoners. Granger, Jonah decided, had an obsession with building monuments to his ambitions.

As he stepped onto the first row of the pyramid's large dusty blocks, a red and black scorpion appeared above Jonah on the steps. The giant insect, at least three times as big as him, scuttled down the stepped sides of the pyramid, priming its tail to strike. Jonah groaned at the sight of its stinger glowing blue and buzzing with a searing, electric sound.

Granger could've warned me about this, Jonah thought. But then he realised that maybe Granger hadn't mentioned the firewall program on purpose. Maybe Granger, in his twisted, egocentric beliefs, wanted to kill the train. Maybe Granger wanted to die a martyr.

Suddenly, the scorpion pounced. It leapt down, throwing itself at Jonah. He dived out of the way as the scorpion's tale plunged into the blocks of the pyramid. Instantly, they pulsed blue and disintegrated into nothingness.

A deconstruction virus, Jonah realised.

The blocks quickly rematerialised back into place as the scorpion raised its tail to strike again, taking lethal aim at Jonah. The pyramid program was clearly immune to its own firewall. But Jonah knew it would only take one strike to destroy him.

He tried not to panic. Jonah ran up the pyramid, the scorpion swiping its stinger below him, dissolving the blocks beneath his feet. He scrambled up as fast as he could. He had to be quicker than the scorpion, or he was dead.

'Ahhh!' Jonah cried as he slid and tumbled back down to the bottom of the pyramid. He had to get to the top, remove the capstone as Granger had explained in his message, and drop into the Imprint Chamber. But the artificial intelligence scorpion seemed to anticipate his every move.

As Jonah collapsed at the base of the pyramid, he looked up at the impossible summit. The hideous scorpion blocked his view, raising its tail to strike again. This time, Jonah decided to fly.

He rose into the dry air, but the scorpion hovered

over him, snapping with its claws. When Jonah darted right, the scorpion moved in synchronicity with him, then raised its tail to strike. Jonah was saved by something that slammed into it.

'Take that, you AI brute,' called a voice.

Jonah turned to see that Axel's gryphon had kicked the scorpion into a spin. The giant insect slammed into the pyramid and tumbled down the side, zapping away blocks as it slid.

'Axel!' Jonah called with relief and astonishment.

'Always the nick of time with you, eh, Jonah?' laughed Axel, setting himself down on the side of the mighty pyramid. Jonah joined him, very happy to see Sam's father. He hoped that this avatar was live, and not an Uploaded echo of the real man.

'You are alive, right?' asked Jonah.

'And kicking!' snapped Axel.

Suddenly, above Axel's shoulder, Jonah saw a new scorpion materialise.

Jonah opened his mouth to shout a warning, but Axel must have read the urgency in Jonah's eyes. The gryphon didn't hesitate. Axel soared into the air as the second scorpion smashed its deadly tail into the blocks where Axel had just been resting. Jonah flew further up to join him.

'And always a close call with you, Axel,' Jonah said.

Both scorpions darted upwards, chasing Axel and Jonah into the sky. Two more avatars appeared in the desert, flying through identical doorframes that hovered in the air – copies of Granger's short cut. The moment the new avatars appeared, Jonah spotted a third, and then a fourth scorpion pixelate into existence.

'I've brought friends,' boasted Axel, 'to give you a distraction.'

As more avatars appeared, they were matched one for one by AI scorpions.

'The security program is generating one defender for every intruder,' shouted Jonah, as he and Axel flew around the pyramid, attempting to outrun their deadly pursuers.

'Don't worry, we'll keep them busy,' said Axel, 'while you get inside and let everyone out.'

Jonah and Axel twisted around each other in the air, confusing the scorpions. Below them at least fifty new avatars had appeared, each causing a new scorpion to pop to life from nowhere. But it looked to Jonah as if the more scorpions, the more they – ever so slightly – slowed down.

The program wasn't designed to defend against so many intruders, Jonah thought. Each AI scorpion required processing power, and the more of them there were, the more demand on the power. The defence program was virtual, but it had physical limits. It could cope with hundreds of intruders, thousands or million even, Jonah guessed. *But could it cope with billions?*

'Sam, can you hear me?' shouted Jonah.

'I'm right here,' she said. Jonah wanted to see her face again through the pop-up window, but didn't dare distract himself while the killer scorpion was so close to his fleeing avatar.

'Can you send that copy of Granger's short cut to more avatars?' Jonah asked.

'Of course,' she replied. 'To who?'

'Everyone!!' he said.

'What?'

'Send it to every single online avatar, all seven billion of them. Tell them to step through if they want any chance of getting out. We're going to crash the artificial intelligence defensive systems!'

Jonah darted through the desert air, criss-crossing with Axel, until they were above the pyramid's pinnacle. He attempted to dive-bomb the capstone, but the scorpion swung below him and halted his approach. So long as the AI was operational, Jonah couldn't get inside. So he kept flying. Jonah soared, zigzagged and weaved through the sky, avoiding the stinger and hoping that Sam could muster enough avatars to wear down the defences.

When Jonah was high above the pyramid, arms outstretched to his side in the bright blue sky, he saw them appear on the horizon. From way up high, the new avatars looked like ants swarming towards an anthill. There were so many of them that they blended together into one pulsating mass. But Jonah knew they were millions, hopefully billions, of individuals with hopes, dreams and right now, very real fears. They were the people that Jonah had pledged to save, and they had appeared in the desert to give him that chance.

Jonah dived back down to the pyramid, the scorpion slowing in pursuit. As he touched down on the top of the great monument, the scorpion smashed into the blocks below. The foul insect slowly scuttled up the side, but slid back down, unable to keep a foothold. Sluggish and uncoordinated, the scorpion slumped and its dangerous tail fell limp. Jonah's plan was working.

All around, the scorpion defenders were struggling; their responses were slowing until they crashed out.

Sam had done it. She had sent in enough avatars to force the program to match their number with AI defenders; too many for the system to handle. It forced a full-scale crash of the program that governed it all.

Jonah had no doubt that Granger would've coded a reboot protocol, so he knew he didn't have long. Taking his opportunity, Jonah slid off the capstone. It was a heavy sandstone block, shaped like a miniature version of the massive pyramid. The apex stone hovered in the air, as if waiting to be slid back into place. Jonah felt a whoosh of stale air blast his face as he stared down into the darkness.

And then he jumped.

39

Sam watched as Jonah disappeared through the top of the pyramid.

The capstone slid back into place, sealing Jonah in. Sam tried to follow him, but the meta-window wouldn't allow it. The pyramid must have had a blocker program to prevent uninvited eavesdropping. Unable to see Jonah's online humatar, Sam looked down at his real-world face; eyes closed, completely vulnerable in her lap. It was then that she heard a rush of wind from the front of the car and the clickety-clack of train wheels rolling on the tracks.

She looked up to see a hooded figure stepping into the car through the forward door. She removed her hood and Sam saw a young woman, only a few years her senior. She had long black hair and sunken eyes. Her lips were ruby red, the only colour on her pale, gaunt face. The intruder stared at Sam down the long, narrow corridor between the stacked servers. She wore the long, flowing cloak of the Quesnel Lake commune.

'What are you doing, Sister?' the woman asked. In the dim light, she looked like a ghost with her pale face and haunting black eyes.

Sam hesitated, working out what to do and what to say. The woman clearly believed that Sam was one of Tomorrow's Children – she wore the robe, of course. Sam decided to try a Jonah technique: play the facade and stall for time.

'Our brother is online,' said Sam, nodding at Jonah's peaceful body. 'Checking that everything is in order for the new dawn.'

As she said the words, Sam's skin crawled. She didn't know this woman, but she knew she hated her. She knew she wanted to kill her.

'I am Alexa, but I don't know you, Sister,' the woman said, removing her hood and kneeling down beside Sam. 'And I don't know this *brother*.'

'We came from Quesnel,' Sam said, deciding to inject truth into her lies. 'We have been with Sal Vator and came to lend support to the cause in these final hours.'

'Minutes, Sister,' Alexa corrected. 'We are mere minutes away from salvation and the new tomorrow. And there's nothing you can do to stop us.'

Sam's eyes widened just enough to be caught out.

'If Sal Vator had sent you two, I would have been informed,' Alexa said. 'Besides, I've spent too long embedded with the Millennials not to know Samantha Kavanaugh and Jonah Delacroix when I see them.'

Alexa sprang to her feet and tugged at Jonah's Ethernet cord.

Jonah fell through the darkness until he landed in a massive reclining chair.

The chair glowed with a deep red and rested at an incline. It reminded Jonah of trips to the dentist he took with his mother when they could still afford it. He always felt so small, so vulnerable lying in the dentist's chair. Jonah realised that this chair was coded to be large enough for Matthew Granger to occupy. His eight-legged avatar was much larger than Jonah's slender humatar. What was unusual was that this recliner had an enclosed ring, like a thin slice of a tunnel, where the headrest should've been. To Jonah, it looked like a red exit halo.

Jonah shuffled himself up the incline to place his head inside the ring.

A pop-up message appeared:

AVATAR NOT RECOGNISED

Jonah had known deep down that only one avatar would activate the chair. He slid back, understanding what he needed to do. He needed to release the captured, Uploaded avatar of Sal Vator. Only his unique avatar sequence could control the Imprint device and unlock the halos.

Jonah rose from the chair and opened his inventory space with a flick of his hands. He pulled out the bear trap. Inside, Sal's immortal avatar waited to be released.

Sam reached up and grabbed the cable, stopping it from coming loose from the servers. If Alexa pulled out Jonah's cord, there'd be no way to reunite his mind and his body, because to do so, Jonah's aimless avatar would need to be pushed back through his exit halo. But right now, all the halos were locked.

As Sam steadied the cable, her guard was down.

Alexa kicked her so hard that Sam's head smashed into the plastic server housing. She lost her sight for an instant, and slumped onto the ground. Sam tasted the blood flowing down her face and into her mouth. It was salty and warm and there was too much of it. But her bleeding face was the least of her concerns. She had to protect Jonah.

As she stumbled to her feet, Alexa kicked her again, sending Sam's head smashing into the opposite wall of servers. She couldn't take another blow like that. Somehow Sam had to regain the advantage in this narrow corridor. She rose up again, her head still reeling, but focused her adrenaline on fighting faster and smarter.

As Alexa surged forward, about to step on Jonah's comatose body, Sam leapt into the air and grabbed the tops of the servers, suspending herself in the air. She held tight, and swung her legs back, unleashing a fierce kick that knocked Alexa down hard.

Sam jumped to the floor, careful not to crush Jonah. She landed with her legs on either side of his body. Alexa was momentarily dazed at the end of the car, and Sam snatched her chance to advance. She threw three quick punches, a jab and two crosses, into Alexa's face. She wanted the young woman to feel pain before she killed her.

Sam reached out with her left hand to jab again, which Alexa blocked. But while Alexa's arms were protecting her face, Sam guided her right and forward and pulled at her cloak, catching her off guard. She swept at the back of her enemy's knees with her feet, destabilising her, and grabbing Alexa's torso as she fell forward. Sam forced Alexa down, holding her body parallel with the floor. Then she rushed to the back of the train, ramming Alexa's head into the rear door.

Alexa's body hit the floor, but Sam wasn't finished with her yet. If she stayed alive, on this train, Sam knew Alexa was a deadly threat to Jonah. She couldn't take any chances. She opened the door, and a rush of noise and wind flooded the car once more. Sam stepped over Alexa and pulled her onto the narrow platform between the last server car and the crane car.

'You can't st-stop us,' stuttered Alexa. 'Our destiny is—'

Sam didn't allow Alexa to finish her sentence before she threw her off the train.

She'd had enough of Sal Vator's proselytising parroted by his followers. She felt no remorse as Alexa's body bounced off the rail bed into the shimmering lake below. Anyone who threatened Jonah, she decided, would receive no mercy.

Sam rushed back to Jonah's body, not stopping to close the door. The corridor was deafeningly loud, but Sam ignored the noise as she inspected Jonah's Ethernet.

The plastic clip in his back had broken, but the connection was still live. Sam slumped beside his body in relief, catching her breath. Jonah was safe, for now, in the real world. But Sam had no idea of the danger he faced in the virtual one.

40

Jonah tried not to see his father in the red dragon staring back at him.

He knew the avatar was a copy, a digital fabrication that Sal Vator had somehow filtered and fused to his own avatar to disguise his true online identity. And yet, the dragon haunted Jonah like a ghost. He wished his father was still alive, in one form or another, and for the first time since he'd jumped to Sam's side over the frozen Arctic, he felt very alone.

He knew Sam would be watching over his body. He was thankful to have such a devoted and focused guardian, but right now it seemed to Jonah it was not his but Sam's body that was at risk. He was making a dangerous gamble. If Sal usurped his avatar, and awoke in the real world in Jonah's body, Sam would be an easy target for Sal's rage. His only hope was to let Sal take over his body enough to satisfy his hunger for life, but not enough to lose himself to the immortal predator. But first, Sal needed to take the bait. And Jonah was hoping that the confined surroundings would arouse the dead man's hunger for life.

'You are a foolish boy,' Sal snarled. 'It's just you

and me in here and only one of us will leave this chamber.'

'I'll stop you,' said Jonah.

'You will fail,' whispered Sal into Jonah's left ear. The dragon's head twisted his scaly neck around Jonah's human-shaped avatar. Jonah turned his head to see the dragon's snout appear on his right side. 'Like your father did.'

The mention of Jonah's dad, combined with the costume this madman wore, enraged Jonah internally. But this time, he kept his cool. He waited as the dragon slithered around him, taunting him.

'You miss the real world,' said Jonah. 'That's what all of this is about, isn't it?'

'Creating fake worlds inside computers is a distraction from the plight of our species, the plight of our planet. You Guardians and Millennials are equally guilty in ignoring the real problems while you fight over a virtual world built on ignorance.'

Jonah didn't want to waste any time debating, but he needed to spark his hunger. If Sal didn't bite, then Jonah couldn't use his avatar sequence to release the halos. He decided his best bet was to keep the dragon talking about the real world; after all, usurping Jonah was Sal's only ticket back.

'What will it be like, then?' asked Jonah. 'The new real world, once you've trapped and killed seven billion people?'

'It will be darkest before the dawn,' hissed Sal. 'The ßetas will activate their real mission, their true purpose, to cleanse the Earth of the hold-outs and off-liners. They will not stop until the great flood of human blood has drowned those who believe themselves to be survivors. They will bury the bodies, return them to the soil of the planet. Life will grow from their death.'

Unstoppable killing machines, thought Jonah. He bit his tongue. He wasn't here to antagonise Sal. His role was to entice him. *Let the maniac speak.*

'And once the great purge is complete, and the wickedness of mankind is eliminated, then, and only then, can we begin again,' said Sal. 'The ßetas will plant new growth, seed forests where cities once stood, and deconstruct and decontaminate the worst of the toxic installations. Tomorrow's Children will grow up in a new world.'

'I bet you'd like to see it,' urged Jonah.

Sal snapped back, pressing his snout into Jonah's face. The dragon sniffed and puffed, his breath clouding Jonah's sight.

'I would,' he replied. 'I truly would.'

'I can arrange a pop-up window,' Jonah said. 'You could watch the rebirth of the planet from in here.'

The dragon's eyes widened, and then narrowed. 'That's not enough.'

Without warning, but without surprise, Sal Vator

spread open his jaw and swallowed Jonah whole.

He had taken the bait.

Granger surveyed the steel trestle bridge over the white-watered creek below. In another life, he might have marvelled at the beauty of this manmade structure joining two sides of ancient rock. But this wasn't another life. Matthew Granger had chosen his path, and it was going to end here. He wasn't here for beauty.

He was here for destruction.

Granger placed four packets of C-4 explosives along the bridge. His plan had been to detonate them remotely, but he'd found the wireless signal was unreliable in this valley. He was going to have to blow them by wire.

He had enough tripwire in his backpack from the armoury to link them together, but not to give himself a safe distance from the blast radius. But the job had to be done.

His palms were sweaty with nerves as his secured the final explosive brick to the steel structure. Once he was satisfied the bombs were well placed, he climbed onto the bridge to wait with the tripwire. He sat on the wooden beams and waited. He waited for the train to curve around the mountain and trundle onto the bridge. He wasn't used to waiting. Granger was used to making things happen, making others wait. But now, with everything he loved taken from him, all he could do was wait. He was waiting to die.

His attention was distracted by a small insect crawling along the rail tie in front of him. This tiny creature had no idea of the destruction about to occur. Granger was raising his hand to squash it, when his mind flashed to another insect; a scorpion.

He realised that he'd not warned Jonah about the firewall program at the pyramid.

Did I not warn him on purpose?

Perhaps he wanted Jonah to fail, he realised. He admired the boy, respected him as an adversary, but was also envious of him. Granger had raw intelligence that Jonah could never know, but Jonah had something Granger lacked; selfless resilience. Jonah put others in front of himself and risked his life to save strangers. He didn't do it for fame or money; he just did it. He did because it was who he was. Matthew Granger admired Jonah for it, but somewhere in a dark part of his heart, he also hated him for it.

But since Granger's world had crashed down around him, he knew he had to move beyond hate. He had a chance to be reborn, to become a new man. While he'd never be young again, he could graft some of Jonah's youthfulness, both optimism and naivety, and live and die a selfless man.

Granger frantically reached for the square communicator, hoping to catch a signal to contact

Jonah and Sam. Jonah would be taking his short cut into a trap. He had to contact him before it was too late. It might already be. As he pulled the shiny glass communicator from inside his parka, it slipped through his fingers. He reached to grab it with his left hand, but was too late.

He watched, as if in slow motion, as the communicator, his only link to the outside world, dropped between the rail ties and plummeted into the raging water below.

Matthew Granger was cut off from the rest of the world. He was alone. He could not follow the progress of Jonah and Sam's mission, he could not discover whether he should implement his fail-safe or not.

Jonah was resourceful and intrepid, and Granger had finally learned not to discount him. But with no way of knowing if he'd succeeded or failed, he felt he only had one choice. He couldn't risk the human race, whatever belief he had in Jonah's abilities. With just minutes remaining on Sal Vator's countdown to genocide, Granger had renewed his commitment to his plan. He was going to blow up the bridge as soon as he spotted the train.

41

Jonah's mind was under assault from within.

He had successfully fought off mental invaders before. He had learned how to expunge hungry usurpers, keeping his mind whole and his consciousness his own. He had trained his brain to fight off any attack, brain cell by brain cell. But something about Sal's immortal mind was different.

Somehow Sal was beating him at his own game. Jonah's memories were being invaded by foreign thoughts and he couldn't hold them back. The more Jonah defended his sense of self, the more under attack he felt. It was like pieces of his life were being ripped away; meat stripped from a bone.

Jonah was reliving moments of his young but eventful life. Some of his memories were small, just glimpses, moments even. Others were major, sometimes traumatic memories. Jonah recalled the paper cut he got on his first day of primary school, handing out activity sheets to his classmates. He remembered the beating he took on his last day at real-world school, pummelled by a gang of bullies until the police were called and his parents took him out of school and into the Chang Academy. But Jonah remembered each event twice, like double vision. The first version played out exactly as he recalled it, but the second was invaded by an unknown stranger.

At once, both virtual and real-world attackers thrashed at Jonah's memories. These invaders took every form, every shape. While he was shielding himself from the punches and kicks in the corner of the schoolyard, the gang was attacked by two men Jonah had never seen before. They dispensed with Jonah's bullies and then turned on Jonah. He fought them back, confused about who they were, where they'd come from.

Then, as Jonah remembered a class debate with Mr Ping in his Chang Academy classroom, the room was rushed by four geometric avatars: a green square, a silver cone and two hexagons – one translucent and the other bright orange. The shapes burst into the room like a colourful tornado and bounced off the walls, floor and ceiling; knocking his classmates out of existence.

Except that had never happened. These strange shapes were infecting his memory, beating it into something else; like someone else's memory.

Amid the barrage on his brain, Jonah tried to concentrate. He tried to locate the man who was driving the invasion, Sal Vator. But he couldn't.

There were too many invaders running rampant across his mind. A motley menagerie of avatars acted as foot soldiers in Sal's campaign to suppress Jonah into submission.

It felt like his mind was being starved of oxygen.

Jonah's reactions grew sluggish and strained. He watched as his own memories were stripped away, changed, or replaced altogether. Moments with his mother, his father and even his Uploaded grandmother were torn to shreds before his eyes. This attack was different from what he had expected, but Jonah wasn't going down without a fight.

He focused his concentration on defending his memories, defending his conscious soul. And that's when he realised what was so different about Sal Vator: he was just like Jonah.

Jonah had long believed that he had the only brain capable of holding more than one conscious avatar at a time. Yes, others could filter the facade of another avatar, pretend to be someone they were not, but only Jonah could hold the full consciousness of another human being in his brain. It's what allowed him to keep, hold and eventually Upload his father from his mind.

Jonah had come to think of himself as unique, as possessing a special power that made him immune from usurping. He counted on this power to capture Sal's consciousness in his brain long enough to control his invader, turn the tables on him to release the halos, thereby rescuing everyone trapped in the Metasphere.

But as a barrage of strangers chipped away at his consciousness, Jonah faced the fear that he was no longer unique.

Somehow, it seemed that Sal Vator was able to store and control a thousand consciousness avatars in his own brain. These unexpected avatars, captive in his brain, were his menagerie and his army. They travelled with him in his head while he was alive and Uploaded with him when he died.

Jonah was overwhelmed by the numbers and the force of these strangers in his head. They were grinding him down, beckoning him to join them in a collective prison housed within Sal's consciousness. They called to him, taunted him. A thousand voices rang out through his mind, and as Jonah tried to quieten them, focusing his remaining thoughts on fighting back, one voice rang both softer and louder than the rest. Jonah knew that voice from anywhere, but it was the one voice he never expected to ever hear again.

'Jonah, my darling,' called his mother.

42

Jonah was startled by the memory of his mother, but shocked that it wasn't a memory at all.

At first, Jonah thought he was simply recalling his mother from his childhood, one memory out of a countless collection he had of her. But her voice wasn't a memory. Miriam Delacroix was a ghost.

'Jonah, my darling,' repeated her soft, reassuring voice. 'Why are you fighting me?'

Jonah concentrated, focused his mind on the source of the voice and found himself on a windy cliff overlooking a choppy sea. A picnic blanket was laid out on the grass, with a spread of fresh food just waiting to be eaten. The sea was dark, reflecting the low clouds over the water that were threatening to make landfall.

Jonah recognised the scene. He must've been only six or seven when his parents took him camping in Devon. He didn't remember everything, just flashes and moments, like fighting with his mum to be allowed into the Metasphere on the long drive down to the campsite, roasting marshmallows over an open fire, taking cover in the tent as his father warned off a homeless tramp who'd discovered them, and this; this cliff-top picnic that Jonah knew would end in torrential rain.

'Mum?' asked Jonah. 'How is it…*you*?'

Miriam Delacroix's avatar was a white dove. She floated in the humid air above the cliff edge. But as Jonah looked at her, he didn't see her as digital. He only saw her real-world self. He saw her sad eyes and long dark hair. She wore the flowing white dress with daisy-like embroidery on the hem that she kept for special occasions. He saw the same woman who pushed him out of the window of the City Tower, just before it exploded. Just before she died. And yet here she was, in Jonah's memories, alive and conscious.

'It's me, my darling boy,' she said, pulling him into an embrace that he never wanted to end. 'But what are you doing here? Has he trapped you in here too?'

'Where is *here*, Mum?' Jonah asked.

He pulled back from her hug, looked into her darkened, sad eyes. She looked like she was about to cry. And Jonah could no longer stem his own tears.

He had flown to safety while his mother burned to death on what Jonah had come to consider the first day of his insane new life.

That same day he'd filtered a copy of his father's avatar, and Matthew Granger had mistaken him for his dead father and sent assassins to kill him. That was the day he lost his home, lost his mother, and lost all semblance of the innocence that once enveloped his childhood.

A copy, Jonah realised. Jonah had filtered a copy of his father's avatar, a copy that was created by Sal Vator. His father created a back-up version of himself in case anything happened to his real-world self. It was that back-up copy, that duplicate version that Jonah filtered and eventually Uploaded. But Jonah had no idea that his mother had also made a back-up copy of herself.

'We're in the mind of the One,' she said. 'We are many, but he is *One*. And he is in control of us all.'

Suddenly, from the tree line, a wave of ghostly avatars approached, racing across the waving grass.

'They're coming for you, my darling boy,' she said, urgently.

'Who are they?'

'The One has copied many,' she said, 'and taken us into his own mind, trapping us in here. They do his bidding and they will hurt you until you join us.'

Jonah didn't know how it was possible for Sal Vator to hold these avatars in his mind, but he knew enough to know danger when he saw it.

'I can fight them,' said Jonah, pushing his mother behind him, sheltering her from the approaching onslaught. He scanned the horde and figured there were at least five hundred avatars bearing down on him.

'That's what I thought too,' she said. 'That's what

we all thought. But he's too strong. He controls us all. Even now, seeing you, loving you, I can feel him inside me telling me to take you over, bring you into our world, our prison within his mind.'

Jonah felt the raindrops spray his neck. The sheeting rain came off the sea at such a low angle that it was nearly horizontal.

'The picnic!' gasped Jonah's mum; an echo of what she'd said that day.

Jonah remembered it clearly now. He and his parents had scrambled to save the blanket and the food and raced into the woods to take shelter in their tent. Soaking wet, they unpacked the sodden food and laughed as they ate under the tent's green canopy. It was a happy memory, one Jonah hadn't revisited in years. But it was just a memory. Now, on that same cliff-top plateau, with hundreds of demented avatars trampling the picnic, doused in rain, Jonah was living in the present. This was the battle for his brain, for his very soul.

'You can jump from here, Jonah,' said Miriam. She moved his body to the steep edge, ready to push him into the surging sea below.

In a flash, Jonah was back on the sixty-first floor of the City Tower. His mum strapped him into the escape glider and looked him directly in the eyes. She steadied his shoulders, urging him to relax. She instructed him to jump then pull the red ripcord.

She was telling him how to save his life even as she knew that meant certain death for herself. But Jonah lost his balance and his mother shoved him out of the window. Saving his life, condemning her own.

Back on the rain-soaked cliff, Miriam was preparing to do it all again.

'No,' said Jonah.

Miriam's eyes widened in fear as the angry avatars approached. She was going to sacrifice herself again. Jonah hugged his mother one last time.

He wasn't going to let history repeat itself. Jonah grabbed his mother and shoved her over the edge.

Miriam's white dress fluttered in the wind. The human look of his mother morphed back into her avatar; and spread her wings. The white dove took flight, flapping her wings against the rain. She soared over the raging sea, safe from the onslaught. But the avatars were now upon him. Jonah rose into the air to face his attackers.

He wasn't going to fight them. He was going to recruit them.

43

Jonah spotted the same saddened, dark eyes on each of the approaching avatars.

As the horde of humatars, animals and shapes bore down on Jonah, they thrashed at his clothes, tore at his hair, and piled onto his body. These ghostly prisoners were held captive in Sal Vator's mind, and now that Jonah was inside with them, he was going to set them free.

Jonah knew that most people only used ten or eleven per cent of their brain. Perhaps, in holding both his father and himself in his head, Jonah had learned to stretch his grey matter's muscle, using more than the average person. He was counting on it.

The mob of avatars surrounded Jonah. They clawed at him, teasing memories from his mind. His head ached as they tore at his consciousness. They were pummelling him into submission, but he knew what to do. Jonah Delacroix was going to flex the only muscle that really mattered. He was going to use his mind as an Ark. He was going to collect these avatars and deliver them to digital salvation.

'Come with me,' he said calmly. 'Come with me and I will set you free.'

Jonah pushed up against the pile of angry avatars on top of him. He rose into the air as the attackers slipped off his soaking body. The avatars were stunned by his strength.

He hovered in the wind and promised his attackers a different path. 'Come with me, and when I separate myself from the One who holds you, I will give you a tomorrow that is different from today.'

'That's impossible!' spat a snail.

'We are trapped, forever! And you are trapped with us,' added a trembling zebra.

'Don't fight us, don't resist,' urged a mass of vines.

Two jellyfish bobbed in the air, their tentacles intertwined, and spoke in unison, 'There is no out, there is only within.'

But Jonah wasn't giving up. He closed his eyes, focused his concentration, his mind, on opening himself up to these entrapped souls. They were in his head now, all of them, and if they joined with his consciousness, they could sever their link to Sal. They had come aboard his mind, hoping to hijack it. But Jonah was opening up his brain to them as a lifeboat; an Ark.

Jonah held out both of his arms and waited.

At first, he remained alone in his own darkness. He kept his eyes closed, focused himself in his own mind, building a new home for these captives. And then he heard it, the flutter of wings.

From behind him, the gentle flapping of a bird's wings soared over the sound of the falling rain. He felt a gentle tap on his right shoulder; a bird landing and perching on him.

'Who will join my son?' asked the dove. 'Who will join Jonah, our saviour?'

A furry paw took his left hand. Jonah squeezed it with a reassuring pulse. One of the slimy jellyfish tentacles wrapped around his right hand. Jonah resisted the urge to pull away, recalling a time a when he'd been stung by jellyfish as a boy, and simply closed his grip gently around the outstretched slimy offering.

Jonah allowed himself to open his eyes. Around him, the avatars formed a massive circle on the cliff's plateau, each holding hands, or whatever counted as hands, with each other. They were trusting Jonah, giving themselves over to him. As he prepared to open his mind, to accept them inside, he looked to the pearlescent white dove on his shoulder.

'Thank you, Mum,' he said. 'For everything.'

'I'll see you when I wake from here,' she replied.

Jonah suddenly realised that his mother didn't know she was dead. She would have copied her avatar at the same time as Jonah's dad; probably just over three years ago, he reckoned. This white dove, this digital copy of his mother, had no idea what'd happened to Jason, to Jonah, or to herself. She was hoping to wake from the recesses of Sal's mind to slip back into a life that no longer existed.

Jonah doubted himself. He wondered if he was doing the right thing at all. His mother, and all of these avatars, had been stuck in Sal's head for years, some for decades. Was it right to free them into a world that had moved on? He didn't know what to do. But his moment of reflection was interrupted by a storm of fire.

The red dragon burst through the low clouds and screamed.

44

Jonah faced his foe as it floated in the circle of avatars.

'They're coming with me, Sal,' said Jonah.

He knew whatever risk there was of bringing them out of Sal's head, it was worth it. They'd been prisoners in his mind for so long, but they deserved to be free.

'You are mistaken, boy,' the dragon replied. 'I am taking you over, just like I took each of them.'

Jonah opened his heart, opened his mind. He pulled his hands down and felt each avatar fuse within him. The relentless flashes of memories were overwhelming, but Jonah kept control.

In the flashes, he saw lives lived and lives lost. He saw children playing on a beach. He saw two lovers kissing on a park bench. He saw an old man in a hospital, closing his eyes for the last time. He caught a glimpse into a thousand different lives as they boarded his consciousness.

A young girl chased a ball. A father kissed a baby. A solider shot an enemy. A fisherman jumped into the water to save an overboard shipmate. A woman in a dress threw a glass of wine at a man. An old lady learned to dance.

They were memories, secrets and moments of lives lived.

One by one these avatars disappeared from the now scorched plateau as Jonah internalised them. He welcomed them into his mind. He felt them re-emerge inside the ninety per cent of his brain that would be their Ark.

He witnessed a thousand lifetimes in a matter of moments. They were all inside him except for one. His mother, the dove, perched on his shoulder.

'It's time,' Jonah said.

'Take me to a better place,' she whispered.

'I promise,' he replied, meaning to keep his word.

The white dove spread her wings and flew down to land in Jonah's palm. He gently cupped his hands around it and whispered, 'I love you, Mum.'

The bird disappeared from view, but not from existence. She was now nesting inside his mind, with a thousand others, safe from the captor that Jonah now faced. Both Jonah and the dragon hovered in the rain-drenched sky, staring at each other. There could only be one victor.

'It will do them no good to live within you,' scolded Sal. 'Don't forget that I usurped you; I am in control of your mind, and soon over your body. And I will walk among the living again.'

Jonah channelled his thoughts inwards. He spoke silently to the thousand souls aboard his cerebral Ark.

I need you.

We must pull the One inside; trap him as he has entrapped you.

Reach out and envelop him; usurp him from within my mind.

He would need the strength of the avatars to overcome Sal Vator's dominance. He would need them all to usurp Sal from within.

At first only silence answered.

Outside, floating above the charred grass, Jonah stared at the red dragon. Sal Vator laughed, mocking Jonah for trying.

'You're a foolish boy,' he said. 'Your father would be ashamed.'

Jonah's confidence faltered. The mention of his dad from Jason's own avatar was too much to bear. He closed his eyes, saddened and defeated.

But then faintly he heard his mother's voice in a distant corner of his mind.

'He was proud of you. I am proud of you. We are all proud of you. And we are with you.'

He felt their unifying courage rising inside him. Jonah looked at Sal and smiled. He felt the power of a thousand souls united within him.

At once, he opened his mind. The avatars flew from his digital body, surrounded Sal like a tornado. The dragon fought against the flurry of digital beings – kicking, flailing and blowing fire over his liberated captives. But Sal was overwhelmed by their numbers and their resolve. They caught him in the eye of their tornado, held him motionless in their unnatural force. The swarm of avatars were in tune with Jonah; they knew what he needed. Jonah's mind directed the vortex, a magnetic force that Sal was unable to resist. The avatar swarm tightened their whirl and pulled Sal back inside Jonah's brain.

He had usurped the usurper.

Jonah was alone on the scorched cliff-top of his own mind. As quickly as it started, the rain stopped. Jonah thought back to his own memory, to the day he and his parents scooped up the picnic and ran to their tent. The rain had ended that day as abruptly as it had started.

It was time to leave this place within his mind now that he was in control of Sal's Uploaded avatar. Jonah ran into the woods and spotted the green tent gently wavering in the breeze. It was a symbol of a happy memory. It was a symbol of an innocent time long before death and devastation became the Delacroix family business. As he approached the tent, he longed to go back to those days. He wished to return to the time when they could shelter him from the world. But of course, as he pulled back the flap, the tent was empty.

He stepped inside that happy place. He used it to anchor his consciousness so that he wouldn't risk getting lost amid Sal's thoughts. Jonah willed himself to emerge back where he began, in the Imprint Chamber. Now he reappeared inside the pyramid, but wearing Sal's stolen avatar.

He opened his eyes, took in the digital screens that surrounded him and did something so instinctive that it startled him. Jonah Delacroix stretched out his wings; his father's scaly, red wings. This digital body was so familiar to him that it felt like an extension of his own. Wearing it now, he realised that he missed the dragon's strength and size. But it wasn't who Jonah was. This was his father's avatar, and Jonah was his own man now. Where once he longed to try on his dad's digital skin, now the avatar felt foreign and ill sized. But it was time to do what he came to do. It was time to release the halos.

Jonah looked outwards, through Sal's yellow eyes, in full control over his Uploaded avatar, and reclined back onto the Imprint Chair. Controlling Sal's mind, living inside his avatar, meant that Jonah could access the chair as only Sal could.

At once, the walls of the chamber sprang to life with moving images from the panicking Metasphere. The countdown read 00:04:22. In just minutes, the Metasphere would sever all connections with the trapped avatars – killing over seven billion people.

Jonah slipped the dragon's head up into the red ring. The Imprint chair hummed and vibrated, as it verified his avatar.

It's me, Sal!

Jonah wanted to release the halos immediately, but the program was taking its time.

Jonah could see the virtual world from all angles. There were millions of scenes, each playing out in a different part. The countless number of sequences made Jonah feel dizzy and overwhelmed. He focused his eyes, narrowing his gaze on one scene at a time, trying to make sense of what he was seeing.

The Imprint Chamber controlled the exit halos, and Jonah was peering into the virtual world through the digital looking-glass of the sealed-off halos. He was spying on a population desperate to get out before it was too late.

In one scene, an amphibian avatar banged on his dim halo, croaking for mercy. Jonah spotted a group of geometric avatars crying at a candle-lit vigil. In another corner of the Metasphere, in a jungle clearing, at least a hundred avatars prayed in a religious-looking ceremony. They bowed their hands and then in unison held up a glowing blue pill. For a moment, the scene was beautiful, this group of colourful avatars each holding what looked like a turquoise firefly to the night sky. But it wasn't beauty; it was desperation.

'Don't do it,' shouted Jonah, too late. 'I'm going to—'

His promise came too late. The congregation

swallowed their pills. They had Uploaded themselves before Jonah could save them. He widened his gaze, taking in the whole messy melee of life stuck online again. This time, the dizziness and disorientation was replaced with a sickening feeling of futility. All across the Metasphere, living avatars were giving up. With Sal's deadline looming, Jonah had to release the halos right now to stop more users Uploading. But as his mind interfaced with the programming code of the chamber, it awoke the last command that Sal had installed in the system.

Suddenly, Jonah felt an overwhelming, unstoppable urge to kill himself.

45

Matthew Granger leaned his ear to the iron track and felt the vibration of the coming train.

The explosives were in place, ready to blow up the bridge that spanned the gorge. It was his last stand, his last chance to stop the dragon from killing everyone stuck inside his world. He was on his own.

Ever since he was young, since he first went to live with his uncle in an apartment decorated only with computer servers and pizza boxes, Granger had been on his own. But as he looked across the vast gorge, the valley between two mountain ranges, isolated by nature and ready to destroy in order to save, he felt just fine about it.

There was no more Louise Thorne to be with. Gone was the chance to live with her in Hawaii – like she'd asked for so many years ago, when Granger had put her off, wanting to shore up his position as unequivocal controller of the Metasphere. Anything else he viewed as a distraction. But now that she was gone, he would have given anything for that distraction. He was alone.

Jonah felt the urge to die by his own hand. What

struck him about the urge, however, was that it seemed to come from within. Jonah was at once aware of his position in the Imprint Chamber and lost amid consuming thoughts of suicide. He knew this directive was an imprint, a message designed by Sal Vator, programmed into the Chamber to be broadcast through the halos.

But Jonah's awareness of its origin allowed his brain, and his heart, the space to consider the directive for what it was – an implanted desire that ran opposite to Jonah's own, inner, quest for survival. He understood the directive was a command, not a desire. Jonah imagined his future, and the first element that clung to his heart was Sam. She was his future.

He yearned to survive this, this suicidal directive, this MetaWar, this seemingly non-stop struggle for control over the world, to build a future with Sam.

He loved her. He imagined them living away from the chaos of the world, somewhere secluded and safe. He imagined swimming in fresh water, eating food they'd grow together from the land, and looking up to watch the stars slowly parade across the night sky for them. He had too much to live for to give into the echo of Sal Vator's murderous suggestion.

Jonah was in control of Sal, not the other way around. He searched Sal's memories, scanning a lifetime of bitterness and revenge-driven planning, and discovered the programming to the Chamber. He watched as Sal hacked Granger's code, reprogramming it to be responsive only to his stolen avatar sequence. Now that Jonah was wearing that avatar, from the inside out, he swung a wing in the air and opened the commands. A pulsing red release button hung in the air above his head. Inside it was the one message that Sal Vator had programmed to broadcast into the halos: *kill yourself*.

Jonah swiped that awful message away, leaving a hole inside the release button. All he had to do now was press the button and free the world's halos. Over seven billion users, the ones who hadn't given up and Uploaded themselves, would be able to log off and…

And what, Jonah wondered. *What would they do next?*

Would they have learned from their captivity? Or would they, perhaps after a period of shock and recovery, simply go back to the ways things had always been? Would they soon seek solace from the crumbing real world in the Metasphere?

Jonah was suddenly convinced that the cycle of violence would commence anew. The Guardians and Millennials might be gone, but there would be another Granger, and perhaps another Jonah, fighting for a vision of how people should live in the virtual space. If the real world was escapable, then people would always choose escape. People tended to bury their heads in the sand, even the tar sand, instead of facing real challenges with real solutions. *But what if*, Jonah thought, *what if there was no escape from the real world?*

What if everybody chose to live *for real?*

That was it.

That was the new imprint message that Jonah would instruct. He would give the captive users one simple, single message as they logged off. They would pass through their halos, and as they did, Sal Vator's suicidal message would be replaced with Jonah's urge for freedom; freedom from escape.

He would force the world to face its problems in the real world because there would be no alternative. Jonah loved the Metasphere, he always had. But when he imagined his future with Sam, it wasn't virtual; it was physical. The future for humankind had to be physical too. It had to be *real*. Jonah felt compelled to survive, but he also felt compelled to help the human race survive.

Sal Vator believed that the survival of the species depended on wiping most of it out and starting over. But Jonah believed that he could give the species a gift, a neurological nudge in the right direction; towards a future free from an easy escape. If the human race was going to survive, it would have to cross the freedom frontier. It would have to *live for real*.

At Jonah's command, those three words appeared within the pulsating red button that hovered above him. Those words, and Jonah's sentiment behind them, would imprint in every exit halo in the virtual world.

Without hesitation, Jonah lifted the wing and pressed the button. All around him, he saw the soft golden glow of the newly enabled exit halos wash over the desperate, trapped avatars. Billions of avatars turned to their halos, as they did so seemingly staring right at Jonah, and with looks of relief and bewilderment, they dived through.

Jonah knew these avatars weren't actually looking at him as they dived to their safety. They were looking to their salvation. But like being on the other side of a one-way mirror, he pretended they were looking right at him. He was their saviour, though they'd never know it.

He'd been called a saviour before, and enjoyed the attention that came with it, but this time he was happy to be invisible. He was content to simply watch as one by one they left the Metasphere to start anew in the real world.

The Imprint Chamber, once alight with moving images from the virtual world, slowly faded to static images of an abandoned world as the Metasphere emptied out its avatars.

And that's when the real world intruded on Jonah.

The pop-up message read:
    CAN'T REACH GRANGER.
    HE'S GOING TO BLOW UP THE TRAIN.
    GET OUT OF THERE!!!

46

Sam whispered into Jonah's deaf ear.

'Please wake up, please get out of there,' she urged.

She hated not being able to see him or what was happening inside. Despite its huge risks, she had to trust that Jonah was disabling the halos, safely, but she had no way of knowing. She'd sent the pop-up message because she knew that the longer they stayed on the train, the closer they were to Granger's fail-safe.

As she knelt with Jonah's metatranced body, something caught her eye. On a small access screen on the server bank, there was a flurry of motion. The window showed a busy urban square where avatars scrambled away from their candle-lit vigil. Jubilant and rejoicing, they were diving through their halos. They were giving up their vigil and flooding back to the real world. Jonah had done it, Sam realised. But any relief she felt was tempered by Jonah's comatose condition.

Why isn't he waking up from his metatrance?

'Please, Jonah,' she said, hoping that somewhere inside he could hear her. 'It's time to come back to me. It's time to start our tomorrow, it's time to—'

The hiss of the carriage door interrupted her. Sam

looked up to see four brown-robed people barrelling down the narrow corridor. Tomorrow's Children. The young man leading the charge was grizzled and furious and carrying an axe. Sam quickly glanced backwards to see if the aft door was clear. It was. But she couldn't leave Jonah unattended. He was helpless and vulnerable in his metatranced state. Why wasn't he coming back? She rose to fight. To fight for Jonah. To fight for her future.

Jonah focused himself inwards again. It was time to separate himself from Sal Vator's avatar. He slowed his breathing and found himself, sequestered from the fusion of Sal Vator's Uploaded consciousness. It was like looking at his own humatar and jumping into his own skin.

He held onto everything that made him Jonah: his memories, his hopes, his dreams and his fears. Like packing up his mental belongings, Jonah moved everything of himself from the digital dragon that had usurped and housed him.

Take us with you, they called from the far reaches of Jonah's brain. *Save us.*

Jonah heard the cries of the copies and Uploaded that Sal had hidden in his mind, the avatars that Jonah had saved but who no longer had real-world bodies to return to. Jonah wanted out, wanted to log off, but he didn't know if he could take them all with him.

I'll try, he answered back. *I'll do my best.*

In his mind, he created an Ark; a giant ship for the digital dead to flee. He welcomed them on board, providing a safe haven from the flood to follow. He imagined the giant vessel, offered it to them as a concrete metaphor within his mind. They joined him on the deck.

They were guests in his grey matter. The avatars clung to the mysterious ninety per cent of Jonah's brain that nobody quite understood. But Jonah had unlocked its secrets, unleashed its power. He now used it as a vessel for these scared and desperate ghosts, echoes of living human beings, to carry them with him as he moved back to the real world.

Jonah found himself flying down a long, dark tunnel. The light at the end was faint, but visible. In his mind, the passengers aboard his mental Ark flew with him. They were silent, but Jonah could tell they were there. He could feel them within his essence. As he hovered closer to the mouth of the tunnel, he realised it was actually a mouth.

He was emerging from the long, red snout of his father's avatar. He was emerging from Sal Vator's Uploaded form.

As Jonah tumbled out, onto the cold, stone floor deep inside the pyramid, he looked up to see his father's digital image staring down at him.

'That was quite a trick,' Sal snarled.

'And it worked,' replied Jonah. 'Look around you. What do you see on the walls?'

The dragon turned and twisted his head. The walls, once alive with colourful scenes from the Metasphere, as observed by the sealed-off halos, were now just bare stone.

'You cannot stop me,' hissed Sal Vator.

'I already have,' said Jonah.

'I take many forms,' spat Sal. 'I am unstoppable because I can be anyone.'

Jonah touched his temple. Sal hadn't realised he'd lost them.

'They're with me now,' he said. 'I built an Ark in here and I'm saving them from you. Sal, you will die alone inside this chamber. You won't feel it, but when the electrical current that powers the servers stops flowing, your immortal life will meet its mortality.'

'You'll never turn off the Metasphere. In here I can live forever, and I will be reborn in another body. Then I'll find you in the real world.'

'Sal, it's over. There is no one left in the Metasphere. It's just you and I, and you now know that you can't usurp me, not fully. You tried to take me over and look how it turned out for you. I released the halos. Everybody is free.'

Jonah turned to his own golden halo, pulsing in anticipation of him diving through.

'Goodbye, Sal,' said Jonah as he stretched his humatar arms straight out to fly.

As Jonah entered the familiar dark zone between virtual and real, the nether-space between worlds, he faintly heard Sal Vator say, 'You assume I mean a human body.'

And then Jonah was consumed by darkness and silence.

47

Jonah woke to the sight of an axe swinging over his head.

At first, Jonah though the nausea of returning to the real world was causing him to see things. But as the sharp blade swung above him, he only wished he was hallucinating.

Sparks exploded as the axe slammed into the grey server boxes. A robed figure tried to dislodge the red-handled axe from the plastic casings of the servers.

'Get on all fours!' called Sam's furious voice. She was above him, standing by Jonah's legs in the narrow corridor of the computer-filled train.

Jonah was dizzy and disoriented, but he knew enough to realise that he'd just awoken into a bloody brawl. He also knew to trust Sam. He rolled himself onto his front and perched up on his hands and knees.

Sam leapt onto Jonah's back. Using him as a springboard, she launched herself into the air. Sam kicked the robed man in the face. Jonah heard his nose break on impact and saw the blood drip on the floor in front of his face.

The 'brother' stumbled backwards, covering his bloodied face to stem the bleeding and ease the pain.

Jonah looked up to see Sam dislodging the axe from the metal casing, clearly stronger than the man who'd gone before. She swung it angrily, aiming at the man's jugular. She was going to decapitate him.

'Stop!'

To Jonah's surprise, Sam twisted the axe in her hand and brought the blunt end to the fore. The steel brick slammed into the man's already mangled face, knocking him down. More blood splattered onto the wall of grey. As the man collapsed in front of Jonah, he could tell he was still breathing, still alive.

'Are you all right?' asked Sam, looking down to turn her full attention on Jonah. 'Is it done?'

Jonah nodded, noticing two other robed figures lying unconscious on the floor towards the front of the carriage. 'Better than them, I suppose,' he said.

'I wasn't going to kill him,' Sam said, dropping the axe to the floor. 'As much as I wanted to. But they weren't going to show us any mercy.'

'I know,' said Jonah. 'But we need to be better than them. I think we can create a better Tomorrow than they can.'

'I hope you're right,' said Sam. 'I hope our version of the future is better than their version.'

Jonah jumped up and hugged Sam tightly. He didn't want to ever let her go. When he imagined his future, it was her.

'I didn't think you'd come back to me,' she said, blinking tears from her eyes. 'But you did.'

'I promised you, didn't I?' said Jonah.

Sam looked at Jonah. 'Did you see my father?'

'Yes. I couldn't have got into the pyramid without him.'

'Did he get out?'

'I think so,' said Jonah, hoping it was true. 'I could see across the Metasphere, and everyone left. Everyone that could leave, that is.'

'What about the Uploaded?'

'There's so many now. A lot of people took the suicide pill. They didn't see any hope, no point in waiting for what they thought was inevitable. I don't know how many dead are roaming around in there, but I bet it's a lot.'

Sam placed her hand on the grey server boxes.

'But Axel wouldn't do that,' Jonah said. 'He's a fighter.'

'We need to get to him,' urged Sam, 'to his real body.'

'When the train gets to Vancouver, we'll find a way back up north. We'll excavate the mine, find your dad.'

'Jonah,' said Sam, 'this train may not reach Vancouver.'

'Granger?' asked Jonah.

'I haven't been able to reach him,' confessed

Sam. 'There's no answer. Which means he doesn't know you've fixed it. He's going to blow up the train at Stoney Creek.'

Jonah had freed the living from the Metasphere. If Granger blew up the train, the two billion people that had been trapped in the Northern Corner – trapped in the servers on the train – would be safe, but the casualties would include the slumped cult members on the floor, the driver, the countless Uploaded still online, and he and Sam.

Sam held her datapad, zooming in on the satellite map showing the train rapidly approaching the eastern side of the gorge. They didn't have long.

Jonah let go of Sam and ran.

'C'mon!' he shouted. 'We have to stop this train!'

He flicked open the lever of the carriage door but nothing happened. The door was sealed shut. They were trapped.

'They must've locked it behind them when they came for us,' Sam said. 'We can't get through. But, Jonah, we could jump, before it's too late.'

Jonah thought hard about the option. It was dangerous at this speed, but since the train was snaking besides lakes and rivers, they might be able to jump safely into water. They could save themselves. But there would be other casualties.

The driver, whomever he or she was, wouldn't see the blast coming. The comatose cult members would perish too. Jonah wondered if he could live with sacrificing these people as what Granger would call 'collateral damage'. He knew Sam would have no qualms about their deaths. But there were other victims: the Uploaded. Jonah didn't know how many Uploaded were stored on the servers on the train, but he guessed there were hundreds of thousands, if not millions of digital souls who'd already committed suicide, roaming the abandoned Metasphere. He wanted to protect their afterlives.

'There's another option,' Jonah declared, brushing past Sam and stepping over the slumped bodies before he ran to the rear of the carriage. He opened the aft door and stepped out on the narrow platform between the server car and the crane car. Jonah started to climb the ladder on the rear wall of the container car, the wind whipping. He didn't have to go through the train. He was going over the top.

'What are you doing?' shouted Sam from below.

Jonah kept climbing. The people who had Uploaded did so because they had no hope. Jonah failed to free them on time. He failed to give them hope. He felt the burden of their deaths and the responsibility of safeguarding their digital immortality on his shoulders as he reached the roof of the train and pulled himself up onto it.

The roof was flat and made of thick corrugated steel that reminded Jonah of the shipping containers on the Chang Corporation freighter. It was the vessel that first took Jonah to Australia, a ship that sank in Sydney Harbour.

As he steadied himself on his feet, he noticed the majesty of his surroundings. The mountains on both sides sloped down, covered in a thick jumper of green pines, to meet the train as it chugged alongside a pristine blue lake. Sam was right, they probably could jump into that water and survive. They'd splash in the clean water and watch as the train powered forth to its imminent demise.

'You're sure you don't fancy a swim?' called Sam.

She was right behind him, on all fours on the roof. Jonah turned, smiled, and shook his head.

'All right, then,' she said. 'If we're going to do this, let's do it together.'

Jonah reached out, grabbed her hand and the two of them rose into a crouched position. They walked carefully along the length of the train carriage, trying to keep their centres of gravity as low as possible. Jonah was shaking from the adrenaline or the vibrations of the train below; he didn't know which. It might have been both. He knew one wrong move would kill him so he chose each step so that it wouldn't be his last.

When they finally reached the front of the car, Jonah climbed down and waited for Sam. He helped guide her body down as she descended the steel ladder. The platform was narrow, six inches at best. He set his feet in between hers and held her in place against the wall of the last train carriage. Jonah had the urge to kiss her again, but there was no time for that.

He took one large step and leapt over the rushing tracks below. He tried the door of the next carriage and this time, fortunately, it opened. Jonah didn't want to risk climbing over nineteen train carriages. Now they could go in. Propping himself in the door, he reached his hand back. Sam jumped over the couplers and landed in his arms.

Jonah and Sam raced through the nineteen identical carriages, each containing the lines of servers on either side of their narrow corridor. They ran as fast as they could, carriage after carriage, until they stepped through their final door and into the engine room of the train. Jonah shuffled through the narrow corridor, half the width of the carriages' corridors, until he reached the control area.

The conductor turned, his mouth gaping in shock and surprise. He was a gaunt man with a moustache and eyes that matched his grey hair. Jonah noticed, with relief, that he wasn't wearing a brown robe. Perhaps he wouldn't try to kill them. Instead he wore matching dark blue – a buttoned-down shirt over thick cotton trousers. It was a uniform, but not one that Jonah recognised.

'What – who are you?' asked the driver.

'I'm Jonah Delacroix,' he said, 'and I'm here to save you.'

'You're one of them nutcases,' the man replied, looking at Jonah's brown robe and bloodied face.

'Listen closely,' Sam said as she pointed at the tracks ahead. 'There's no time to chat. You need to stop the train before it's too late. There's someone on the tracks ahead who's going to blow up the bridge.'

'Which one?' he asked, staring ahead.

'Stoney Creek,' said Jonah.

'Then it's too late,' the driver replied. 'We're already there.'

Jonah looked out of the window as the train curved to reveal a vast valley ahead. A massive bridge spanned the expanse below. In the distance, standing on the tracks, Jonah spotted a man; a man with shiny steel legs.

48

As he waited for the train to reach the bridge, Granger grabbed the remote detonator, a small square of glass, from a chain around his neck. He held up the translucent tile and saw that it had no bars of service. He was angry at himself for not thinking of this. Up here in the mountains, there was no cell tower to provide a signal. He shoved the slab of glass back under his parka and gripped the manual detonator tethered to the tripwire.

He let his eyes wander from the tracks ahead. Stoney Creek valley was lush with evergreens and raging white water below. It was a green oasis in an overcrowded world. It was a beautiful place to die.

And he wouldn't be alone. He'd be killing Jonah, killing Sam, killing nearly two billion trapped users. But their sacrifice would ensure his Metasphere lived on for the five billion users trapped online through the servers that used to be the Southern, Western and Eastern corners. With the Northern Corner destroyed, the halos would release automatically. Granger smiled at the irony that his last act would be to grant freedom. He'd fought the Guardians for so long, who'd claimed freedom as their own rallying cry, and now he'd be the one freeing five billion people with his final act.

The vibrations on the track grew more pronounced. His nerves seemed to shake with them. He'd faced death, or at least the possibility of death, numerous times, and had never been afraid. Every day since the emergency workers pulled his wrecked body from the carnage that killed his parents, he felt he'd been living a fortunate parallel life. He never feared death because a part of him, in the parallel reality, had already died. The living Matthew Granger, the one who went to live with his uncle, learned programming code, and eventually created a real parallel world called the Metasphere; that Matthew Granger had cheated death and he knew that it was simply a matter of time before death discovered the oversight.

But as Granger flipped open the safety housing on the detonator and rested his thumb on the metal switch, he felt as shaky as the bridge. The black train trundled into view, curving around a wide bend to straighten out for its final approach. Granger stood up straight to meet his demise. He stood proudly, stubbornly, as the train sped towards him from the opposite side of the deep gorge. When he flipped the switch, the tracks would explode and the train would plummet into the valley. It would all be over.

Of course, he wouldn't be alive to see that. But perhaps in that parallel world where Granger had never survived his childhood car crash, it didn't matter. Perhaps in that parallel, there was no Metasphere, no MetaWars, and no Jonah Delacroix. Maybe, Granger thought, by destroying the bridge and the train, and himself, he'd finally fuse those two parallel lives.

In that moment, as he pressed his thumb against the steel switch, he hoped to see his parents again. But instead, staring down the parallel train tracks of this life, he only saw Jonah Delacroix.

Jonah stood on the top of the locomotive, waving furiously.

Sam was behind him too, signalling to Granger not to detonate. They'd left the driver in the control room below to slow the train as fast as he could. Jonah could tell the velocity of the long train was waning; he just hoped it would stop soon enough.

As the train rolled onto the bridge, Jonah wondered if he should have chosen Sam's plan to bail out before it was too late. But now, it *was* too late.

As they neared, Jonah caught Granger's eye. He shouted as loud as he could, despite knowing the Millennial founder wouldn't be able to hear his words.

'Don't detonate!' he yelled, hoping Granger would read his lips and trust his eyes.

Jonah looked into Matthew Granger's eyes and saw sadness and resignation. Jonah was aware that the train was speeding across the bridge, but time seemed to slow down. His eyes were locked with Granger's. The Millennial founder stared back with a hardened, detached gaze.

Jonah worried that maybe Granger wanted to die. He'd lost everything he'd built, fought for and loved. Matthew Granger was alone now and was obsolete. And as much as Jonah despised the man for what he'd done to his family, and to countless other families, he felt like he understood his drive. There was going to be a new world order, and if Matthew Granger's drive and determination could be conscripted into building the new tomorrow, then Jonah wanted him to know he was not alone. He was not obsolete.

Jonah smiled. He nodded a confident, reassuring nod that he hoped Granger would understand.

Granger nodded back, thawing his icy stare into a look of recognition and relief. He jumped off the tracks and tumbled down on the sloping rail bed.

The train rumbled past him. The locomotive cleared the bridge and was now on firm ground again, and its speed was slowing rapidly. The train was stopping.

Jonah climbed down from the roof and Sam guided him onto the platform at the rear of the locomotive. She pulled him inside as the train rolled gently to a stop.

'We're still alive,' she said, almost robotically, as if she couldn't quite believe it.

'He saw me, Granger saw me,' Jonah shared. 'I think he understood.'

She threw her arms around Jonah and said nothing. Jonah held her close. She was right; they were still alive.

'There's someone coming down the tracks,' called the driver from the control room. 'Are we picking up hitchhikers?'

'He's with us,' Jonah called back. Even as the words left his lips, Jonah couldn't comprehend the full meaning of them: Matthew Granger, *with us*. Granger had been his foe for months, a deadly enemy who'd attacked and murdered at every turn. And then, he'd become an ally of necessity. *But now*, thought Jonah, *he is with us*.

Jonah opened the engine room's side door and leaned out. Granger was walking along the side of the tracks and waved to him. Matthew Granger was wearing a thick parka coat – blue, fur-lined and puffy – over his torso and shredded cargo trousers over his titanium legs. Granger's metal feet wore no shoes as they crunched on the rocky gravel of the rail bed. Jonah waved back.

He helped his enemy aboard with a smile.

'Thank you,' he said, 'for not killing us.'

'Who says I haven't?' asked Granger. He unzipped his parka, revealing enough explosives strapped to his vest to kill them instantly. Jonah staggered back, at the same time trying to keep calm. He reached for Sam's hand, and squeezed it to ask her to do the same.

'What's all that for?' asked Jonah.

'An insurance policy, in case you didn't do what you set out to do,' said Granger.

Jonah nodded. 'I released the halos—'

'But the imprint message!' said Granger. 'It killed Louise. It'll kill anyone who—'

'He changed it,' said Sam.

'To what?' asked Granger.

'Sal Vator imprinted a message of death. He thought that was the answer,' said Jonah. 'And you thought control was the answer.'

'Then what is?' asked Granger, his eyes darting about nervously. 'Some Guardian notion of freedom? That only leads to chaos. That's why I built the Metasphere in the first place. To give the people a way out of chaos, a place to escape to.'

'And now it's abandoned, and will be forever,' said Jonah. 'Now people can live, really live.'

'Live for real,' added Sam.

'That's the message,' said Jonah. 'Live for real. Nobody who heard me will come back into the Metasphere. Ever.'

'You changed the Imprint message?' Granger asked. 'But that's mind control. That's not exactly being a champion for freedom.'

'I whispered into the ear of the world's subconscious

and gave the people a new way to do what Sal Vator sought to do through genocide and you sought to do through control,' said Jonah. 'I played the long game. You taught me that. Remember?'

Matthew Granger frowned – he looked confused. And his confusion worried Jonah. Especially when Granger began stroking the bricks of C-4 attached to his vest. 'No more virtual world, no more Metasphere,' he muttered to himself. 'Everything I built, you just took away.'

'No,' said Jonah. 'I've freed you from it. Don't you see, it was a prison; a prison of repeated behaviour. You and me, Guardian and Millennial, trapped in a cycle of hatred and violence over a world we both loved but couldn't escape. You said you built the Metasphere to be an escape from the real world; well, now I've given you, and everyone else who was trapped in the Metasphere, an escape back to the real world. This is where we need to live now. Live, *for real*.'

'The Metasphere is my life. Without it I...I...' Granger stuttered his sentence, swallowed, and looked hopelessly into the middle distance. And then he looked straight at Jonah and completed his thought: 'Without it I have no reason to live.'

Sam whispered in Jonah's ear, 'We have to stop him.'

'No, Sam,' replied Jonah. 'We have to help him.'

'*You?*' scoffed Granger. 'Help *me*?'

'Why?' asked Sam.

'Because the world needs you,' said Jonah. 'You built a new world, a world so compelling and inviting that everyone flocked to it and ignored the reality they left behind. But the *real* world needs you. It needs your brilliance, your determination, and even your obsession. Play the long game with me, Granger. Build a new world of flesh and blood and clean air and fresh water. Build a new world that can outlive us all.'

'I have nothing left,' admitted Granger. 'If the Metasphere is gone, so is the Millennial Corporation. I'm worthless.'

'The value of your stock isn't the value of your soul,' said Jonah.

'My soul drips with blood,' said Granger. 'You know that.'

'And I'll never forget it,' promised Jonah. He thought about all of the hundreds, thousands, maybe even tens of thousands of people that Granger had killed, but mostly he thought of his mother. She was a casualty of a war she wanted no part in. 'But the planet needs redemption and so do you. And I think you can work on it together.'

'Play the long game,' repeated Granger.

'So here's what's going to happen,' explained Jonah. 'When we pull into Vancouver, Sam and I are going to go north. We're going to get to her father, and anyone else trapped under the mine. And then, we're

314

going to fix the world together.'

'I love your optimism,' said Sam, 'however misplaced it might be. But with what resources; with what money?'

'Sal Vator got the top two thousand wealthiest people to bid for their lives, and then he released their halos with an embedded message to kill themselves,' Jonah reminded them.

'My Louise,' Granger said with a terrible shaking sadness in his voice.

'And I'm sorry,' said Jonah. 'But I am the only living soul who has access to that account.' He had an imprint, an echo of Sal's consciousness burned into his brain. He might have expunged Sal Vator from his mind, but Sal's memories were with him. Jonah had witnessed Sal's entire life, including the establishment and passcodes for the secret bank accounts that now contained over a third of the world's total wealth. And so it was Jonah who was the richest person on earth.

'That's blood money,' scoffed Sam.

'I agree,' said Jonah, 'and that's why we're going to put it to good use, for reconstruction, for dealing with the real-world problems. We'll start by rescuing the people trapped under the Northern Corner and then we'll continue to rescue the planet trapped under its own unsustainability.'

49

Jonah held Sam's hand as the train approached Vancouver.

They stood behind the driver, taking in the forest of gleaming glass towers silhouetted against a mammoth mountain. Vancouver was a city by the sea, and Martin, the driver, explained that unlike most of the real world, its position as Canada's main port for resources and minerals kept it wealthy and vibrant.

The cityscape reminded Jonah of Hong Kong with its vertical glass trophies reaching for the blue sky. Jonah blinked, held his eyes closed, and remembered what Hong Kong looked like when he'd left it: collapsed and smouldering. He hoped never to see such destruction again.

As the train entered its final terminus, the freight yard on the south side of Vancouver Harbour, Jonah feared his hopes were about to be crushed. Sam squeezed his hand. They were rolling into an ambush.

Brown-robed men and women, holding automatic weapons, lined the tracks on both sides. Tomorrow's Children had come for their father.

Granger burst into the locomotive. He had been with the servers for the duration of the trip to

Vancouver, counting the Uploaded in the otherwise abandoned Metasphere. But now he was brandishing a warning.

'There's at least a hundred of them out there,' he said.

'We're outnumbered and definitely outgunned,' observed Sam. 'We don't stand a chance.'

'In a straight fight,' said Jonah, 'no, we don't.'

'You mean surrender?' asked Granger. 'That's not exactly your style.'

'Neither is getting killed,' snapped Jonah. 'They've come for Sal Vator. He's Uploaded onto these servers. They're going to want to secure him.'

'We're not going to let them take that maniac!' asked Sam. 'Even if he's dead.'

With a final hiss and jolt, the train came to a stop. Jonah looked out of the front window and, not for the first time that day, thought he saw a ghost.

Standing before the train, tattooed and gnarly as ever, was Jez. As they locked eyes, Jonah couldn't understand how this was possible.

'We watched him die,' said Sam. 'He killed himself.'

'Jeremy Trundle has an ego even bigger than my own,' said Granger, shaking his head. 'He made you believe what you wanted to believe.'

'Jonah Delacroix!' called Jez, pointing his machine gun at the locomotive window. 'We have come for our

317

father. Open the train and step out.'

Jonah had been tricked. He'd spared Jez's life in the north, and then watched as he killed himself with cyanide. But somehow, it had been a ruse, an illusion. The tattooed traitor stood before them, threatening to take Sal Vator. *An illusion*, thought Jonah. That's what he needed now: an illusion of surrender.

'We need to get them all on board,' said Jonah quietly, so those outside could not hear. He meant to set a trap. If he could lure the gunmen onto the train, then he had one surprise up his sleeve, a surprise that was once strapped to Granger's vest.

'Granger,' said Jonah. 'Can you detonate your explosives remotely?'

Granger pulled out a square slab of glass dangling from a silver chain. It was his mobile remote. He held it up for Jonah to see – the display showed full 8G coverage – and then he nodded knowingly.

'Plant them under the servers in carriage nine, where Sal is stored,' ordered Jonah. 'When you're off the train, blow it up.'

'What about you two?' asked Granger.

'We're going to make them believe what they want to believe,' said Jonah.

'That we're surrendering,' said Sam.

'Go, now,' said Jonah.

Granger raced through the narrow corridor to the rear door and disappeared into the first carriage. Jonah knew he had to stall for time, so he opened the locomotive window to talk to the ghost.

'Jez, I guess you've won,' said Jonah.

Jez nodded. 'There's nowhere to go,' he said. 'Come out and face your fate.'

'What about the fate of the users online, in these servers?' said Jonah. 'I owe it to them to make sure they're safe – both living and Uploaded.'

'Even in the face of death you have a sense of duty and loyalty,' spat Jez. 'You're so predictable, Delacroix. It's pathetic!'

'You want to keep Sal Vator safe? Then why not take the rest, too? Take the entire Northern Corner, it's all on board.'

'Are you negotiating?'

Jonah could see the calculations behind Jez's eyes. Sal Vator might have spoken out against the Metasphere, but Jonah counted on the fact that Jez had spent too many years fighting in the MetaWars to give up on the chance to own a quarter of the virtual world. Jez was demented, murderous and treacherous. But most of all, he was greedy.

'I'm offering it to you in exchange for our lives,' said Jonah. He noticed excited looks on the gun-toting men and women. They appeared to share Jez's interest in owning a piece of the Metasphere. 'Mine, Sam's and Matthew Granger's.'

'Granger's on board?' snarled Jez. 'Then I'll give

you two out of three. Two live. One dies. You decide.'

'That's not a choice,' said Sam. 'That's a—'

'Final offer,' shouted Jez. 'Now get off that train and we'll begin.'

Sam hugged Jonah, pressing her face into his chest. At first, Jonah thought she was scared, distraught. But as she whispered, he realised she was shielding her mouth from Jez's eyeline in case he could read her lips.

'Granger will have planted the explosives by now,' she said.

'I hope so,' said Jonah, holding her close. He took Sam's hand, led her down the narrow passageway behind the controls and pushed the rear door out on its hinges.

Two robed gunmen, barely a year older than Jonah, greeted them with automatic weapons pointed at their chests. Jonah checked behind – the length of the train was now guarded by cloaked terrorists. Jonah called back to the driver, 'OK, open them all up and come outside.'

A sequential hiss travelled down the length of the train as the side doors opened automatically one after another. Jonah and Sam jumped off the rear platform and were flanked by a young gunman with a shaved head and nose ring.

Tomorrow's Children, thought Jonah. *They look like children.*

The driver stepped down and was quickly ushered into the rail yard and out of sight.

Jez approached Jonah and Sam with a look of contempt and disgust.

'So where is he? Where is Matthew Granger?' Jez asked.

Jonah tilted his head, motioning to the train. 'He's back there, guarding over his creation.'

Tomorrow's Children were boarding the train. Jonah knew they'd check the servers, in search of their 'father'. Granger had to get off while the bulk of the terrorists were on board. It was their only chance of overpowering the large group.

'Not his any more,' snapped Jez. 'Mine.'

'He might not give it up willingly,' insisted Jonah. 'You should get him off that train before he sabotages the servers.'

'I'll kill him if he does,' fumed Jez.

There was another voice. A young man leaned out of carriage nine, calling: 'He's in here, we found him!'

'Watch them, Kassim,' Jez said to their guard. The kid obeyed the order, grabbing hold of Sam and Jonah while Jez ran down the outside length of the train to find Granger.

Jonah watched Jez climb aboard and disappear. That's when he was blinded by the explosion.

50

Jonah was blown backwards by the blast.

He skidded on the gravelly ground and immediately reached out for Sam. He couldn't see a thing, but he felt her hand. Aching, he propped his body up on top of hers to protect her from the aftershock.

'Sam!'

The sound of the blast, at first a roar, and then only a ringing silence, meant he couldn't hear himself scream her name. The heat from the train washed over him, and Jonah was worried he and Sam would be roasted on the ground. As his sight slipped back to him, blurry and smoke-filled, Jonah kept his body covering Sam's while he dragged her away from the still-intact locomotive.

'C'mon, Sam!' Jonah urged. The explosion was igniting the train carriages one after another. The fire was raging, and getting closer. Fast.

Kassim, their robed captor, was lying face down in the gravel. Jonah made a split-second decision to leave him there.

It was a mistake.

As he continued pulling Sam away, the kid with the nose ring rose to his knees and grabbed onto

Sam's legs. She kicked, but was disoriented and uncoordinated. Jonah was wavering on his feet, but he knew that they'd all be dead if the fire, racing along the length of the train, caught the locomotive. If that happened, the entire rail yard would be decimated and they would die.

'Let go!' he shouted on instinct, though not able to hear himself. Kassim didn't stop holding on tight to Sam's legs, seemingly unable to stand himself.

Jonah, thinking quickly, picked up a handful of gravel and pounced on Sam's clinging captor. Kassim opened his mouth to shout, but it gave Jonah a chance to strike. He shoved the gravel in Kassim's open mouth. The kid spat and spasmed, finally releasing his grip on Sam.

Jonah pulled his best friend to her feet.

'Can you run?' he asked. Again, his words were silent to him, disappearing in the roar of the fire, but Sam understood. She nodded furiously and grabbed at Jonah's hand. Together, hand in hand, they sprinted around the locomotive and Jonah guided them towards the nearby shore of the harbour on the opposite side.

They jumped over two sets of rail tracks before reaching the concrete barrier separating the rail yard from the water. Jonah looked at Sam, telling her to jump with his eyes.

His message understood, they leapt in tandem. Jonah felt the blast on his back as they hit the waiting water, sinking quickly. Their thick brown robes were absorbing the water and pulling them down, which was a blessing.

Above them, through the water, Jonah saw the blue sky turn bright orange. The flames reached across the surface and Jonah and Sam tried to hold themselves under for as long as their breath would allow.

Jonah felt himself choking on his own lungs. He had to give in – had to pull off his robe to rise to the surface for air. He wriggled free from the cumbersome cloak but Sam was still sinking.

She was trying to undo the knot in her robe's tie, but it was tight and waterlogged. Her eyes were wide with fear. She gulped for air – surely an instinctive but deadly reaction – and convulsed underwater.

Jonah tugged at Sam's right arm, pulling it out of its sleeve. Her body shook and her right hand gripped his arm, pulling him down. He had to loosen her grip and he pried her hand away. Jonah released her left arm from its sleeve and drew and drew the heavy robe over her nearly naked body. He wrapped his arms around her torso and kicked with all of his diminished strength. He had to get her to the surface, to get air. But her body was limp.

Trying not to panic, he changed tactics. He held her with his left arm and continued to kick up as hard as he could, using his stronger right hand to propel himself upwards. Looking up, he noticed the flames had dissipated. There was hope. But was it too late for Sam?

When Jonah broke the surface, he gasped deeply, taking in as much air as his burning lungs would permit. Floating on the choppy surface of the harbour, Jonah pulled Sam's unresponsive body onto his chest.

'Sam, I need you,' he pleaded. 'Stay with me. Stay with me!'

He kicked to the water's edge and found his footing on the small sloping beach adjacent to the concrete barrier. He dragged Sam's body ashore, suppressing his worst fears that it was too late. But fear consumed him.

He couldn't lose her; not after everything they'd been through. He refused to fathom a future without her.

Jonah had never learned first aid, but he wasn't solely relying on his own experiences. His brain flooded with memories that were not his own: CPR training in flight school, saving a choking man in first class aboard a 747 at 37,000 feet, and pumping the heart of a drenched young woman on top of an upturned SUV in Manhattan while a soaking wet teenager. Jonah let his borrowed memories guide his hands and his mouth.

Quickly, he tilted her head back. He cleared her strands of red hair from her nose and mouth.

Don't die on me.

Jonah was depleted and his lungs still burned, but he found strength from within. He placed his hands on top of one another, in the middle of Sam's chest, and pushed. And pushed. And pushed.

Thirty compressions. His arms were already aching.

Please.

He leaned over, cupped his mouth over Sam's. In another reality, somewhere, he'd be kissing her passionately right now. But he lived in the reality of war and violence, not romance. He blew in, watching her chest rise as his air filled her lungs.

Then he returned to the compressions.

Thirty. His arms felt weak.

I need you.

Another breath. Filling her body with air and his heart with hope. But after his own strains he felt like he'd collapse beside her. He reminded himself to breathe, to take in enough oxygen to fuel his weary body. Water dripped down his face, itching his eyes, but he didn't dare take his hands off Sam's body as he continued to stimulate her circulation.

Finally, a cough.

Yes, Sam. Yes!

She sputtered, spitting up water and gasping for air. She was coming back to him.

You're here!

On the pebbly beach beside the burning rail yard,

Sam opened her eyes. She didn't say anything, she just stared at Jonah. The silence made Jonah nervous; he didn't know what she was looking at.

'You said you wanted to jump in a lake,' he managed to joke.

'I think this is a harbour,' Sam said. 'But yes, I did, didn't I?'

Sam crawled into Jonah's embrace. They warmed each other with body heat. From their position below the concrete barrier, they couldn't see the train burning but they watched the massive black billows climbing into the sky. Fortunately, the prevailing winds were waving the smoke away, out over the harbour. Jonah could hear the crackle of fires, but he didn't want to see. Up there was death and devastation; two things he'd experienced enough since joining the MetaWars.

He guessed from the size of the blast that none of Tomorrow's Children would live to see their tomorrow. But he wondered silently about Granger.

'Thank you,' said Sam. The light from the fires above bathed Sam's face in a warm glow. She was beautiful. Her face was filthy, covered in grease and dripping with water from her wet hair, but she was gorgeous.

Jonah thought back to the first time they'd met. They'd collided on a night-time service road in South London. They were strangers, both trying to survive a cruel world. But their bodies clashed and their lives intertwined, connected through friendship and chaos until they both ended up here, laid on the beach, inspecting each other for serious injuries. Jonah checked Sam's body and face for any cuts.

'You're OK,' he said with relief.

'Yes, I am,' she said, pulling Jonah closer until their lips touched.

He didn't want to stop kissing her warm and salty lips – and the only thing that motivated him to stop was to start a new life, to walk away from the burning wreckage of the train, of the entirety of the MetaWars, and disappear. Jonah had a promise to keep, and a burden to bear. He'd promised to find Axel, free him from a frozen grave if he could. And since he'd told the world to *live for real*, he felt an obligation to help them do it.

'But my father isn't,' she said, pulling back from the embrace, her eyes pleading.

'Then we have to go.'

Jonah heard a clank on the concrete barrier, just feet away. He grabbed Sam close, worried that debris was falling from the sky. But nothing struck. Jonah looked over and spotted two unmistakable titanium legs standing over them.

'Is this what you teenagers call romance?' laughed Granger. 'Go on a real date or something.'

So he was alive. Jonah wasn't sure if he was

surprised or not. With Granger, he'd learned the hard way to not underestimate him.

Jonah and Sam rose to their feet, wary and weak. For the first time, Jonah surveyed the full scale of the decimated rail yard. The server train was a charred carcass, barely even a shell. The other trains in the yard were still alight and the brick control building was split in two.

Granger jumped down onto the beach, wearing what looked like tight-fitting black pyjamas over his torso and upper legs. He was holding his blue parka and handed it to Sam. She covered up her shivering body, giving Granger an exhausted smile and a thankful nod.

'And you,' continued Granger, looking at Jonah's skinny frame. 'Eat a real meal for a change.'

Jonah couldn't remember the last time he'd eaten. His stomach was hungry but the confusion in his mind overpowered that. *How did Granger survive?*

'But the explosion?' asked Jonah. He couldn't believe his…Jonah didn't know how to label Granger any more. *His nemesis?* He certainly was. *His mentor?* He had taught him many things, things that kept him alive. *His friend?* Jonah wasn't sure, but liked to hope that maybe, someday, if Granger became a better man, then yes, they could be friends. Jonah couldn't believe Matthew Granger was still alive.

'You were on the train,' said Sam through chattering

teeth as she pulled up the parka hood over her soaking hair.

'The doors on that train open on both sides,' he said. 'And I always leave myself a back door.'

'I thought you'd sacrificed yourself,' said Jonah.

'I would have,' said Granger. 'If I had had to. But as soon as Jez boarded, I knew I had a chance, not just to stop Tomorrow's Children but to do what you offered me; to help rebuild the real world. I think that's a future worth living for.'

'Worth fighting for?' asked Jonah.

'If it comes to that,' he said.

'There's been enough fighting,' said Sam as she leaned into Jonah. 'It's time to start something new.'

He put his arm around her, hoping she meant it.

'We have to get back to the north,' said Jonah. 'Find Axel and any others while they're still alive.'

51

Sam looked down over the destroyed mine with fear, anxious that she'd find only death.

She and Jonah were riding in a hired helicopter circling the wreckage. Below them, an army of excavation workers manipulated diggers and cranes, clearing the wrecked buildings to expose the tunnels. Jonah had remained optimistic when he contracted the crew from Fort Mac, now out of work following the city's destruction and SynCorp's demise.

Sam had been amazed at how quickly Jonah had mobilised the rescue effort, getting the crew and equipment to this desolate place in under a day. But he was now the richest person in the world of course, and money, it seemed, could move mountains. She just hoped it would be enough.

As the helicopter circled, the pilot indicated their descent.

'They found something, someone,' he said over the headset.

Sam was too scared to let her hopes rise. *It might be Axel, but it could be anyone.*

The helicopter touched down on a makeshift landing pad. Sam didn't wait for the blades to stop spinning; she jumped out and kept herself low.

She ran towards a large mobile crane teasing a length of wire out of the rubble. Sam felt Jonah's arm around her as the crane pulled up a metal cage.

'I can't look,' she said, wincing her eyes shut.

'Yes, you can,' replied Jonah, giving her shoulder a squeeze.

Jonah's confident voice encouraged her to open her eyes.

Her father.

Axel was frail and clearly exhausted, but alive. As weak as Axel looked, he was propping up a young man who was outfitted in Millennial black.

Sam felt her knees buckle, and Jonah stopped her from falling. Her entire body shook uncontrollably as she sobbed. Sam felt Jonah's arms around her, steadying her.

Be strong, she told herself.

The crane set the cage down on the blackened snow and Sam rushed to open the cage door. She hadn't thought she'd see her dad again, and yet here he was; plucked from the earth like a diamond. *A diamond very much in the rough.*

Two paramedics rushed to grab the Millennial man and laid him on a waiting stretcher.

'Thank you,' he said to Axel as he was pushed away.

As Axel stumbled out of the cage, he opened his

arms to envelope Sam in a hug. She could tell he was weak, and yet his embrace was so strong. In that instant, she felt only five years old. It was the same kind of hug, the same intensity, that he had given her when her mother died. Axel had never been big on displaying emotions, but on that day, like today, he held nothing back. Her father wept, and Sam rubbed the tears from his dirty face, leaving zebra stripes on his cheekbones above his blackened beard.

'Hiya, kiddo,' Axel said, his voice gruff and low.

Jonah offered him an aluminium bottle of water, which he guzzled, spilling much of it down his chin and in his beard as he struggled to swallow it all.

'Easy does it, Dad,' Sam said softly.

'I didn't think I'd ever see you again,' he said. 'I'd given up.'

'So had I,' Sam confessed. She squeezed Jonah's hand. 'But he hadn't.'

Axel leaned on Sam – it felt good to give her father the support – and pulled Jonah into an embrace.

'Thank you, Jonah,' he said. 'For keeping her alive; for coming back for me. I know I haven't exactly been the warmest to you sometimes, but—'

'It's OK,' said Jonah, cutting Axel off. 'You don't need to explain. I've put Sam in a lot of danger, more than you even know about.'

Her dad raised an accusing eyebrow at her boyfriend, her best friend.

'But we're safe now,' concluded Jonah.

'So what happened?' asked Axel. 'All I know is that the halos opened and I dived through. Is everything all right? Did you stop Sal Vator? Did you save the Metasphere?'

Of course – her father had no knowledge of what had happened, but while there would be plenty of time for explanations later, right now she just wanted him to get warm and well.

'We can explain it all. But, Dad, can I ask, what do you want to do now?'

'More than anything, I want to live,' he said. 'Live *for real*.'

Sam looked to Jonah and they shared a smile.

Jonah piloted his new floatplane over the Y-shaped Quesnel Lake.

He looked down on the sparkling blue and prepared to land. Sam was by his side, admiring the views where the mountains met the water.

After the excavation of the mine, rescuing sixty-two people, both Guardians and Millennials – not that those labels meant anything any more – they parted ways with Axel in Yellowknife and made plans to reconvene in Fort McMurray along with Granger.

Jonah had already established his base of operations there. The 'Jason & Miriam Delacroix Trust', funded by Sal's ill-gotten ransoms, totalled trillions of dollars and Jonah would direct and invest it into projects to ensure humanity's survival. Fort Mac would become the epicentre of the rebuilding, a phoenix from its own ashes. There was a long road ahead, and Jonah intended to conscript Axel into his cause. He was looking forward to mending the wounds of the MetaWars by inviting Axel and Granger to work alongside one another to build a better world; a sustainable world for today's inhabitants and tomorrow's children.

But first, Jonah wanted to return to Quesnel to check on the people they'd left behind. Jonah wanted to know that Tony, Kit, the Lakers and the original Tomorrow's Children youngsters were safe in the mountains.

There was another reason to go back. Quesnel Lake had a store of ßetas. And Jonah was still carrying a thousand refugee Uploaded in his brain. He couldn't commune with them, but he knew they were there inside him. He wanted to set them free.

What was left of the Metasphere was the sole domain of the Uploaded, a land of the dead. The remaining servers – the former Southern, Western and Eastern Corners – were now a closed system where the dead could roam forever. Nobody would bother them; nobody would tempt them with life. But the avatars in Jonah's brain were different.

They'd been trapped inside Sal Vator, prisoners in

a madman's mind. Jonah felt he owed them a second chance, especially his mum. He wanted to transfer them from his brain and into ßeta bodies so that they could *live for real*.

And then he wanted to cleanse himself of everything that had happened in the sparkling Quesnel Lake water.

That water sprayed from the pontoons as Jonah splashed the plane down. He taxied to the dock where he'd first deposited the Lakers to the cult.

'Jonah!' shouted Kit from the tree line. She and her brother, Tony, descended the slope, rushing to greet Jonah and Sam. The other Lakers lurked in the trees; Jonah spotted Kareem, Shaq and at least six others, looking both excited and nervous.

Jonah and Sam deplaned onto the wooden dock.

'You came back,' shouted Tony. He extended his hand to shake Jonah's and then pulled him into an embrace, patting his back with a friendly series of thumps.

Meanwhile Kit was hugging Sam and jumping her up and down, a huge grin on her face.

'Have you come to stay?' asked Kit.

Sam shook her head.

'I wish we could,' said Jonah. He meant it. A part of him wanted to remain here, with Sam. The world was so big, so broken, that at times he felt daunted and afraid of the challenges ahead. It would be so much easier to stay at Quesnel, to live off the land in this secluded paradise. Sal Vator had believed in saving the world by killing off humanity. Jonah knew his fight for the future wasn't over. He believed in saving the world with humanity. He wouldn't shirk from the challenge; he'd meet it head on. With Sam.

'There's so much to do out there,' said Jonah. 'But maybe we can stay one night.'

'We'll get started tomorrow,' said Sam.

'You're always welcome here,' said Tony. 'In our home. Whether it's for one night or a hundred.'

'Thank you,' said Jonah. 'But first, I need to use the computers in the cave. The elders, they haven't touched anything, have they?'

'Nah,' said Tony. 'We contacted the police and they took them away.'

'They even came on horseback,' said Kit. 'Real Mounties!'

Jonah and Sam walked to the mouth of the cavern and re-entered the high-tech cave where Sal Vator had died. The ßeta robots hung motionlessly from their hooks, but Jonah was about to inject a form of life into one sixth of their hanging population.

'They're trapped in here,' said Jonah, touching the back of his skull. 'And that's not right.'

Sam helped him recline in a chair next to the bank of computers. Accessing Sal's memories, Jonah found the ßeta programming and opened a closed-circuit transfer program. When he connected, clicking the Ethernet wire into place in his lower back, he wasn't going into the Metasphere, but the sensation felt the same.

He opened his digital eyes to find himself within the transfer program. It looked like the lobby of an office building, and reminded Jonah of Manhattan. The space was sterile and the marble floor was shiny. Jonah approached the bank of lifts and felt a tug at his consciousness. It was time to say goodbye to passengers who'd been silently travelling in his mind.

The lift doors opened and Jonah summoned an avatar from deep within his brain. A female lion materialised as if from nowhere. But Jonah knew she'd come from a far recess of his brain, somewhere in the ninety per cent.

'Thank you, Jonah,' she purred. 'You are my saviour.'

Jonah began to protest, to tell her that he wasn't a saviour, but the doors closed with a chime and she was gone.

One by one, Jonah repeated this ritual, letting each avatar off his Ark and into the lifts, to a new life within a robotic form. He eventually lost count of them, and lost track of time – Sam had sent him a warning message that he'd been plugged in for over twelve hours – when finally he could sense there was just one more left inside: his mother.

'Mum,' he said. 'It's time to go.'

'I don't want to leave you, Jonah,' said her voice. 'I want to live within you.'

'You do, Mum. You do. Always.'

She appeared, in her avatar form – a dove. She flapped her wings inside the steel lift box, hovering in the air. She looked at Jonah and waited.

'See you in the real world,' said Jonah. And then the doors closed, separating them with a wall of brushed steel.

He didn't feel any different, but he knew his mind was his own again. He'd rescued these avatars, including the copy of his mother, from the same fiery death that consumed Sal Vator's Uploaded avatar, and was giving them a fresh start in the real world. He knew it was what every deceased soul really wanted – it meant something that he could grant the immortal wish to even these few.

When he was done, he looked to his glowing exit halo and dived through, eager to see Sam again.

52

Jonah opened his eyes to see the chamber alive with robotic movement.

One thousand silver robotic ßetas had woken, lifting themselves off their hooks and steadily jolting to life.

'It was as if they just turned themselves on,' said Sam, pulling Jonah with a hand from the chair.

'They're alive, again,' said Jonah. 'In the real world. It's amazing.'

The ßetas were hopping down from their racks, getting used to their metallic bodies. Jonah recognised some of the avatars on the screens that perched atop their steel spines. The female lion spotted him and waved with her new metallic arm. But Jonah was looking for the dove. He was looking for his mother.

'Jonah, darling,' called her voice. A ßeta stepped through the crowd of robots and walked towards them. On its screen, Miriam's dove soared against a black background. The ßeta-Miriam opened her skeletal arms and wrapped them around Jonah.

At first, it felt strange to be embraced by a robot, but then Jonah closed his eyes and remembered all of the hugs, all of the warm embraces she'd given him over the years. Her embrace now was cold and metallic, but in his heart, it felt warm and comforting. Until it didn't.

The hug grew into a squeeze, which quickly became a crush.

'M-m-um,' Jonah stuttered, unable to breathe. 'You, y—'

He couldn't get the words out. The air was being pressed from his body – he was going to faint. Everything went blurry and then dark.

'Stop!' cried Sam. 'You're crushing him.'

Suddenly, he was released. Jonah fell to the hard ground. He opened his eyes to see his mother's metallic feet by his face. He was struck by how similar they looked to Granger's titanium extremities.

'Oh no,' said his mother in a shocked whimper. 'My darling boy.' She pulled him up by his hands, gently. 'I'm so sorry. I'm getting used to this…body, this form. I don't know my own strength.'

Jonah caught his breath, still shocked.

'It's all right, Mum,' he said, but only half convinced by his own words. 'It'll take you time to get used to it.'

'I hurt you,' she said shakily. Jonah could hear the tears in her voice, even though there were no tears from her screen. He looked at her in ßeta form, in robot form, and she looked nothing like his mother. His mum was soft and beautiful. This robot, with its shiny steel skeleton, and flat-screen face, was mechanical and harsh – and potentially very dangerous, Jonah realised. 'And I'm not…I'm not real, am I?'

'You're in a robotic form, but you're real. You're real to me.'

'Jonah,' she said softly, 'I've been in your mind, in your memories. I know everything that's happened to you, and what happened to me.'

'I'm so sorry, Mum!' Jonah cried. 'I shouldn't have left you to die.'

Jonah had pushed the guilt he felt for flying to safety while his mother burned to death in the City Tower so far down, so far back in his mind, in order to survive. But now it surfaced and consumed him. He sobbed uncontrollably, his whole body shaking with an eruption of guilt. 'I'm…so…sorry.'

'You don't have to be sorry,' she said. 'I saw everything through your eyes. And I'd do the same thing again to keep you safe.'

Jonah wiped the tears on his sleeve. He didn't want his mother to be this understanding. But if she'd been riding in his mind, she knew what he knew, felt what he felt. It was true empathy.

'And that's what I intend to do,' she said. 'All of us, in fact.'

Miriam pointed to the mass of robots milling around the cavern. Many had already stepped out from the tunnels, seeing the outside world for the first time in their ßeta form.

'We know what you and Sam are about to do. If you're going to save the world, you're going to make enemies. A lot of them. There are still too many people on this planet that will fight you to keep things the same, as terrible as they are. Some will even want to kill you for your ambition. We can protect you. You saved us. Let us save you. We can be your army.'

'She's right,' said Sam, taking Jonah's hand. 'We're going to need all the help we can get.'

Jonah thought about all of the people he'd met in the MetaWars who fought to bend the world to their vision of the future. And now it was his turn. He hoped that he could use courage, not violence, to inspire change; but he'd seen too much to be naive any longer. He would need protection. The MetaWars were over and a second version of the world needed to be forged, a better version; a beta version. If Jonah was going to save the planet, he would need all the help he could get.

'I love you, Mum,' said Jonah. 'You have no idea how happy I am that you're…'

He was about to say 'back', but caught himself. 'That you're here.'

'You have no idea how much I love you, Jonah,' she replied. 'And you probably won't until you two have children of your own.'

With that, she turned away and, her metallic feet clinking on the concrete floor, disappeared from the chamber to join the others in the sun.

'Children?' asked Sam.

'Of our own?' repeated Jonah, looking at Sam with disbelief.

He and Sam followed the robots out of the chamber and watched as they explored their new surroundings, the real world.

'I'll check in with Granger in the Trust's offices to arrange transport for them,' Jonah said. He'd conscripted Matthew Granger into the long game of healing the planet, and Jonah felt fortunate to have Granger's vision – and occasional obsession – focused on such an important and complex task. 'The ßetas can start by helping with the reconstruction in Fort Mac.'

'Do you really want to go back there?' asked Sam.

'No,' said Jonah. 'I don't want to. But I feel that we have to.'

'I love you, Jonah Delacroix. I'm glad you slammed into me that night.'

So much had happened since Sam had run into his path. He thought he was racing for his life that night, but really he was racing into a new life.

With her.

'Wait a second,' he teased. '*You* slammed into *me*.'

That night, after a barbecue on the beach with the Quesnel kids, Jonah and Sam stayed awake to watch

344

the stars. They sat for hours by the dwindling campfire, talking and gazing at the sky. The night air was cool, but they kept warm wrapped in the brown cloaks that were once the cult's uniform. And in each other's arms.

Jonah spotted a light moving fast across the star-scape. He hoped it was his father, encased in his satellite and enveloped in the love of the Uploaded avatars Jonah had left him with.

'This is perfect,' said Sam, tenderly holding Jonah's hand.

Jonah kissed her gently. 'When the sun comes up, it'll be a new start.'

But there was one more thing Jonah wanted to do before daylight interrupted their seclusion.

Jonah stood, slid off his shoes, and dropped the cloak to the ground.

'Race you in,' he said, heading for the dock.

He heard the scramble of Sam following him, felt her by his side as she caught up.

Jonah and Sam raced down the wooden planks of the dock. Their bare feet tapped the planks in a chorus of percussion as they ran towards the waiting water. Jonah reached out his hand and felt Sam grab it. He gently squeezed as they both leapt into the air. As they flew, Jonah looked down over the still water and caught a reflection of himself in the liquid mirror; holding Sam with the bright starlit sky behind them. He never wanted to let go of her.

Jonah's body was flying, but his heart was soaring.

THE END

Acknowledgements

There are many people to thank for helping me bring MetaWars into the world.

At my publisher, Orchard Books, Sarah Levison first believed in this project enough to take a gamble on a bold concept. My incredibly talented editor Catherine Coe championed it as if it were her own acquisition, becoming my trusted guide through all four books. Georgia Murray and Caitlin Drake, thank you for shepherding the project across shifting sands. And thank you to Rosie Turner for brilliantly copyediting each book, making them ready for readers. Thy Bui created the striking visual motif of MetaWars. But great editorial and eye-catching design are no good unless they land in bookshops. Mariesa Dulak, Andrew Nolan, and Louise Grieve, thank you for guiding the book to the market. Les Phipps, Paul Litherland, and Helen Bower convinced booksellers to take a chance on an unknown author. Megan Larkin and Rebecca Frazer, thank you both for keeping the faith in Jonah's journey. And Rebecca Hearne, thank you to you especially for your tireless support and enthusiasm in our never-ending quest to connect with readers in a meaningful way. Your unique energy and positivity has kept me moving forward.

There are three key people who helped guide and shape the project in its early form. Thank you Nancy Miles, Caroline Hill-Trevor, and Steve Lyons for your support. And thank you to Neil Blair and Zoe King for seeing the potential going forward; and to Rick Jacobs for playing the long game with me.

While so many wonderful people contributed to the MetaWars journey, the saga started at home. So my most significant acknowledgement is to my darling wife, Sidonie. I love you for everything that you are and for encouraging me to pursue this dream. This project was an ambitious, oftentimes unwieldy creation that intruded on our lives for years but I hope I have made you proud. Caden and Torin, you are both too young to read these words as I write them, but I look forward to reading these stories with you as you grow. My sincere hope is that the world you grow into is far brighter than the one I have painted on these pages.

I also need to thank my Mom and Dad who gave me a grounding of love and support. As a father now, I can see how easy it is to take a parent's love for granted. Much of Jonah's journey has been for him to see his mother and father as real people and not just as parents.

Lastly, I must recognise, acknowledge, and thank

you, the reader. These stories are for you. I hope you enjoyed Jonah's quest, and seen something of yourself in his struggles. The world is an amazing place, filled with many manmade wonders, but I hope you find a way to strike a balance: interfacing through technology while living *for real*. There will be many challenges in our world that you will have to face. Different people will compete to align you to their agenda. You will have the chance and the responsibility to decide what kind of world you want to live in. You will have to choose: *Whose Side You Are On?*

I look forward to your choices. Please be in touch through www.jeffnorton.com.

Jeff Norton,
Canada, August 2013